Stone Woman

By Veronica R. Tabares

Hardcover Edition

Cover by Bridgitt Tabares

Sun Break Publishing

Published by Sun Break Publishing, Seattle, Washington.

Library of Congress Control Number: 2022909601

ISBN: 978-1-60916-023-4

Publishers note:
This book is a work of fiction and a figment of the author's imagination. Similarities to actual characters, places, names, or events are purely coincidental.

As my children's momma likes to say,

"Was gonna never won the lottery!"

Chapter 1

"No, no, and again no!"

As Nicole tossed the words over her shoulder she tripped and nearly fell. Irritated, she twisted around to glare at the tall man following her on the jungle path— as if the man had somehow been the cause of her near fall—before resolutely plunging ahead.

The path was not an easy one, although, to be fair, in the bright light of day it might not have been that bad. But there was no daylight because it was night, and in the dark, the jungle saw no reason not to play impish tricks if it wished.

And it did wish. The game it had chosen to play with Nicole was the jungle version of peek-a-boo. Every ten feet or so, that mischievous jungle would pop up a root or vine in her path, just to see if her feet could find it.

And her feet did. Over, and over, and over again.

Nicole thought she could not take even one more minute of this torture when something wonderful happened. She had just bulldozed her way through a nasty bit of extra-thick jungle brush and shoved her way over a clump of tall grasses, when, miracle of miracles, Nicole stumbled into a clearing. A clearing!

If it had been during the day—the time most sane people chose to tramp through the jungle—the clouds would have parted, and a happy ray of sunshine would have bathed her in its glorious warmth. But it wasn't day, it was night. No sun.

Luckily, the lack of a fiery ball in the sky did not spoil her mood. A wondrous volcano of joy erupted somewhere near her navel and flooded her body with happiness.

Because for the first time in over an hour—it honestly had seemed more like several days—she was free of the jungle's creepy crawlies. In the clearing, there were no vines to tangle her feet or brush across her face. No giant insects to drop from overhead branches onto her shoulder so they could scuttle toward the neck of her blouse. No roots to spring up out of nowhere, intent on snagging her feet and making her fall flat on her face.

She was done with all of that. She had successfully traversed the jungle. She had beat it, and now, she could relax.

The euphoria lasted exactly 7.5 seconds, then reality reared its ugly head. Sure, she had pummeled that jungle trek and beat it into submission, but unless she planned to sleep all night in this clearing, tentless, there was still the return journey to make. The hotel was on the other end of the trail, and the trail twisted its way through the same jungle that had snagged her hair, tripped her feet, and showered her with critters of all shapes and sizes.

Nicole could feel all that lovely joy draining away. And right about the time the last drop drained out of her right big toe, an epiphany hit.

The nighttime jungle trek was not the real problem, it was a symptom of the problem. The true problem was that her honeymoon was not going as planned.

Although Nicole had not expected the honeymoon to be perfect—she was not as naive as that—every romantic movie she had ever seen had convinced her that honeymoons should be romantic and relaxing.

It only made sense. The entire purpose of a honeymoon, after all, was to create a plethora of happy memories that would bond the new couple together and build emotional glue strong enough to hold them together through good times and bad.

This jungle trek had done nothing to bond the newly married couple. What it had done, instead, was make a tired, cranky Nicole wonder who, exactly, she had married.

A year ago, when she and Michael had taken the scary step to start planning their wedding, Nicole's brain had formed a habit of daydreaming about the honeymoon. Leisurely days holding hands. Sunset walks on the beach. And her favorite, candlelit dinners with soft music in the background. Each scenario was the perfect backdrop to gaze into her new hubby's eyes while they planned their future together.

Those daydreams were glorious. So much so that she became addicted to them and had had trouble pulling herself out of them when she needed to rejoin the real world. It was only after she got a C+ in a class that she should have aced that she shut down those lovely flights into daydream land.

All was wine and roses, until the day an excited Michael announced that he had been promised exclusive access to his favorite archaeological site. At night, no less, which would allow him to finally check out his pet theory.

It was an archaeologist's dream and an archaeologist's new wife's nightmare.

Now, instead of holding hands, she found herself bogged down with a heavy backpack. In place of a sunset stroll on the beach, she was trapped in a nighttime tramp through a bug-infested jungle. And the candlelight dinners of her dreams had given way to poorly wrapped sandwiches, mosquito bites, and those ever-present howler monkeys that refused to be quiet.

As a matter of fact, as soon as they arrived in Belize Michael somehow managed to shoot down every romantic idea she suggested and replace it with all things archaeological.

But Nicole was an artist, not an archaeologist. And she was on her honeymoon. She wanted the romance.

Still, Nicole put on a brave face and soldiered on. After all, she had known Michael was a budding archaeologist even before she fell in love with him.

So, she put on her hiking boots, slathered on a disgusting-smelling mosquito repellent, and reluctantly followed Michael and their guide into the dark jungle. And then, forty-five minutes into the hour-long trek into the jungle, too far away from the hotel for Nicole to safely return alone, Michael informed her that—horror of horrors—the plan was for her to climb the Mayan ruins with him.

Nicole stopped dead in her tracks as her brain raced to process this new information. A multitude of emotions welled up inside her, and she had to work particularly hard to tamp down a gigantic gush of panic, the most dangerous emotion of them all. When she had her emotions reasonably under control, she raced to catch up with her husband. After a deep, calming breath she thanked him for the offer and declined it. She had a paralyzing fear of heights that she had had since a young child, she explained to him. For her, climbing the temple would not be a treat. The very thought of it filled her with terror.

Michael laughed his jolly laugh and told her not to be silly. Nobody in their right mind would even think of turning down such an opportunity.

That was the moment Nicole wondered if Michael truly was the man she thought he was. It was also the moment a very large, and very loud, argument began.

Signs of trouble had been there all along, but Nicole had been too in love to pay attention to petty little things like the way Michael always thought he was in charge. Of everything. Their schedule, choice of restaurant, mode of transportation—a few times even the clothes Nicole wore.

At first, Nicole had found it cute and reasoned it was because he was tall while she was petite. Maybe he thought his height gave him added authority. He was also two years older than her, which might have led him to assume he was wiser.

Whatever the reason, from their first date forward, Michael always glibly insisted he have the final say in all decisions.

So, when he proclaimed that Nicole was going to climb to the top of the temple with him, Nicole had had enough. She was tired of being treated like a child rather than the full-grown woman she was. No matter how loud she had to yell, Michael would learn that at twenty-two, she had earned the right to make decisions in her own life. She had a brain. She had likes and dislikes. She deserved to have a say in where and when she spent her first days as a married woman.

And she absolutely, positively, was not climbing to the top of that Mayan temple!

Michael—irritating man that he was—was unfazed by her impassioned pleas for understanding. Even worse, the more she yelled, the broader he smiled.

Frustrated, Nicole turned her back on Michael to stare up at the Mayan temple looming over the clearing. Backlit as it was by a near-full moon, it was several degrees more ominous than she had expected. Panic made her stomach do a flip flop, which, in turn, fueled her anger. Needing an outlet for all that anger she stomped to the center of the open space and slammed her backpack angrily to the ground.

Michael—who had used his long legs to nimbly step over the brush to follow Nicole into the clearing— grinned as he watched Nicole's antics. *No doubt about it,* he thought. *My wife is as cute as a button. Let her pretend to be cranky all she wants. She's mine, all mine! What's a few silly little temper tantrums?*

Besides, he mused, as he moved to stand next to his wife, *she looks so darn cute standing there with her arms crossed, tapping her foot to the beat of the cicadas. Kind of like an angry puppy.*

Grinning more widely than before, he removed his Indiana Jones fedora, and calmly placed his backpack next to Nicole's.

"C'mon, Nikki," Michael coaxed with a voice as smooth and sweet as honey, "I—"

"Don't call me Nikki!" Nicole yelled. And to make sure he understood she was serious she kicked her backpack repeatedly before she moved it a foot away from Michael's. "I hate that name!"

Michael should have remembered that it was bears that liked honey, not puppies.

"And just in case you're wondering." Nicole pointed to the top of the temple that loomed nearby. "I am NOT climbing that!"

Michael took a step toward his irate, but cute, wife and held his arms up pleadingly. "But Nicole, a good wife would—"

"Ha!" the word exploded from Nicole's mouth like a cannon ball. "You're dreaming."

Snatching up her backpack, Nicole stabbed Michael with a don't-mess-with-me glare. Then, to send home the message she was angry, she repositioned her backpack another two feet away from Michael's.

"Aw, Nicole, c'mon!" Michael complained.

Moving slowly, as if not to startle a wild animal, Michael gently lifted his backpack and cautiously placed it next to Nicole's. His movements were careful and restrained, so much so that an onlooker might assume he was a lion tamer attempting to pacify an angry lion with a fresh piece of meat.

But it was a good thing Michael was not a lion tamer. He would not have made a very good one. Because if Nicole were a lion, she most likely would have had him for dinner.

Michael, who by nature leaned toward self-centeredness, lacked the ability to truly read body language. Nicole was standing still—except for the tap, tap, tap of her foot. *Great*, he thought, *she's calm.*

He was so caught up in what he wanted that he failed to notice Nicole's angry glare, which shot arrow, after arrow, of rage in his direction.

"You know," he wheedled, "all you need to do is one climb. And I'll be there the entire time. I won't let you fall."

It was unfortunate Michael was among the many who were unable to tell the difference between controlled anger and passivity. He had no clue about the depth of Nicole's anger.

But he was about to find out.

Nicole managed to hold her tongue for another five seconds.

"Some honeymoon!" she yelled.

The words seemed to free her from her immobilization. She jerked her backpack from the ground and tossed it four feet away. She stomped over to it and put her hands on her hips, then turned to Michael. "What's next? Ditch digging?"

"Nicole, Nicole, Nicole!" Michael crooned, in a vain attempt to lessen his wife's anger.

He slid his backpack a foot closer to Nicole before he continued his argument.

"My dissertation, Nicole. We talked about this. Just a few shots. It won't take long. It'll be fun."

"Fun!"

As the word exploded out of her mouth her face registered shock. How could she possibly be expected to think climbing a dark temple in the middle of the night was fun?

"It's dark," she whispered, and no one could mistake the fear in her voice, "the middle of the night, right?"

Michael certainly recognized the fear and felt a sudden twinge of empathy. He had not meant to scare his wife. He would do better.

But as he pasted a grin on his face that was meant to cheer her, his calculations were off. The face he turned to Nicole looked more like a smirk than a smile. To make matters worse he snickered a bit as he slid his backpack another foot closer.

"It's not that tall," he said reassuringly.

This was too much for Nicole.

"Oh, Michael," she wailed, as her shoulders lost their stiffness and drooped like a piece of wet spaghetti. "Why can't you get it?"

"Why can't you?" Michael returned stubbornly.

Taking advantage of Nicole's moment of obvious weakness, he lifted his backpack and quickly planted it firmly beside Nicole's backpack. Then he subconsciously tried to gain the upper hand by adopting Nicole's previous stance of crossed arms and tapping toe.

Nicole slowly turned her head, taking in first Michael's backpack, which was now so close to her own that it was hard to define where one started and the other stopped, and then at Michael with his tapping toes.

Anger bubbled up and over as the meaning of Michael's pose sunk in. He was mocking her! There he stood, arms crossed and tapping his toe. It was the exact same pose that had been used to make fun of her for years.

The noodle that had been her spine was instantly replaced by a rod of steel, and no one, not even Michael, could mistake the anger in her eyes. She snatched up her backpack, stomped several feet across the clearing, and slammed it to the ground.

The battle of the backpacks was far from over, even if it wasn't much of a battle, or even about backpacks. Michael needed to get over always needing to be in charge.

Besides, Nicole was perfectly willing to give a little when it came to other areas of their newly minted marriage. But not heights. With heights, there would always be a battle. No matter what Michael wanted, or why.

Why did Michael have such a total disregard for her deep-seated fear of heights? She could understand if she had complained about sitting on a tall chair or a high stool. But this was a very high, very steep temple. And it was the middle of the night. Could he not see the danger?

"Look, Nicole," Michael's voice interrupted her train of thought, "I've got to do this."

"Well, I don't," Nicole retorted.

Michael took one look at the stubborn set of his wife's chin and shook his head sadly.

18

Michael was fearless, and being fearless, he simply did not understand how anyone, particularly someone as close to him as his wife, could pass up the opportunity to explore an ancient Mayan temple in the middle of the night.

Fear of heights? There was no such thing! It was made up to keep kids from climbing tall trees. His parents had tried to convince him that heights were dangerous, but it hadn't worked. He had climbed all the trees in the neighborhood, anyway.

Why could Nicole not understand how important this was to him? It was, truly, a once-in-a-lifetime opportunity. It had taken him eons to get permission from the government, and then several more months to find a guide who would agree to take him.

"I thought you'd want to help," Michael said wistfully.

Hearing the sadness in her husband's voice, Nicole snuck a quick peek at his face. The disappointment she saw there nearly broke her heart. As her face crumbled and tears began to flow, she turned her back so Michael wouldn't see that she was frantically searching her backpack for a tissue to mop up the sodden mess that was her face.

It was at that moment that Walter, the middle-aged, Belizean guide who had succumbed to Michael's pleading and bribery, gingerly stuck his head through the bushes. After suffering through more than a mile of constant bickering between the young couple, he was determined to do everything in his power to remain out of earshot if there were any further confrontations.

Not hearing raised voices, Walter slipped through the overgrown bushes and joined the couple. He was ready for a break. And quiet time. But when he placed his pack near Michael's, the tension in the air warned him that the war between the young couple had not ended.

The two men silently watched the tearful woman search her backpack until Michael broke the silence.

"What are you looking for?" he asked, disappointment making his voice gruffer than intended.

"Tissue."

"Nicole, you're stronger than you think," Michael scolded, as he rolled his eyes. "Certainly, stronger than your fear!"

Nicole found one of the elusive tissues and blew her nose loudly as she huffed across the clearing away from her pigheaded husband. She took one quick look back at him, then plopped down on a large, carved stone. All the while she was careful to keep her ramrod-straight back to the man she had married, a few short days ago.

"C'mon," Michael moaned, frustrated by Nicole's stubbornness, "we can't fight on our honeymoon."

"Wanna bet?"

Michael studied Nicole as she sat stiffly, her back firmly aimed in his direction.

"You're serious, aren't you? You're going to let your silly fear keep you from climbing."

Nicole did an excellent imitation of a statue in the middle of a wilderness. There was no indication she had heard her husband's words.

"Fine," Michael blurted, his frustration turning to anger. "No climb for Nicole."

But after another look at his wife, the anger drained away. Michael ambled over to take a seat beside her.

"C'mon Nicole. Let's make up."

Nicole maintained her statue-like stiffness, so much so that if a pigeon had happened to fly by it would have happily perched on her head.

"Nicole. You know you're not mad at me."

When Nicole still gave no response Michael cautiously wrapped his arms around her stiff shoulders. All he got for his troubles was a shove and a glare.

"Okay, maybe you are mad at me," Michael growled in a burst of anger. "In that case, I'll go alone."

Michael failed to see the glance Nicole sent his way, nor did he notice her shoulders sag in dejection.

But Michael was the sort who rarely stayed angry for long. In less than a minute all anger had dissipated, and he was back to his normal, happy-go-lucky self. This was far from the first argument he and Nicole had had, and it wouldn't be the last. Besides, he loved her dearly and hated the thought he might be causing her more stress than necessary. It would be better if she stayed in the clearing, and he climbed alone.

"I'll be back in a bit," he said decisively. "Walter will stay with you. He'll keep you safe."

"No!" the word shot from Nicole's mouth, as she grabbed her husband's arm. "You need him with you."

"What about you?"

"I'll survive."

Michael grinned pointedly at the claw grip Nicole had on his arm.

"Does this mean we're not fighting anymore?"

Nicole released Michael's arm like it was a hot potato and her hands were made of butter. Then, making a quick decision, she picked up her backpack and placed it gently beside her husband's.

"If you fall off that temple I'll never, ever, forgive you," she whispered, gazing deep into her husband's eyes.

"He's safe," a voice a few feet away declared.

The voice belonged to Walter, their intrepid guide, who Nicole had totally forgotten about. She tore her eyes away from her husband's face and turned to the guide.

"The Stone Woman hasn't been seen in years," he continued.

"Stone Woman? Who's she?" Nicole asked, only half interested after being lost in her husband's eyes.

"The ghost of the temple. An ancient Mayan woman who brings death to all who see her."

"When you say ghost—?"

"He means," Michael interrupted, with a loving kiss to Nicole's forehead, "that susceptible tourists are easily fooled."

Maybe it was a reaction to the jungle trek. Or maybe it was because Nicole honestly loved Michael deeply and did not want to be mad at him. But at the touch of his lips on her forehead, the last vestiges of anger melted away and she fell deep into a daydream in which the two of them were buying their first house together. Both would be done with their degrees by that time, and they might even be thinking of starting their family. Together they would—

Nicole smiled dreamily at Michael as she planned their future together. But the look Walter gave Michael was anything but dreamy.

"The ghost is real," Walter insisted firmly, standing as tall as his 5'3" stature would let him.

"Walter, you don't have to put on an act for me." Michael chuckled, slapping the diminutive guide on the back. "I'm not one of your tourists."

"It's no act," Walter said flatly. "I lost an uncle to the Stone Woman. She always brings death."

As the word "death" penetrated Nicole's consciousness her goofy, daydream-induced smile slipped off her face. What was the guide saying? Was Michael in danger?

"And just where does this spooky, old ghost show itself?" Michael did his best to hide his disbelief. After all, it was obvious a belief in ghosts was normal in this man's life. It would be rude and unprofessional to show disdain for any part of his culture.

"There. Near the top, on the right side of the temple."

Walter gestured at the temple as he reluctantly dug a camera and two flashlights out of a backpack. After a slight pause, he slid the camera strap over his head and tossed a flashlight to Michael. Then, with a shrug, he continued to dig in the backpack.

"Great," Michael said, with a grin, as he shoved the flashlight he'd just caught into his pocket, "'cause that's just where we're heading!"

Walter froze, then turned to stare at Michael, a strange combination of fear and defiance on his face.

"Come on, Walter!" Michael wheedled gently. "You're not scared, are you?"

Walter paused for a moment, then gathered all three backpacks to carefully stack them in the middle of the clearing.

"Halfway," he whispered, but the word came out garbled, as if it had tumbled over several boulders as it escaped his mouth.

"What?"

Walter cleared his throat and spoke in a loud, clear voice. This was important. He wanted to make sure the American understood.

"I'll take you halfway."

"But you were hired to—"

"I have a family," Walter stated flatly. He raised a shaky hand to halt Michael's words. "I will take you halfway."

Michael, confused by Walter's sudden stubbornness, looked at Nicole, who was busy fidgeting and slapping at the mosquitoes on her legs. Then he looked up toward the top of the temple, the place that held the secrets that could make his career as an archaeologist.

If only he could get there.

"Halfway, huh?" Michael studied the guide as he weighed his options. "Okay then, maybe I should pay you halfway?"

"I guide you to this clearing. I guide you back." Walter walked over to Michael and crossed his arms stubbornly. "I earn my pay."

"The top," Michael countered, and to show he was equally intent on getting his way he stood tall and crossed his arms to match Walter's stance.

"Halfway," Walter said firmly. He took a step closer to Michael, which somehow upped the ante. Now, the two men were so close their elbows were touching.

It was a funny sight, the two men facing off, nose to chest, like mismatched roosters after the same worm. Michael looked very tall and fit next to the short, pudgy guide. He should have easily dominated. But Nicole had little doubt Walter would win this battle. As much as Michael wanted to get to the top of the temple, Walter's fear of the mythical ghost was stronger. Superstition always won. Fear would trump ambition.

After several, painful minutes, Nicole squeezed between the two stubborn men to wrap her arms around Michael. She had to. Michael was stubborn enough to spend the rest of the night fighting this challenge to his authority.

"You know, Michael," Nicole stood on her tiptoes to whisper in Michael's ear. "He has a family. You can't take away his pay."

Nicole's breath tickled Michael's ear. His stiff shoulders relaxed a bit, and when he shifted his eyes away from his opponent, he found that Nicole's eyes were filled with compassion and love.

Suddenly, winning a battle of wills against Walter was not nearly as important as it had been five seconds earlier.

"I wouldn't actually do that," he assured his new wife.

"I know."

"It's the principle of the thing," he explained, wanting her to know he was not a monster. "We hired him to take us to the top."

"I know. But I'm tired, Michael." Nicole rested her head on Michael's chest. "Aren't you tired too?"

Michael looked at the top of Nicole's head, grinned, and wrapped his arms around her.

"Right. Wait right here."

Michael looked over Nicole's head at Walter.

"You'll take me halfway?"

Walter turned his eyes to Nicole with her head resting on Michael's chest. He was old enough and wise enough to recognize this was her way of helping. He sighed. As much as he wanted to avoid running into the ghost, he now felt obligated to stick to the original deal.

Besides, young love was a beautiful thing. He'd always been a sucker for it.

"I'll take you to the top," Walter sighed, "for your wife."

Then, mostly in reaction to the grin on Michael's face, he speared the young man with a glare.

"But only the left side," he declared with finality.

Michael released his wife to slap Walter on the back, happy to have that settled. Then, after giving Nicole a quick kiss, the two men headed off to the left side of the temple.

CHAPTER 2

Nicole stood alone in the clearing as she watched Michael and Walter slip around the left side of the temple and out of sight. She was wondering how she should pass the time until they returned, when a loud rustling in the bushes to the right of the temple startled her.

Her mind was not slow to provide her with a whole slew of visions of what could be making that noise. Jaguars, wild boars, snakes, or even unfriendly beings of the human variety might be waiting just out of sight, to rush out of the jungle and grab her.

Or, and this was quite likely hopeful thinking, it could be Michael. Michael was very fond of jokes, after all.

That was it. It had to be. Michael had run all the way around the temple and planned to jump out of the bushes to scare her. That was so like Michael!

"Michael?"

Nicole had intended for her voice to sound commanding and authoritative, but instead, it came out more like a squeak. If it was Michael hiding in the bushes it wouldn't matter, but if not, well, that was not a sound that was likely to scare away non-husband critters. She grabbed a flashlight from her backpack and shone it toward the bushes, desperately hoping to see her husband's elfish grin shining back at her.

But the flashlight revealed nothing. No mischievous grin, no happy-go-lucky face, no Michael.

"Hey!" Nicole yelled. Fear gave her voice an unexpected strength, so she continued with, "Who's there?"

The bushes rustled ominously.

A cold wave of terror flooded Nicole's bones and instinct took over. She ran to the left side of the temple, as far from the rustling bushes as she could possibly get without leaving the safety of the clearing. She reached out to touch the cool stone of the temple wall and realized she was shaking like a bowl of her mom's favorite gelatin dessert in a bumpy car ride. Turning her back to the temple, she leaned against it for support as she shakily shone her flashlight into the darkness that had recently consumed her husband.

"Michael?" Nicole whispered. The whisper wasn't very loud. Too soft, in fact, to have any chance of being heard by her husband. But it was the best Nicole could do. She was terrified that whoever, or whatever, was hiding in the bushes would hear her call.

"Michael," she whispered again, "I think somebody's here."

When there was no response from her husband Nicole threw caution to the wind and yelled at the top of her lungs.

"Michael! Come back!"

Immediately the bushes directly in front of her began to rustle and sway.

Nicole gulped. The last thing she wanted to do was confront a wild jungle creature or a robber. She was alone. There was no one nearby to help her.

Nicole blinked several times as she realized that something very odd was happening. A wild creature, or even a robber, would have struck by now. What purpose would there be to hide in the bushes, making them shake? It made no sense.

But it did make sense if it was her prankster husband. It was exactly the type of thing he loved to do. He often took pranks one step too far.

Yes, that was it. It was Michael in the bushes after all. Had to be.

"Okay, Michael," Nicole said in her sternest voice, "I get it. You're playing a joke. Good joke. Come out now. I know it's you. I'm not scared."

When there was no response, not even a spooky rustle of the bushes, Nicole's fear returned full force. As much as she wanted this to be Michael, it didn't feel right.

"Michael? Are you there?"

More frightened than she would ever admit, even to herself, Nicole kept her eyes on the bushes as she slowly backed away from the temple. When she finally reached the middle of the clearing, she swung her flashlight around, focusing it on random spots, hoping to catch her jokester husband in its light. She would much rather find that her husband did not know when to end a joke than discover she was being stalked by…well, by whatever it was out there.

"Michael, please tell me this is a joke," she pleaded. "I won't be mad. I promise."

A strong breeze suddenly whipped through the clearing almost knocking Nicole off her feet. She shivered and wrapped her arms around her body. But the shiver was not from cold but from fear.

She was suddenly struck by memories of all the times in the past she had cowered in fear. There had been scary movies she had unwillingly watched with her sisters, amusement park rides her parents had taken her on, and cross-country trips on narrow, mountainous roads and steep curves. She had survived them all. There was no reason to think she would not survive this one moment of terror.

"Okay, whoever you are, you got me," Nicole said infusing her voice with a touch of boredom she did not feel. "I'm scared. You can come out now! Great joke."

Instead of the hoped-for laugh, a loud growl from deep in the jungle paralyzed Nicole for several seconds. Then, forcing her legs to do her will, she jumped back, away from what was most likely a large cat stalking its prey. But instead of springing gracefully away from danger, her foot clipped a backpack and she landed unceremoniously on her rear.

CHAPTER 3

Michael and Walter climbed onto a three-foot-wide ledge near the top of the temple. Walter, leading the way, looked around nervously.

"The glyphs are just up ahead," Walter whispered uneasily.

"Where?" Michael's voice was loud and strong, and the sound of it made Walter visibly cringe.

In answer, Walter pointed a shaky arm to a spot about 20 feet away. "There. Near the corner. That spot," he paused to gulp, "the spot in the deepest shadows."

Michael looked toward where Walter was pointing. Seeing his goal so close he rubbed his hands together eagerly and smiled. Someone who did not know him would be forgiven for mistaking his avaricious look for that of a treasure hunter, rather than an academic.

"I've been waiting for this for a long time! Do you need to lead the way, or can I go first?"

Walter closed his eyes to gather his courage. Then, after sucking in a quick, sharp breath, he opened them and moved his right foot a step forward. A slight grin spread on his face, and he lifted his left foot for a second step. But the foot froze mid-air and would not move forward. The grin fell away as he realized any further steps were impossible. Something inside him absolutely would not let him move even one inch closer.

"Walter?"

Walter slowly placed his foot back on the ledge and took a step away from the deepest shadows. That step made him feel much better, so he took another step, then another. Before he knew it, he was practically standing on Michael's toes. He looked around nervously, and his eyes strayed to the deep darkness further along the ledge that had been their goal.

"Walter? What's wrong?"

Walter looked Michael in the eye and inched around him. Then he took another step away from their goal and sighed in relief.

"Walter?"

"I thought I could do it. I can't."

"Do what?" Michael's forehead crinkled in confusion. They had settled this issue of Walter going with him on the ground. At least he thought they had.

"Face the ghost."

"What ghost?" Michael peered around in all directions, looking for something that in the darkness might look like a human form. All he saw were the stone walls of the temple and darkness. This part of the temple did not even have the glyphs traditionally used by the ancient Mayans. There was nothing visible that Walter could mistake for a ghost.

With another sigh, Walter planted his feet, stood as tall as his diminutive stature would let him, and stuck out his chest.

"I will wait here," he declared with finality. Then he noticed how close to the corner he was and pointed to the corner. "Around the corner. I'll wait around the corner for you."

"Look Walter, I'm paying you to take me to the glyphs, you're supposed to help me—"

Walter raised his hand, palm out, to interrupt.

"I took you to the glyphs," the guide stated firmly. "They are there."

"But you won't come any closer?"

"No."

Michael studied the little man. Walter's arms were crossed tight across his chest and his jaw looked like it was made of steel. Even his lips were pinched together firmly.

Michael had taken several psychology classes early in his educational career before he decided his calling was archaeology. But even if he had not, he would have recognized stubbornness when he saw it.

He had married Nicole, after all. He loved her dearly, but early in their relationship, he had discovered that she liked to have her own way.

It wasn't so much a stubborn streak as she seemed to be made of stubborn. It was a part of her DNA. From the top of her adorable head to the end of her cute, little toes. Stubborn. Every inch of her. Stubborn. He would suggest to her that she change her middle name to Stubborn, except she would stubbornly refuse to make the change. Stubborn. Stubborn, stubborn, stubborn.

Michael smiled to himself as he thought back on the many instances when he had had to overcome Nicole's stubbornness. It had almost stopped them from coming on this trip.

Yet here they were. Exactly where Michael wanted to be.

Funny how often it happened that way.

But luckily, Michael was a reasonable man. Once he made up his mind about something, he persevered until he reached his goal. When he decided to marry Nicole, he had taken the time to study her and figure out how to get around her stubbornness. Now everything was as good as gold.

He sized up Walter. Maybe he had been using the wrong tactics on the guide. If coercion and bribery failed to work, humor and comradery might do the trick. It would certainly hurt nothing to try.

Michael schooled his face into a friendly smile and slapped Walter on the back. A slap on the back from one dude to another was a great, friendly gesture. It symbolized comradery and mutual respect.

"Really?" Michael chortled. He infused his words with a touch of laughter. "You'd let me go on by myself, all because of some legend of a ghost?"

"It's not a legend," Walter declared majestically. He straightened his back until it resembled the flagpole outside the police station. "It's the Stone Lady."

"The Stone Lady?"

Michael could see that Walter was dead serious and tried to make sure it was a smile on his face and not a smirk. This was hard, because to Michael, most things in life were a joke. Particularly anything that had to do with superstition, which he viewed as quaint.

But Walter's body language told Michel that the guide would be offended if he thought his beliefs were being viewed as quaint. Michael needed to rein in his natural skepticism and humor. Or, at the very least, hide them from Walter.

"Yes," Walter said gravely. "To see the Stone Lady is to see death."

"You don't actually believe that!"

"I lost an uncle to the Stone Lady," Walter carefully took another step toward the corner.

"Walter—"

"I will guide you back down when you are ready."

Michael looked at the resolute set of Walter's jaw, then at his shadowy goal.

"I could use your help taking the pictures." Michael hung his head trying to look humble. "Together we could get it done in half the time. I need you."

"Sorry." Walter sounded far from sorry. Instead, he sounded like a man who couldn't care less what Michael wanted or needed. "I have to think of my family. They need me more."

"But Walter, you can't believe all this superstitious nonsense! You've been to college!" Michael blurted. He had not meant for his thoughts to come out as words, but he truly could not understand how an educated man could allow himself to be afraid of shadows.

"Going to college made me more educated," Walter raised his chin high and speared Michael with a challenging glare, "not stupid."

"But—"

"I will be around the corner. I will not leave you. When you're done, I will guide you back down. Take care, the ledge is narrower in some places."

Walter saluted sharply before he slipped around the corner. Michael shrugged. He knew he was beaten. There was nothing for it but to go on alone. He gave a second, little shrug and sauntered alone along the ledge.

"Of all the superstitious nonsense," Michael muttered, but too softly for Walter to hear. It would not do to offend the little man. It was not his fault he had been raised in a culture that promoted a belief in imaginary creatures like ghosts and monsters.

When Michael reached the darkest shadows, he pulled out his flashlight and shone it on the glyphs carved into the stone walls.

"Ah. Here they are."

At the sight of the glyphs, all irritation melted away. Who cared that Nicole refused to be a supportive wife and follow him up the temple? Why should he mind that Walter, his guide, was a weak-minded fool who was afraid of ghosts? All that mattered was archaeology and that he was about to find the proof he needed to back up his dissertation.

He carefully looked over the glyphs. These were very like the ones he wanted, but they weren't them. The ones he wanted…

He spotted a unique group of shadows, unlike any others, on the temple. The stones had been placed in such a way that the light of the moon highlighted certain glyphs, while allowing others to remain in darkness.

"I knew it!" Michael whispered. As much as he wanted to shout for joy, it seemed wrong to make a lot of noise here, in the dark.

He set his backpack carefully on the ledge and searched through it for his camera. Then the fun began. He made sure to use a flash for the first picture, so he could use it as a reference. Then he turned off the flash to preserve the full effect of the moonlight highlighting certain glyphs.

He snapped picture after picture into the shadows, the camera set to its highest pixel level. All the while he was careful not to get between the night sky and the glyphs. And, of course, not to take that long step off the ledge.

"This is it!"

His smile held just a touch of gloating as he thought of his accomplishment.

"This is the stuff that will make me famous. No one else has ever done this."

He changed the setting on his camera. He had more than enough moonlit pictures. Now it was time to turn on the flash and document everything he could about this historic moment.

"No ghost is going to keep me away from the discovery of the century," he muttered.

Maneuvering around the narrow ledge he took more pictures, mostly focusing on the temple wall.

"Ghosts!" Michael scoffed. "Some people will believe anything,"

Michael paused to contemplate the silliness of superstitious people. It was unbelievable that so many allow fear to stop them from reaching their goals.

He snapped a few more shots of the temple wall.

A man like Walter, for example. Walter was on the spot and could have accessed these glyphs whenever he wanted. He could have easily made a name for himself. Yet, he let a local legend scare him away.

"Whoooooo!" Michael smiled as he made the ghostly sound used in every silly paranormal movie he had ever seen. "Watch out, or a ghost might get you!"

He moved in for a close-up of the glyphs. He doubted this opportunity would ever come again. These glyphs were in a restricted part of the temple where foreign archaeologists were rarely allowed.

"I should probably thank the ghost," Michael snickered to himself. "It did keep the other archaeologists away."

With a shrug, he continued to snap pictures. The steady clicks rent the air as Michael aimed and snapped like a fashion photographer hired to photograph an elusive supermodel.

Finally, he had gotten what he wanted. All was well with the world. Sure, he had expected Nicole by his side as he made the discovery of a lifetime.

He could imagine how her face would have looked. He was sure it would have glowed with pride at his accomplishment, and maybe even a touch of awe. He would have been her hero. That would have made his day, to see her look at him like he was the best man in the world and could do no wrong.

Too bad she had that silly fear of heights!

At least Walter had been nearby to see him make history. It was always nice to have an audience when you did something amazing.

Though, if he were being truthful, Walter was a poor substitute for Nicole.

Not that it mattered. Ultimately, he had attained the prize. Maybe it was better that he was alone. No chance he would ever have to share the glory.

"Bad luck for them, good luck for me!" He chuckled gleefully. And by 'them', he meant all the other archaeologists in the world. He honestly would not have minded sharing whatever glory he earned with his wife.

He pulled his thoughts back to the here and now. What more could he do to document this grand discovery? Maybe a few shots of the surrounding countryside in the darkness, in case he needed or wanted them. He flattened his back against the temple wall and began to shoot panoramic style.

"Ghosts! Ooh, I'm so scared," he snickered.

It was a good thing that Walter was too far away to hear. Michael was bursting with pride in his accomplishment, so much so that he had become physically unable to hide the sarcasm in his voice. He twisted around in his perch to get a different angle and continued to snap away.

"Some people are so naive."

Snap, snap, snap.

"I can barely believe it. Walter believes in ghosts?"

He smiled gleefully as he paused to check the shots he'd captured with his digital camera. As he swiped through them, he sometimes whistled, sometimes grunted, and sometimes nodded his head happily. The pictures were exactly what he needed to finish his dissertation. With the data he had gathered here, he could prove—

All thoughts of his dissertation fled as an image on his screen registered.

"Where did that come from? I don't see..."

He looked over the ledge, saw nothing, then moved forward several feet. Still, all he could see were the tops of trees.

"Where was I standing when I took it?"

He studied the screen for seconds, repositioned himself, then again looked over the edge into the darkness.

"Nicole?" Michael whispered in shock.

Gone was his pride of accomplishment. Also gone were his usual sarcasm and humor. The only emotions he could muster were horror, and a fear more powerful than he had ever before felt.

He was in shock, frightened, and unable to make sense of what his eyes showed him.

Because what the picture had captured, and what Michael now saw with his own eyes, was Nicole, in the distance. She was sitting on the ground staring up at a figure five feet in front of her. A figure of a woman all in white.

The woman was translucent and was emitting a soft, eerie glow.

CHAPTER 4

In the clearing, Nicole was sprawled half on the ground and half on a backpack. She probably would have been cowering too, had she not been too busy gawking, open-mouthed, at the translucent figure of a woman who loomed over her.

A crash in the jungle drew her eyes away from the ghost—to Nicole it sounded like a hungry elephant intent on breakfast—and when she looked back at the ghost it was barely in time to see the woman fade completely away.

Nicole scrambled to her feet. She was reasonably sure the elephant crashing through the brush was Michael, and by the sound of it, he would reach the clearing soon. She might as well use the next few seconds to make herself presentable. With a shaky hand, she carefully began to brush dirt from the seat of her pants.

Michael's head and torso exploded through the bushes and he craned his neck to search the clearing. He could see a lot of it, but there was too much greenery in the way to see it all. As he stood there, gasping for breath, an epiphany rocked him to his core. An epiphany about Nicole, and what she meant to him.

At the top of the temple, when he had seen her in danger, every thought left his head but one—he must protect Nicole. He ceased to be an archaeologist intent on making his way in academia. He was Primal Man intent on protecting his mate. His brain had no room for petty trivialities—his camera was attached to a lanyard around his neck, or he probably would have left it behind—he had one purpose in life and that was to protect the woman he loved.

Gone were all thoughts about his dissertation or proving his theory, he only cared about Nicole. Which meant, Nicole was more important to him than archaeology. Michael had always believed archaeology was his life.

It was mind-blowing.

But where was she?

A new surge of panic flooded his veins and his heart raced uncontrollably. He had to find her. He had to find her fast. She could be hurt, or scared, or—

"Nicole!" he bellowed, fear making his voice squeak a bit at the end.

"What?" came back the irritated reply.

It was Nicole, and she was close. Although she didn't sound the least bit frightened, Michael still had an irresistible urge to find and save her. He shoved his torso further past the thick limbs of the bush and looked to his right. Nicole was only a few feet away. The sight of her flooded his body with energy and without a second's hesitation he bulldozed his way through the bush and scooped up his wife. He immediately enfolded her in a huge bear hug, and only then did his heart begin to slow down to a more reasonable rate.

"Are you hurt?" he mumbled into her hair. The poor girl was shaking just like his golden retriever always shook every time a thunderstorm rolled through town.

"Put me down, Michael," Nicole ordered.

Her voice sounded strained. Michael realized he was probably squeezing her a bit too tight, so he gave her one last little squeeze and set her down on her feet.

"Did you see her?" Nicole asked, as her feet touched the ground. "Did you see the ghost?"

"Ghost?" Michael scoffed, his civilized brain reasserting itself. "Right."

Michael had a very clear memory of seeing Nicole in danger, with a figure looming threateningly over her. But his brain refused to accept that the figure had been translucent and had changed it to a solid form.

"Michael!" Nicole was not very happy about Michael's dismissive tone. "It was right in front of me. I saw it."

Now that Nicole was safe and adrenaline was no longer flooding Michael's brain and body, his native humor and skepticism returned. All he could think was that his wife was just so darn cute when she was mad.

"No!" Nicole yelled, as she noticed the condescending grin on Michael's face. She took a step away from him and lifted her chin. "I saw a ghost. It was right here. It *was* a ghost!"

Michael chuckled good-naturedly and shook his head.

"They certainly fooled you, didn't they?" Michael expected Nicole to laugh with him and failed to notice her scowl. "Be careful or they'll sell you some authentic artifacts next."

The comment was more than Nicole could handle. She had experienced something strange, and scary. She wanted to share it with her husband.

But all he wanted to do was make fun of her.

With a glare supreme, she snatched up her backpack and moved it several feet away from Michael's backpack.

"Nicole!" Michael moaned.

CHAPTER 5

The hike back to the hotel was long and awkwardly quiet. Nicole not only refused to say even a single word to Michael, but she kept her face pointed rigidly away from him as well.

Normally Nicole's coldness would have worried Michael. But he decided not to worry about it because all that mattered was that she was safe. He could turn all his brain power where it belonged, on those wonderful moonlit glyphs at the top of that temple.

Nicole would eventually forgive him for not believing she had seen a ghost. She always forgave him.

Once in their room, the young couple took silent turns washing off the dirt of the jungle before plopping down in a couple of armchairs. Since ignoring Michael's existence was having no effect on him, Nicole decided to change tactics and use him for eye-dagger, target practice, instead. That's when she discovered he had drifted off to sleep and was snoring softly.

The new wife was not sure what she should do. She was far from ready to let her husband off the hook for not believing in her. Especially since he had laughed at her, actually laughed, as if she had been telling a joke.

It made her worry about their future together. What kind of marriage would they have if he dismissed everything she said as a joke? It seemed to Nicole that Michael had reacted more like an adult to a child than a husband to a wife. Not good. Not good at all. This was something that needed to be fixed. Pronto.

Nicole practiced throwing her eye darts for several more minutes, but eye darts are useless when the target is asleep. Frustrated, she sprang to her feet to pace. Step, step, turn. Step, step, turn.

The room was a small one and the pathway she could pace was rather restricted. A couple of steps in each direction pretty much covered it.

After several minutes of taking the same few steps back and forth, Nicole decided to take it up a notch by stomping. This silent pacing was somehow less than satisfactory. Unfortunately, bare feet on a carpeted floor don't make very much sound. This was turning into an epic fail.

Nicole paused to stare at her sleeping husband. In no way was it fair for him to sleep while she was forced to fume in silence. He had caused her stress, he needed to be a part of her reaction to it. But how…?

"Got it!" Nicole muttered, as she rearranged her path so that she would 'accidentally' bump into Michael's chair.

"What?" Michael moaned groggily, as Nicole's body slamming into his chair jarred him awake.

Nicole plopped into her armchair, eye darts engaged, arms folded angrily across her chest.

"Come on, Nicole," Michael groaned, as his eyes focused on his wife. He was exhausted, but through his exhaustion, he could see that Nicole wanted to talk about the incident in the clearing. "It was just a woman in a costume."

"I could see through her. And she glowed, Michael." Nicole's jaw jutted out stubbornly. "GLOWED!"

"Fluorescent paint," Michael muttered, with a dismissive flap of his hand. Then he made a rookie-husband move that was most likely the worst thing he could have done. He drifted off to sleep in the middle of what his wife considered an important argument.

As Michael's gentle snores filled the room, Nicole's level of frustration skyrocketed. How dare he fall asleep while they were talking!

Here she was, stuck in a hotel room in an unfamiliar country, in the middle of the night, with a husband who was too ignorant to know that he should believe his wife.

Nicole stayed in the chair for several more moments, silently fuming. Then she hopped out of her chair and stomped over to her suitcase. She dug through her suitcase, making as much noise as possible, until she found her laptop, then she slammed the suitcase closed and slapped the laptop onto a nearby table.

But instead of waking so Nicole could talk to him further about what was bothering her, Michael yawned and snuggled deeper into his chair.

With a loud, long sigh, Nicole opened her laptop and began a few random internet searches. She pounded the keys with as much force as she dared, her eyes darting to

Michael every few seconds to see if it had any effect. But it was to no avail. Michael was truly exhausted. He slept on.

After several, long minutes of these frustrating tactics, Nicole realized she was frankly too tired to be on the computer. With another loud sigh, she let her hands fall to her side as she studied her husband. How was she going to make him believe her? How could she make him understand she had been face-to-face with a real live ghost? Or, at least, a real dead one?

Suddenly she could hear the tick, tick, tick of a nearby clock. Tick. Tick. Tick.

It got louder, and louder, until it filled her brain, and she could no longer think. Frustrated she did something she had not done since she broke her foot in seventh grade. She kicked the leg of the table with every ounce of her strength.

Michael snorted awake, wiped his mouth, and stretched. Nicole straightened as she watched him hopefully. All she had to do was wait for the first sign of true consciousness, and she could open a dialog to straighten out their misunderstanding.

And then, she too could rest. She had always heard it was bad for a marriage to go to bed angry. Nicole was very, very angry.

But Michael's eyes stayed closed as he yawned, stretched his arms over his head, and stumbled to the bed to fall into it.

"Love you, my good wife. Night!" he called sleepily. Then he clicked off the bedside lamp.

His snores filled the room almost immediately.

Tears formed in Nicole's eyes. Even asleep, Michael had taken the time to use his pet phrase and tell her he loved her. Maybe their marriage was not over after all.

She tiptoed over to the bed to gaze down at her softly snoring husband. He looked so peaceful, so sweet. Her heart did a flip flop as love gushed from it into her veins, displacing even the tiniest molecule of anger. She loved Michael too much to stay mad at him. He was her soulmate.

With a sigh, she tiptoed to her side of the bed and climbed and snuggled contentedly next to her husband.

Michael was right. This was a time for sleep. Ghosts could wait for another day.

CHAPTER 6

At a time when the ancient temples of the Mayan were new and shiny, a tall and beautiful woman sat in regal splendor. Her seat of choice was a white throne that had been built halfway up the main temple, and she loved the way the brilliant white made it stand out from the deep red of the temple stones.

Her name was Ix Tzutz Nik. At the age of 32, she was the youngest woman to rule a Mayan city. Ever.

Torchlight frolicked on her smiling face as warriors performed the complicated ritual dance around a bonfire in the public area adjacent to the temple. Behind her stood a handsome man in his late 30s. At her side were three, small children, five and six-year-old boys and a two-year-old girl. It was very much a party atmosphere.

Drums and laughter filled the air as Ix Tzutz Nik enjoyed the performance. Then, noticing that her youngest son had begun to fidget, she smiled mischievously.

Reaching over, she tickled the two boys. That this was a game they had played many times was obvious by the way they laughed and scrambled behind the throne to escape their mother's wiggling fingers. Having entertained her sons, she then snatched up the little girl and hugged her tight. The toddler smiled up at her mother, then snuggled into a comfortable position so she could close her eyes in sleep.

Ix Tzutz Nik smiled lovingly at her daughter. The man behind her, her husband of more than ten years, stepped forward to place a hand on her shoulder. She had just smiled up at him when a change in the tempo of the drumbeats pulled her attention back to the cavorting warriors.

The two boys peeked around the throne to see if their mother's tickling fingers were no longer wiggling. Ix Tzutz saw them, then nodded to her hands to show they were being used to keep the girl from falling out of her lap, then nodded again, this time at the arms of the throne.

The boys immediately scrambled onto the throne to sit beside her, one on each side. Ix Tzutz Nik smiled contentedly.

Life was good. Things were going well in her city, and even better with her family.

The dazzling jade necklace she wore around her neck glittered merrily in the firelight.

CHAPTER 7

Sunlight poured through the open curtains of the hotel room that was serving as a home away from home for Nicole and Michael. The night before had been fraught with tension, but all that had deserted the young couple by morning. The healing power of time, and a good night's sleep, had worked its magic.

Michael smiled mischievously as he retrieved a jade necklace from his backpack. Intrigued, Nicole noticed that the trinket had an interesting patina of age. If she had not known it was impossible, she might have mistaken it as a valuable artifact old enough to have been worn by an ancient queen of the Mayans. But procuring antiquities for personal use was not Michael's style. He was all about museums, research, and doing the right thing.

Besides, there had been very few queens in the male-dominated culture of the Maya. At best, the necklace was a replica of a gift given by a high-ranking official to his wife. Maybe to make up for some silly argument they had had.

Sunlight from the window struck the necklace and for a moment it looked new. Nicole gasped in awe at its sudden beauty. At that moment, more than anything else, Nicole had a craving to wear that piece of jewelry.

Michael saw the spark in her eyes and hurried to place the necklace around her neck. The clasp was a little tricky, and it took him several moments before he managed to secure it properly. Then he kissed his wife's shoulder, which brought a smile to her face.

It's beautiful!" Nicole whispered, as she turned to wrap her arms around her husband's waist. "Where'd you get it?"

"A vendor. Outside the temple." Nicole could hear the uncharacteristic shyness in his voice. "Thought you'd like it."

Her heart did a little flip at that small sign of vulnerability. It made her love Michael even more.

But she couldn't let him off that easily.

"Did they tell you it was an authentic artifact?" she asked, and her tone was that of a strict teacher to a naughty student.

"Ha!" Michael grimaced at the thought. "As soon as the guy heard I was an archaeologist he bent over backwards to assure me that it is NOT authentic."

"Then I love it!" Nicole blurted. Although it would have been fun to tease Michael further, she loved the necklace. Why pretend any different?

"Forgive me?"

There was that touch of vulnerability again. Nicole sighed as she pulled away enough to lock eyes with her husband.

"Believe me?"

"If you say you saw a ghost, then it was a ghost you saw."

The response was everything Nicole could want. She wrapped her arms around Michael's neck and planted a firm kiss on his cheek.

"Thank you!"

"For the necklace?"

"Yes, for the necklace."

Nicole giggled as she took several minutes to cover Michael's face with kisses, then she pulled back to lock eyes with Michael.

"But more for believing in me."

She rounded out the avalanche of kisses with a big, exuberant one on Michael's mouth.

"With a little training," Nicole teased, "you might just turn out to be a good husband after all!"

Michael rolled his eyes and tickled Nicole until she could barely breathe. The shadow of a person walking by the window caught his attention and brought him back to matters at hand.

"What time is it?"

"Almost seven."

"We'd better hurry. I want breakfast before the guide arrives. I'm starving!"

Michael gave Nicole one more final tickle, for good luck, and turned to his suitcase to dig through it for some clothes. Nicole, for her part, skipped over to the closet, where she had hung her clothes, to pick out her outfit for the day.

"Do you mind if I watch the news?"

"Go ahead," Nicole la, with a shrug. She pulled out a shirt and held it up to herself as she looked in the mirror. "Won't bother me."

Michael tossed a pile of clothes on the bed and switched on the big, flat-screen TV attached to the wall. He flipped through a few channels until he found the local news.

"Ah, great! I want to see what the weather will be like today. We've got a long hike ahead of us." He tossed the words to Nicole, but she failed to catch them. She was caught up in a conundrum. Hiking was hard work, and she wanted to be as comfortable as possible. But she also wanted to look good at the end of the hike, when she would have sweat pouring from every pore and bugs, twigs, and dirt in her hair.

What she wore today was an important choice. It was, after all, a honeymoon. The fond memories of these few weeks would help the new couple through any tough times they encountered in their future together. Nicole was determined that when Michael flipped through his memories of this trip, the pictures in his head would have her stylish and pretty. Not dirty and sweaty.

It was imperative she pick out the perfect outfit. Her future married life depended on it.

No pressure. No pressure at all!

Michael, unaware of the crucial wardrobe choices happening on the other side of the room, kept one eye planted firmly on the screen even while he dragged the first shirt and pair of jeans he found onto his body. When

the words BREAKING NEWS flashed across the screen
Michael did not hesitate to hop onto the edge of the bed
to watch whatever exciting events would unfold on the
screen. To save time, he was rather hungry and was
looking forward to breakfast, he continued putting on
his shoes and boots as he watched.

He had put on both socks and one boot and was in the
process of putting on the second boot, when he froze,
mesmerized by the scene playing out on the screen.

"Do you think I should bring a jacket?" Nicole asked,
as she tossed a lightweight sweater onto the bed.

She turned away to grab a few more selections from
the closet, so it was several moments before she realized
that Michael had not responded. Instead, he was sitting
perfectly still, oblivious to her presence, gaping at the
television screen.

"Michael!"

She thought her raised voice would get his attention.
When that failed, she marched the short distance to the
bed to stand beside the irritating man.

Was ignoring her becoming a habit?

She leaned in close and used her breathy voice in his
ear, the one that Michael said tickled.

"Do you think we'll still be out after dark?"

Nothing. It was as if he could not see, hear, or feel the
tickle of her breath on his ear.

She studied her husband's face. Gone was his normal
happy-go-lucky smile. In its place was a look of shock.
Pure shock.

Whatever was on that screen had caused that shock.
Almost against her will, she slowly turned to look at the
TV screen. What she saw there made her plop down on

the bed beside Michael, every bit as shocked as her husband.

Because on the screen, in full jungle color, were hordes of police. And those police were milling around a temple. The same temple Nicole and Michael had visited the night before. Two men, in baby-blue jumpsuits, wheeled a covered body on a gurney to a van and placed it inside.

Nicole watched avidly as the camera cut to a newsroom where an anchor, a beautiful woman in her thirties, said in her melodic voice, "Authorities believe the murder occurred between the hours of 10 p.m. and 3 a.m. last night. As yet they have no suspect in custody, but a local guide has come forward with information about a tourist who paid to visit the site after hours."

They split the screen to show the anchor on the left, while on the right was the temple clearing, where Walter, their guide, stood with a reporter. He was not the same calm Walter who had spent the day tromping through the jungle with the young couple, but a nervous man who did not seem sure he was where he wanted to be.

"Tell us what you've found, Mario," the anchor requested, and the split screen went away, leaving all the focus on Mario the reporter at the clearing.

Mario flashed his pearly whites at the camera like he was the star of a toothpaste commercial. He held that pose for several seconds, then turned to Walter, who was standing beside him. The temple, which was crawling with police, formed the backdrop for the interview.

"You were here," the reporter prompted into the microphone, "on the scene of this horrendous murder last night?"

Mario shoved the microphone in Walter's face, but Walter failed to notice. He was hypnotized by the camera and could only stare straight into the lens. Mario waited several seconds, in case Walter needed a little thinking time, then rephrased the question.

"Were you here, last night?" the reporter asked again. But this time he gave Walter a little nudge with an elbow to the ribs.

The pain was enough to break the hypnotic fascination of the network camera. Walter transferred his gaze to the microphone.

"Yes," Walter stated flatly to the microphone. "Yes, I was."

Walter's lips snuggled in dangerously close to the microphone. With an extreme patience only found in seasoned, on-the-spot veterans, Mario held back a well-deserved eye roll while repositioning the microphone out of harm's way. It was not the first time an interview had resulted in spit-soaked equipment. It was amazing how many people thought they needed to eat a microphone to make it work.

"Tell me what you saw," the veteran reporter calmly continued, knowing that if he could get the witness talking all the gory details would be revealed. He had yet to meet a witness who could resist the temptation of instant fame.

"Nothing," came the unexpected reply, "I saw nothing."

Mario blinked several times as he processed this bombshell. He had been told he was to interview an eyewitness who could give juicy details, not some goof, off the street, with no information and even less camera savvy.

With an internal sigh, Mario continued. He was a professional and would do what all professionals did. Keep going and make the best of things.

"You contacted the police," slogged on the intrepid reporter, "when you heard that Dr. Morgan, the archaeologist, had been killed."

Walter nodded, as if nodding to a waiting microphone was the preferred method of communication. The reporter's eyes jumped skyward for an eye roll, but he managed to regain control in time and turned it into a long blink. With a tiniest of sighs, he continued with the oh-so-painful interview.

"What made you go to the police with your story?"

Though he expected nothing to come of it, as a reporter he felt obligated to ask the question. He was on air, and he needed to give the watchers something to watch. Not that it would be easy, he had interviewed bumbling idiots like this before. They were so caught up in getting their few seconds of fame that they became a bundle of nerves who could barely put two cohesive words together.

While he waited for the witness to dredge up a few words, he allowed his thoughts to skip ahead to when could head back to the station and get a cup of coffee. Then he would have a long, hard talk with the new guy at the information desk who had given him the tip about this story.

But first, coffee. He needed coffee. He and his friends had met at a bar the night before. After several drinks, they had made the unwise decision to—

"Dr. Morgan was my friend."

Walter's words interrupted Mario's thoughts and brought him back to the here and now. That was when the newsman realized the demeanor of the man in front of him had changed. The robot with a dead battery had miraculously been energized. Walter had come to life.

"I will do anything I can to bring his murderer to justice," Walter stated gravely.

The reporter looked at the pain in Walter's eyes. There might be a story worth reporting here after all, if Mario could get the story out of the man without him shutting down again.

"Do you think you know who killed your friend?" Mario was careful to speak calmly and gently. The last thing he wanted to do was spook the man back into silence.

"The American," came the firm reply.

"The American?" the reporter asked in surprise. No one had mentioned anything about an American before.

He straightened his tie and stood tall as he realized the international importance of this interview. This could be his chance. He had never had the opportunity to report on a story with international ties before. It was time to shine.

He cleared his throat and rephrased his question.

"You were saying something about an American?"

"Yes," Walter replied. "I brought the American to the temple last night, after hours. He paid me extra to come after hours."

Walter turned to glare into the camera.

"He claimed to be an archaeologist," he said, and the contempt in his voice was unmistakable.

61

"And you think he killed Dr. Morgan?"

"Yes. Why else would he want to go to the temple so late at night?"

The reporter waited several seconds, hoping Walter would continue. When it became obvious the guide had no more to say, Mario asked the only question he could think of to extend the interview.

"What do you hope will happen?"

"I want the American brought to justice," Walter growled, and he looked fierce as he directed his anger at the camera.

With a smug, little smile—it was always a win when a reporter could elicit strong emotions on camera— Mario snatched the microphone out of Walther's hand and motioned for the camera to bring the focus back on him.

"And there you have it, a tragedy of international importance. The question is, will our police be able to protect our citizens from the foreign invaders who are here to loot our country and terrorize our citizens?" He raised an eyebrow and pasted what he hoped was a thought-provoking expression on his face and held it for several seconds. Then his face split into the toothpaste-commercial grin. "Back to you."

As the camera switched back to the anchors in the newsroom, Nicole turned a shocked face to Michael.

"Isn't that—?" Nicole's words came out more as squeaks than words. She took a deep breath to calm her nerves and began again. "Isn't that Walter?"

"Yeah." Michael nodded his head, but his eyes remained glued to the television screen. He hoped that after the anchors completed their segment on the importance of dental cleanings they would return to Walter and the temple.

"He's saying he took a tourist to the temple last night."

"I know."

"But that was us!" Nicole yelped. She grabbed Michael's face and turned it toward her. "We went to the temple last night. Walter took US!"

"I know," Michael admitted. His voice was calm, but his forehead crinkled the way it did when he was doing a jigsaw puzzle.

"But what does it mean?" Nicole demanded. She held tight to Michael's face. She could feel the muscles tense as his eyes tried to return to the screen, but she was not having any of that. This felt wrong and scary. She needed to understand what had happened. She needed to know how this might affect her and Michael.

Michael fought against the pull of the television as tried to keep his eyes on Nicole's worried face. He knew she was frightened, but if she would just give him time to watch the rest of the news story, maybe, just maybe, he would understand what had happened. Then he could explain it to her.

A tear escaped out of the corner of Nicole's left eye, which brought Michael's attention fully back to his wife. He gently took her hands from his face and held them.

"I'm sure it's all a mistake," he gently assured her. "Walter—"

Before he could get out another word the door burst open. In swarmed an army in full battle gear, armed with rifles, who positioned themselves around the room.

At least, an army was what it seemed like to the young couple. An army deployed to the villain's den, intent on taking down the bad guys.

In this case, Nicole and Michael were the bad guys.

The stench of eight men wearing heavy gear in the hot, Belizean climate nearly brought tears to Nicole's eyes. Or maybe they were tears of fear, she truly could not tell. Because each man was poised to shoot, and each rifle was pointed directly at the young couple.

As petrified as Nicole was—having a battalion of guns pointed at her face was a terrifying first for her—she was more petrified by the possibility she was going to vomit all over the men. Few people reacted well to vomit, but the combination of her nerves and pungent sweat were doing a number on her stomach. Thinking fast she retrieved her hands from Michael and used them to cover her nose.

There sat the young couple, Nicole with her hands over her nose, and Michael blinking at a rifle pointed at his face. It was a snapshot of fear, frozen in time, until Chief Rudy Valente, the man in charge, swaggered into the room.

He was fifty-five, overweight, and carried a chip on his shoulder the size of a car battery. He had more power in town than was good for him, and he hated whatever and whoever he could not control. Most of all, he had a deep, unreasonable hate for Americans.

He paused just inside the doorway to look over the situation and give his badge a quick shine with his sleeve. Then, with a satisfied smirk on his face, he sauntered over to the two young newlyweds perched on the edge of the bed.

"Michael Quinn, you are under arrest for the murder of Dr. Morgan."

Both Nicole and Michael blinked in shock. Murder? He was arresting Michael for murder?

"You are to come with us," the chief continued.

"Michael, what's happening?" Nicole whispered. But since her hands were covering her face, all that could be heard were garbled hisses. She realized this and pulled her hands away from her mouth to grab Michael's arms. She needed comfort, and maybe a little knowledge from her husband.

The police, on their part, must have assumed it signaled an intent to resist, because several of them unceremoniously grabbed Nicole and tossed her to the side, leaving Michael alone on the edge of the bed.

"Hey, we're American citizens—," Michael's attempt to stand was halted by a multitude of rifles shoved closer to his face.

"Quiet!" Chief Valente growled.

"I demand to speak to—," Michael's demand faded away as the rifles moved even nearer.

"I said quiet," Valente barked.

"But—," Michael's third attempt at speech was rewarded by a butt of a rifle to the stomach. As he doubled over in pain, another of the policemen jerked him to his feet while the third pulled his hands behind his back and cuffed him.

Michael threw a glance at Nicole. She had been raised in a protected environment, and other than TV shows, had never been exposed to violence. He could not imagine how she would deal with her world being turned upside down like this. He suspected she would be so shocked her brain would cease to function properly.

Luckily, one of the policemen was standing on the corner of her shirt, and she was busy struggling to free it so she could stand. She had missed the entire rifle butt to the stomach incident.

"What about my wife?" Michael asked quietly.

"What about her?" Chief Valente threw a dismissive glance at Nicole who was still trying, unsuccessfully, to tug her shirt out from under the heavy boot. "We don't want her. We only want the killer. You."

"Look!" Michael gulped. He was doing his best to remain calm, but it was hard to keep his cool with rifles pointed at his face and his hands cuffed behind his back. He took a deep breath, let it out slowly, and started again. "Look, this is a mistake. I've never killed anyone in my life."

"Every murderer I've ever arrested said exactly those words." Chief Valente's sneer increased at this lame attempt to avoid arrest.

"But—"

"Save your breath, or we might have to hurt you."

Chief Valente gave a hand signal. His minions moved as one to close in around Michael and whisk him to the door.

As the heavy boot lifted from the edge of Nicole's shirt she jumped to her feet and brushed away a nasty clump of dirt. Only then did she take the time to look around and take in their current situation.

What she saw shocked her to her core. Michael, cuffed and seemingly in pain, was being marched out the door by armed guards. As the full gravity of the situation sunk in her heart began to beat erratically. She opened and closed her mouth several times as she tried, unsuccessfully, to gain control of herself so she could speak.

Michael caught sight of her ashen face and planted his feet stubbornly. He was determined to speak to his wife before he took another step.

"It'll be okay, Nicole," he said kindly. Then, his mouth snapped closed as he used the last of his willpower to keep from yelping as one of the guards jabbed the cold barrel of a rifle into his ribs.

"Michael," Nicole squeaked, finally making her voice work. "What should I do?"

"Call—"

"No talking," the chief growled. And in case Michael didn't understand that 'no talking' meant 'keep your mouth shut or you're going to be in a lot of pain', several of the police raised the butts of their rifles and aimed them at Michael's soft parts.

Michael looked from the men prepared to use him as a punching bag to Chief Valente's steely gaze.

"Michael?"

Nicole's voice betrayed her fear. But Michael had to ignore that fear and turn away from his wife, toward the door.

"Michael!" Nicole groaned in terror. She took a step toward her husband but two of the policemen immediately stepped sideways to block her. "Please, Michael, you have to tell me! Who do you want me to call? What should I do?"

"Little lady," Chief Valente snorted with disgust at her obvious weakness, "if you want to talk to your husband, you'll have to do it at the station. That's where we let murderers talk to their families before trial."

"No, wait! Michael—"

Chief Valente gave a signal to his men, and they marched Michael through the door. Nicole tried to follow, but it was the chief who stepped sideways to block the doorway.

"Same old story," Chief Valente smirked. "You Americans think we're just a tiny, third-world country so you can do whatever you want."

Before Nicole had time to process the chief's words his smirk turned to a hateful glare. He leaned forward until he was almost nose-to-nose with Nicole. She instinctively took a step back.

"But no one," he continued, venom dripping from each word, "commits murder in my town and gets away with it. Especially not a spoiled American."

With that parting shot, he stepped out of the room and slammed the door. The bang was hard enough to make the shutters rattle.

Alone in the room, Nicole wilted onto the bed.

"Oh, Michael!" she whimpered.

Nicole was alone in a strange country. Her wonderful husband had been snatched away and accused of murder. There was no one to help her. Everyone hated her—

Nicole threw herself across the mattress and sobbed tears of utter despair.

CHAPTER 8

Several days later, Nicole's daily visits to the jail to see Michael had become the norm.

Not normal, of course. It could never be normal for an upstanding, good guy like Michael to be framed for murder and locked up in a Central American jail.

But it was the norm. In an amazingly short amount of time, Nicole had made it so. Every day she showed up at the jail as soon as visiting hours started and stayed until they threw her out. She was now well known at the jail, so much so that they no longer made her sign in, but simply waved her through.

Nicole's goal of a romantic and memorable honeymoon had morphed into a duty to spend as much time with her husband as possible. She could imagine the two of them telling friends about it at a future dinner party. Michael, stoic and brooding, was supported through his trying time by an ever-present Nicole, whose very presence provided much needed emotional support and comfort.

Only...Michael seemed to not want her there. Her first visit to him had been fine, but by the second one a giant, invisible wall had sprung up between the young newlyweds.

It bothered Nicole, but she decided it was most likely caused by a mistaken belief, by Michael, that Nicole needed to be protected from the horrors of jail life.

But Nicole had no intention of letting Michael's misplaced machismo deprive her of a memory-making opportunity. Something had to be done to redeem this honeymoon.

She convinced herself to believe this, until common sense butted in. As the couple sat side by side on Michael's uncomfortable cot inside the uncomfortable cell, holding hands but avoiding each other's eyes, it was glaringly obvious this was not a bonding experience.

The Central American adventure they had planned for their honeymoon had turned into a veritable nightmare with no way to wake up.

When Nicole snuck a quick peek at Michael's face it nearly broke her heart. Michael, her upbeat, jovial, fun-loving husband, looked like a rooster who had fallen off a truck in the middle of a busy highway. All he knew to do was watch for the next car so he could scuttle out of the way.

She knew he had to be scared half out of his mind, and that he was too proud to let her know. It was part of what made Michael, Michael. Since there was exactly zero likelihood she could change this integral part of his nature, the least she could do was cheer him up. No one else was going to do it.

"I'll find someone, Michael!" As she broke the silence she pasted a smile on her face for her husband's benefit, hoping it was a confident one and not a grimace. "I promise."

"What about my parents? Any luck yet?"

Nicole stared at the back of Michael's head as her brain busily translated his garbled words. With his face turned away and his voice barely above a whisper, he was a bit hard to hear.

"No answer," Nicole admitted, when she finally figured out what he had mumbled.

"Your parents?" he asked, this time a bit louder.

Nicole shook her head, momentarily forgetting his face had been stubbornly turned away from her since she had arrived ten minutes earlier.

She wondered which emotion dominated Michael's mind while he was trapped in this jail with the threat of a life sentence hanging over him. Was he more upset, or disappointed? Did fear rule the day, or anger? Did he blame her—?

"Nicole, did you get in touch with your parents?"

It was still a mumble, but at least it was louder this time.

Nicole, caught up in her own thoughts, again shook her head. Then her eyes focused on the back of Michael's head, and she remembered that Michael was refusing to look her way.

"No good," she admitted to him. "I couldn't reach them either."

Without any warning whatsoever Michael sprang from the cot and paced like a tiger in a cage. Nicole had once been to a dinky, little zoo that had later shut down due to lack of funds. The tiger in that zoo had paced exactly like her husband was now pacing.

Nicole caught sight of Michael's eyes when he glanced at her, they were haunted, and in pain, just as the zoo tiger's eyes had been.

That tiger had paced for hours. Michael had less patience than the tiger and grabbed the bars of his cage to shake them with all his might. But no matter how many times he tried to rattle the bars, they stayed firm. He loved to tease Nicole that he was her superhero who would always save the day, but he was being shown that he was just a man. A normal man.

After several moments of testing his strength against steel bars, he finally turned to face his wife, his closed his eyes in anguish.

"Oh, Nicole," he wailed, leaning his head against the bars, "how could anyone think I'm a killer?"

With those words, everything clicked into place and the wall came tumbling down. Of course, Michael was afraid, anyone would be. But he had always been known among the archaeology community as an upstanding guy. That he had been accused of murder devastated his ego. Add to that that the victim was another archaeologist, a colleague of sorts, and the weight of the pain he felt nearly crushed his soul.

"They don't know you," Nicole assured him softly. "We'll get you out. Don't worry."

In the distance, the cellblock door squeaked open, energizing Michael into action. He crammed his face against the bars to see who was walking down the hall. After a few seconds, he hotfooted to Nicole and pulled her to her feet.

"They're coming back to take you out of here," Michael whispered frantically. "Promise me you'll find help. Fast!"

Where Michael's hands touched her hands, Nicole's hands tingled, as if Michael was a live wire sending a current of energy from his hands to hers. It was an odd sensation, one that left her blinking in confusion.

"Nicole, listen to me."

"Of course, I'll get help, Michael, I'm not a total idiot!"

Michael's words had offended, laced as they were with the accusation of failure.

Outrage surged through Nicole, so the eyes she raised to her husband contained no softness, only the hard glare of anger.

What did the man want? She was here, wasn't she? Keeping him company in this disgusting cell most of the day. And when she returned to the hotel, did he not know she spent all her time trying to reach their parents?

It was not her fault neither set of parents would answer their phones. She was doing all she could. Couldn't the man give her credit for trying?

"An idiot, no, I didn't mean that!" Michael softened his voice when he realized he had hurt Nicole's sensitive feelings. "But you have to admit, you're not exactly used to dealing with things like this on your own."

A storm began to brew on Nicole's face.

"Nicole, please!" Michael pleaded. "I don't want to stay in jail for the rest of my life."

That note of pleading was all it took. One look at Michael's distraught face instantly quelled the storm.

"Oh, Michael!" Nicole's anger turned to guilt so quickly she didn't even register the change. "I'll find someone. Don't worry."

All of Michael's stoicism melted into a loving smile as he wrapped his long arms around Nicole. And just like that, the tension that had separated them moments before disappeared. Gone, without a trace.

"Go get 'em, Nikki!"

Michael tickled Nicole's underarm. Nicole giggled in response. Her eyes, which had been shut, flew open, then zoomed to Michael's face. As their eyes locked, it no longer mattered where they were. A dark jail cell with bars between them and the sunshine? Neither of them cared. They were in love, and they were together. All was right with the world.

Michael leaned down to kiss his wife. As his lips touched her lips a loud throat clearing rudely reminded him of his surroundings.

While Michael and Nicole were distracted, two police officers arrived at the door of the cell. There they stood with the door open, impatiently waiting for Nicole to leave.

"I guess you should go," Michael whispered.

Nicole gave a little nod, then wrapped her arms around her husband's neck and looked deep into his eyes.

"I love you, Michael."

The newlyweds remained in that position, eyes locked with arms wrapped around each other, for several minutes. Finally, one policeman got tired of waiting, so he rolled his eyes and firmly tapped Nicole on the shoulder.

Nicole pulled herself out of the depths of her husband's soul and sighed. With a sad shake of her head, she withdrew her arms and blew a kiss to Michael. Then she straightened her back, threw back her shoulders, and stomped through the door.

She had barely cleared the cell door when the policemen slammed the door shut with a loud *clang*. Startled, Nicole shoved her arm through the bars and tried to touch her husband.

"Michael?"

Michael rushed to take her hand.

"It'll be okay," Michael assured her. "Try the Embassy. They should be able to help."

"No, Michael, they're only open during visiting hours!"

"Nicole—"

"My place is here, with you!"

"Nicole, I need you to—"

"I want to be here every moment I can."

"Please, Nicole. I'd rather spend time with you out there," Michael motioned toward the tiny window, "than in here."

Michael's words finally broke through to Nicole. She gave a dismal, little nod as she realized the reasonableness of what he was saying.

"And Nicole," Michael's signature, crooked smile made her heart beat a little faster, "I love you too. More than you know."

Michael released her hand. As Nicole turned to shuffle dejectedly down the passageway a sad smile flitted across her lips. Her entire life she had been protected by family and friends. Never had she handled anything more important than buying a concert ticket by herself.

Now it was time for her to stop being the protected and become the protector.

Michael was stuck in jail. And, based on the snippets of conversations she had overheard while walking through the police department, these people planned to make sure he remained stuck. Forever.

There was no one for her to lean on. If she wanted to save her husband from a life in prison, she had to be the one to get him out of jail. And since she was not very handy at digging tunnels or picking locks, she would have to do it the legal way.

Problem was, she had no clue where to begin.

* * *

The next day, Nicole found herself in a bureaucratic nightmare of an office, perched on an uncomfortable metal chair, surrounded by cheap furniture, staring at the turquoise blue leaves of a fake tree.

Why, Nicole wondered as she reached out a finger to flick a thick layer of dust from a plastic leaf, do people in the tropics feel the need for fake trees? Do they not realize they are practically surrounded by jungle? All they had to do was step a few feet outside of town, and there was all the flora they could possibly want.

Nicole sighed as she tried to find a more comfortable position on the uncomfortable chair. She had slept horribly the night before.

To be honest, she had slept horribly since Michael had been thrown into that nasty jail.

Normally she was a calm, sound sleeper. She would wake up every morning refreshed and ready for whatever the day might bring.

Now, well, now she apparently spent her nights learning the Samba. Every morning she woke to find herself on the floor, wrapped so tightly in her sheets that most museum goers would mistake her for a mummy.

Last night had been the worst night yet. Most nights, lately, she had somehow managed to catch at least a few hours of sleep. Last night she had been plagued with the memory of Michael's dejected face. He had looked more than sad. He looked like he had given up.

No, haunted as she was by her husband's sad face, the night had certainly not been a restful one.

Yet, as dawn broke in the morning sky, she had unwound herself from the sheets and somehow managed to find in her heart a hidden gem of courage. It was what was needed if she were to succeed. It would take everything she had left to march into the embassy and demand a diplomatic key that would release Michael from jail.

When Nicole arrived at the embassy—the beacon of hope to Americans in trouble in foreign countries—she found a woman behind a desk, wearing a badge with the name Maria, who spoke only enough English to tell her to sign in and take a seat.

To say Nicole was disappointed was an understatement. The embassy was far less impressive and a lot seedier than she had expected. But she had nowhere else to turn, so she took a seat and waited.

The next hour was excruciating. Every time her mind wandered in the slightest, she was haunted by the image of Michael's face. And not the normal, happy-go-lucky Michael, either, but Michael as he had been yesterday, depressed and broken.

It brought tears to her eyes every time. Her only recourse was to wage a constant war against her tear ducts. The little imps in charge of opening the flood gates persisted in charging forward, and she had to use every ounce of self-control she possessed to fight them back and keep those gates closed.

To keep her mind occupied she resorted to contemplating strange, philosophical mysteries, like the time-honored question of why human beings in a jungle decorated with fake trees.

After a full hour of being tempted to give up and try again another day, a poorly dressed middle-aged woman in glasses shuffled into the waiting room from the back regions. She checked the sign-in sheet, shot a quick look at Nicole, and exchanged a few words with the receptionist. Her back was turned to the room so Nicole was spared the sigh, as well as the effort it took for the woman to paste a smile on her face.

"Mrs. Quinn?" the older woman asked, as she turned to face the younger woman.

Nicole eagerly rose to shake her outstretched hand.

"Are you the ambassador?" Nicole asked hopefully. She searched the woman's face for a sign that she was there to help.

"No. I'm afraid he's busy today."

The woman bit her lip and her eyes darted around the room as she searched her brain for something further to say.

"But he wanted me to relay to you his sincere concern about your husband."

"Oh."

Nicole's face dropped as she realized that the ambassador, the person most likely to be able to help Michael out of this mess, was too busy with other matters. As if anything could be more important than saving Michael, her wonderful Michael, from a lifetime jail sentence.

As she looked at the ambassador's flunky—the woman continued to beam her fake smile even while condemning Michael to a lifetime in a dank cell—Nicole suddenly realized that relying on the embassy for help was about as productive as relying on a fake tree to grow fruit.

Nicole reached over to a plastic branch and flicked it, sending dust particles shooting through the air. As she watched the dust settle, a flush of anger infused her cheeks. How dare these people try to brush her off like this! The ambassador and his lackeys were put here by the American government, to help Americans in need.

Michael was an American, and desperately needed their help. And they were going to give it, no matter how busy they thought they were.

Nicole straightened her back and turned a resolute face in the direction of the woman in front of her. If she couldn't see the ambassador now, she'd make do with his flunky.

"Fine," Nicole said, sounding much more confident and self-assured than she felt. "I assume you were sent to help me. I want my husband out of jail as quickly as possible."

"Understandable," the woman replied, her smile brightening to a level that surely was meant to mesmerize. "But as diplomats, there is only so much we can do."

"What do you mean?"

Nicole was not exactly sure why, but panic was quickly replacing that hard-won self-assurance.

"I have some information." The woman gently took Nicole by the arm and turned her toward a door. "Information you might find helpful."

"Information?"

"Yes," the woman continued, her voice modulated to the perfect pitch to encourage calmness. "Will you come this way?"

Nicole, at the end of her emotional rope and floundering, followed the woman into a back office.

CHAPTER 9

Later that day a very tired, very discouraged, Nicole visited Michael in his jail cell. As she stood leaning against the bars, her husband slouched on the cot, she noticed that his face had grown an entirely new set of stress lines. He now had so many they had obliterated any sign of his normal, carefree self.

"So, because of the political climate," Nicole continued with the day's update, which had unfortunately been responsible for quite a few of those horrible lines, "all they can do is give us a list of attorneys and wish us luck."

Michael squeezed his eyes tightly closed as he shook his head. Things were not going well. Not well at all.

He stayed that way for several minutes as Nicole looked on with pity. Then, catching sight of Nicole's face, he pulled himself together and put on a reasonably good reproduction of a brave face.

"Can't they do anything else?"

"No," Nicole grimaced. "They said that their hands are tied."

As a plethora of emotions surged through his body — fear, by far, the most abundant—Michael sprang from the cot and began to pace like a caged tiger. He even felt what a caged tiger would feel. Frustrated to be confined in a small space, trapped by walls and bars, and ashamed to have lost hope of eventually being free again.

"This isn't going well," he muttered, just loud enough for Nicole to hear. Then he turned to his wife, and admitted, "I think they plan to keep me here a long, long time."

"Michael!" Nicole gasped as she realized she agreed with him.

But then she also realized it was her responsibility to cheer him up, so she pasted a smile on her face, and said cheerily, "Innocent people don't get locked up. We'll get through this."

Michael continued to pace as if he had not heard her. Worried, she closed the gap between them and put a hand on his arm to try to get him to stop. He did stop, but when he looked at her, instead of the expected smile, there was an unexpected glare.

"Are you sure," Michael glared down at her suspiciously, "you've done everything you can?"

"Of course!" Nicole answered. The question, combined with the glare, made her feel as if she had been slapped in the face.

"Did you speak directly to the ambassador," Michael continued, raising one eyebrow, "or did you let them shove you off on some flunky?"

"I asked for the ambassador," Nicole answered evasively.

"And?" Michael prodded.

"He was too busy," Nicole admitted. "They wouldn't let me talk to him."

Michael jerked his arm away from Nicole's hand and restarted his pacing. As he made the fourth turn past her, he paused to scowl down at her as his frustrations came tumbling out.

"I don't understand you, Nicole!" he growled. "Don't you realize that this is my life that's at stake here? How can you let them do that?"

Nicole stiffened at the criticism.

"If our positions were reversed, I'd be walking on water to get you free. No one could stop me."

The pacing recommenced, but this time, slower. As if he were that same tiger, but old. Old and tired and devoid of any hope for freedom.

"You should make them let you talk to the ambassador," Michael suggested half-heartedly. "Make them listen."

Then, as he threw a look of anger Nicole's way, the young tiger returned.

"I'd do it if you were stuck in here," he muttered. "I wouldn't stop until you were free. I wouldn't let them palm me off on some underling."

"Look, Michael," Nicole began, but Michael ignored her as he continued to pace. Now it was her turn to be frustrated. She grabbed his arm to force him to stop. They stood, stiffly, face-to-face.

"Michael, I—"

Michael jerked his arm away, which angered Nicole.

"I'm doing the best I can!" she yelled, and now her glare matched his. "It wasn't my idea to climb that stupid temple in the middle of the night!"

Now, it was Michael's turn to feel like he had been slapped.

"Are you blaming me for this?" he gasped, taking a step back in shock.

"Why not? You're trying to blame me!"

The hurt on Michael's face jolted Nicole out of her snit. Without a further thought, she threw her arms around her husband and squeezed for all she was worth. He was stiff and tense, it was like hugging a statue.

"I'm sorry, Michael," Nicole cooed softly, "it's just I'm scared."

Those simple words were all it took to demolish Michael's anger and allow his protective nature to reassert itself. For the moment, at least.

"Me too," he whispered, as he wrapped his arms around his wife. "But we'll get through this together."

"That's just it," Nicole shot back. "You're stuck in here. I have to do it alone."

Michael squeezed Nicole tight before kissing her gently on the forehead.

* * *

The next day found Nicole stepping even further out of her comfort zone. Because on this day, she was determined to hit the pavement until she found a lawyer for Michael.

She quickly discovered that pavement was a luxury the town could not afford. As soon as she left the one street that housed the shops catering to tourists, the streets turned to dirt, with no sidewalks. Even worse, the street with all the lawyers was a depressing place lined with old, worn, and dilapidated buildings.

Luckily, for some reason unknown to Nicole, every third building or so had a door painted with a bright and cheery color. Those doors were the saving grace of the street and livened the place up a bit.

Still, Nicole found herself cringing as she walked down the dusty street. Her first look at the ground showed her this was not the clean dirt found in a grassy field or a dirt road in the country. No. This was dirty dirt. The kind of dirt only found in cities or towns where humans couldn't care less about hygiene.

In her hand, she held a piece of paper which she checked often. The night before she had compiled a list of every lawyer in the town. Today, she planned to go down the list and talk to each of them until she found a lawyer who would help her husband.

But the first step was to find them. It was amazing how poorly some of these buildings were marked. She paused in front of a building with a bright red door, rechecked the paper, squared her shoulders, and entered.

Almost immediately she exited the building and shivered, as if to shake off a bad memory.

She looked again at the paper, studied it for several seconds, then looked up and down the street. After a slight pause, she headed for the next building. Standing in front of it she rechecked the address, licked her lips, and entered.

Again, she returned to the street almost immediately, only this time there was no shiver because the disgust she felt was directed at herself. Just inside the door was a plaque proudly proclaiming the presence of a lawyer in office 102. But instead of heading to 102, she had hightailed it outside.

She was a chicken. She might as well admit it to herself.

But she would not admit it to Michael. And there would be no need to admit it to her husband if she simply marched back in there and talked to that lawyer.

If he could not, or would not, help her, she would talk to another one.

"I can do this," Nicole muttered. "I have to, for Michael."

She took a deep breath, turned to face the rickety building, straightened her shoulders, lifted her chin, and pasted a smile on her face.

"Well, here goes nothing!"

After taking another deep breath, the intrepid young woman entered the building, intent on letting nothing, even her own fear, keep her from finding the help her husband needed.

* * *

Later that day, while catching the last thirty minutes of visiting hours with Michael, she found him in a strange mood. He was beyond bored, beyond worried, and beyond restless. He had spent too much time focusing on his situation, and the frustration had built up to a dangerous level. He appeared ready to turn himself into a rocket and shoot through the roof if he did not get out of that cell soon.

They sat facing each other on the lumpy cot that had seen better days. Trying to be as honest as possible, she only left out how long it had taken her to walk into that first office. As Nicole patiently explained what she had done during the day she expected to be rewarded with a smile of appreciation for her efforts. Instead, Michael was less than impressed.

"Did you talk to every lawyer?" Michael asked, after she told him about a lawyer who had suggested she skip town and leave Michael to fend for himself.

"Nearly all," Nicole answered. She snuck a peek down the passageway. It was unclear, even to herself, if she feared interruption or was in hope of a rescue.

"Nearly?" Michael sneered, clearly unhappy with her response. "Tell the truth, how many lawyers did you actually talk to?"

Nicole jumped to her feet. When Michael was angry his chin was much too firm for her taste. Standing she could look down at him rather than up, which would give her a better angle. She turned to her husband.

"I visited almost half. Some of them were in a scary part of town. And I mean scary."

Michael, too, jumped to his feet, thwarting Nicole's plan to avoid his stern chin.

"Nicole," Michael's agitation made his voice harsh and judgmental, "you can't be such a chicken!"

"Such a chicken!"

"Yes. Chicken. You must keep trying. Go to every single one if you have to. Even if the lawyer is in a scary place."

Nicole took a close look at his face and stepped back a step. She would have stepped back two steps, but the bars were inconveniently in her way.

"Are you blaming me again?"

As if by magic, all of Michael's irritation drained away. In an instance, his innate goodwill shattered the wall of tension that had built up between the young couple and his Puck-like smile regained its rightful place. He grabbed Nicole and gave her a huge hug. It felt to Nicole that he was trying to squeeze every last drop of worry out of her.

"Not on your life, Nikki! You're a good wife, you'll find a way to get me out of this, this..."

Nicole reached up a hand and gently clipped his chin with her fist.

"This less than stellar honeymoon accommodation?"

Michael roared with laughter as Nicole snuggled comfortably in his arms.

* * *

The next day Nicole returned to her search with renewed energy. If Michael could laugh while locked up in that dungeon, she could overcome her chicken-hearted tendencies and find him a lawyer.

As Nicole walked down the sunbaked street lined with offices, she stopped every so often to check her list. She was looking for lawyers she had skipped the day before because they looked too sketchy. Today, she vowed to leave no door un-knocked, and no plea unsaid.

A particularly vibrant, turquoise door drew her eyes, and she checked her list. Yep, she had skipped this one the day before. She remembered that as she had approached the door several shady-looking men had exited, and instead of leaving, they had hung around the entrance smoking and chatting. She had been too intimidated to push her way through the group, so had scurried away in fear instead.

Today there was no group of disreputable-looking men. She would have forced herself to plow through them if they had been there, but it was easier when the way was clear. All Nicole had to do was straighten her shoulders, pull open that vulgar door, and sashay her way inside.

Nicole was not in the least surprised to find that the seediness of the office inside perfectly matched the tone set by the lounging men of the day before. Minus the smoking, thankfully.

A secretary, who had never heard of an iron, sat at a wooden desk pecking away at an old, manual typewriter. One lonely letter at a time. Peck...peck...peck.

It would take a full year to type a contract or a will, she typed so slow. And by the way she squinted, Nicole was sure the woman was in dire need of glasses.

The glasses theory was proved correct by the length of time it took for the woman to notice Nicole's presence. After she stood just inside the doorway for several seconds, waiting for the woman to notice her, Nicole finally realized she needed to move closer. She took several steps into the room, then several more. Finally, she had taken so many steps that she was directly in front of the desk.

But the woman still had no clue that she was no longer alone.

Frustrated, Nicole cleared her throat. Loudly.

The woman barely acknowledged her. She merely glanced at Nicole and continued her slow-paced typing.

Nicole cleared her throat even louder and was rewarded with a will-no-one-leave-me-alone type of sigh from the secretary.

"Yes?"

"I would like to talk to Mr. Soto?"

The secretary looked Nicole up and down, clearly unfazed by the statement that ended like a question.

"You have business?"

"Business?"

The secretary looked pointedly at the wedding ring on Nicole's finger, a nasty smile blossoming on her face.

"You need a lawyer," she said, with a nod. "Is your husband, yes?"

"Yes! You see my husband —"

The secretary threw up her palm to stem the flow of any further words.

"Wait here please," she said.

Opening a door located next to the bookshelf, the secretary poked her head through and quietly spoke to someone out of sight. That person turned out to be Mr. Soto, and Mr. Soto was hungry for a new client. So much so that the greasy-haired, middle-aged man in a cheap suit bulldozed his secretary out of the way as he rushed into the waiting room, hand extended.

Nicole was taken aback when he grabbed her hand. And her heart began to beat a bit faster with fear as his hands tightened in a vise-like grip around her hands. She tugged a few times, and nearly panicked when she realized he had no intention of letting her go until he was good and ready.

The secretary, used to being shoved out of the way, sneered once in Nicole's direction before she escaped into the back office, leaving Nicole alone with Mr. Soto.

"Welcome!" Mr. Soto yelled. Then in a slightly lower voice, "How can I be of help?"

"I'm looking for a lawyer," Nicole gulped. She could do this. She knew she could do this. "You see my husband—"

"Yes. I understand," Mr. Soto smirked. "Sometimes husbands do tend to stray a bit."

Nicole opened her mouth to explain that her problem was quite different, but before she could continue Mr. Soto jumped in.

"I agree, at your age, it is best to make a clean break and start over."

"But—"

"Now, now," Mr. Soto squeezed Nicole's hands so hard she could feel her fingers knotting like pretzels. She tried to pull them away, but Mr. Soto's grip was too tight. "There are things you need to know about getting a divorce in Belize. You are American, right?"

"Yes, but—"

"Fees for Americans are a bit higher, more paperwork to do." Nicole could practically see dollar signs glowing in Mr. Soto's eyes as he said this. "But I'm sure you'll have no problem with them. A little money can solve any problem."

Mr. Soto let go of Nicole's hands and grabbed her elbows. She looked down at them for a split second, and when she looked up again, she realized the greed in the lawyer's eyes had been replaced by lechery. Nicole froze in horror.

"And if you don't have the money," Mr. Soto leaned in to whisper in Nicole's ear, "I think we could work something out."

Nicole's eyes widened in horror as his hand slowly moved up her arm. Panicked, she gathered her courage and jerked her arm away.

"I am not looking for a divorce!" Nicole yelped. She stepped away from Mr. Soto and therefore danger. "I want a lawyer who will get my husband out of jail."

"I see. Well, I could do that, too."

Mr. Soto took a step in Nicole's direction and lifted his hand toward her until he was struck with a thought.

"What's the charge?" he asked, as he speared Nicole with a serious look.

"Murder," Nicole answered. "You see, there was this archaeologist who was killed—"

"Stop!" Mr. Soto bellowed. He raised his hand and scuttled to the other side of the desk. "Your husband's name?"

"Michael," Nicole answered, relieved, yet confused, by Mr. Soto's sudden need for distance. "Michael Quinn. We came her for—"

"It was nice meeting you, Mrs. Quinn," Mr. Soto scuttled to the door and jerked it open. "But I can't help you."

Nicole blinked several times, surprised by the abrupt change in tactics.

"Good day," Mr. Soto said pointedly.

"But I don't understand," Nicole stammered. "Why can't you help?"

"It's not possible."

"Please!" Frustration caused tears to form in Nicole's eyes, and she feared one more set-back would cause a flood. "I've visited every lawyer I could find, and not one will even think about taking our case."

Mr. Soto kept his eyes averted from Nicole's face as he continued to point out the door.

"At least tell me what's going on."

Mr. Soto was not a good guy, but he wasn't a bad one either. He had just gotten into the bad habit of taking advantage of anything, and anyone, he could.

So, when he made the mistake of looking into Nicole's pleading eyes his cold, greedy heart melted a bit. He sighed, shrugged, then moved to the door to poke his head out and look around. When he saw that no one was outside, he shut the door and turned to Nicole. But this time, instead of lechery or greed, there was actual humanity shining out of his eyes.

"My advice to you is to get an American lawyer." He shook his head at the sadness of it all. "One that has no ties to Belize."

"But why?" Nicole asked. "Shouldn't—"

"That's all I have to say." Mr. Soto looked quickly toward the door, as if he expected someone to burst through at any moment. "Just know that no Belizean lawyer will help you."

"But—"

"Go," Mr. Soto interrupted. "Your business here is done."

Nicole examined his face and realized that the glimmer of humanity she had seen was now gone. It was time for her to leave.

"Have a nice day, Mrs. Quinn."

Mr. Soto opened the door once again and motioned for Nicole to leave.

Which is exactly what Nicole did. Without any further look or word, she left.

CHAPTER 10

"None of the attorneys will take my case?"

It was a frustrated Michael who slammed a fist against the bars, hard. Then, immediately after the slam, it was a pained Michael who howled as he shook the hand like it was on fire. "What kind of country is this?"

He closed his eyes for a split second. When he opened them again, he looked at the injured hand and noticed that a red welt was forming across his pinky. He shook his head in disgust. The human body was entirely too fragile. He stuck the pinky in his mouth and plopped heavily next to Nicole on the cot.

Nicole's eyes dropped to her lap. It was her fault Michael had hurt his hand. She was a grown woman who had taken care of herself for a couple of years, now. She should be able to get her husband the help he needs.

Michael was right. If the roles were reversed, he would have been able to gather an entire army of litigators by the first day. She had failed him. Failed him utterly, and completely.

A sad, lonely tear escaped the corner of Nicole's eye and splashed onto her hands. Michael saw it and was able to make a pretty good guess what Nicole was thinking.

He wiped his hands on his pants—he had yet to see any cleaning done in the cells and guessed he was spending his days in the worst kind of petri dish—and took both of Nicole's hands in his.

"Look, Nicole," Michael's voice was sterner than he meant it to be, but he kept talking nonetheless, "snap out of it. They haven't beaten us yet."

Nicole's head whipped up so she could study Michael's face. Was he mad, or—?

A bubble of hope formed around her as she realized her husband was not angry at her, nor had he given up.

She watched his face closely as he sat looking back at her and almost jumped for joy when she spotted the tell-tale upward spike of the left side of his lips. She had seen that look before, it meant he had solved a difficult problem of some kind. Surely, in this case, it meant that her brilliant husband had managed to come up with a plan that would get the two of them out of this mess.

Thank goodness! Michael was a master at coming up with workable plans. He would tell her what she needed to do. Then they could—

"You'll just have to get a lawyer from the States," he continued matter-of-factly.

With those simple words that lovely bubble of hope burst, and all the safe feelings flittered away. Michael did not have a plan, or at least, not one that she had not already thought about. The quirk of the crooked smile had let her down. Nicole sighed.

"What?" Michael asked, as he watched Nicole's shoulders slump in despair. He had thought the suggestion was a good one, that having a new avenue of attack would brighten her day.

"I've already been calling lawyers in the States," Nicole burst out, as she shook her head in frustration. "It's not as easy as you might think, Michael. Nobody wants to—"

"Just keep trying, Nikki. I have faith in you."

Michael tickled Nicole but it was a halfhearted attempt at a tickle. Nicole, for her part, tried to play along, to smile and maybe giggle a bit, but the corners of her mouth refused to cooperate, and the giggle got stuck in her throat.

Not wanting Michael to see how truly discouraged she was, Nicole rose slowly from the cot and moved to the cell door to catch a guard's attention. She needed to leave, quickly, before Michael realized he was putting his trust in the wrong hands. How could she succeed when failure emanated from every pore of her body?

"I'll do my best," Nicole managed to say. She even managed to fake what she hoped was a confident smile.

She must have succeeded, because when she glanced at Michael, she saw a confident smile reflected there. It gave her courage, and she straightened her shoulders as she marched past the other cells and through the door to the lobby of the police station.

As the door clanged shut, the smile on Michael's face slipped a bit. He managed to keep it together for a few more seconds, then he gave up and allowed his face to show what he truly felt, which was utter despair. Because no matter how much he tried to fool himself, he did not honestly believe Nicole would be able to find a lawyer who could get him out of this jail. Not when every citizen in Belize believed him to be guilty.

Luckily, Nicole did not see any of this. She went back to her hotel room believing that Michael was in good spirits, that his belief in her ability was strong. So, when she laid down to sleep that night, instead of the sobs that normally soaked her pillow, she only shed a few tears before she drifted off into a restless sleep.

The next day, after spending the entire morning making more phone calls than her budget would easily allow, Nicole returned to the temple. She had, again, failed to find a lawyer who would help her husband. And although she could not understand why no one would take his case, lawyers from the States seemed to have the same revulsion to the case as the Belizean lawyers, she had to accept it as a fact.

Which was why she had decided to shift gears. Instead of looking for someone to help her husband in a court of law, she would make it so he would never have to go there. She would pull a Nancy Drew and uncover a clue that would prove her husband's innocence. She knew it must exist, that the police must have missed it.

After a short conversation with the hotel staff, she found she could take a taxi all the way to the temple site. It seemed there was a fully functioning road that ran right by the site, but Michael had thought a nighttime jungle hike would be fun.

Nicole arrived rested and ready to break through whatever bureaucracy she needed to break through to get the chance to snoop around. After all, they had to let her look around a least a little didn't they? She was the wife of the accused. They had had several days to look for clues. It was only right that she would have a shot.

But when she arrived at the entrance and paid off her cab driver, she was confused. The entrance was wide open, without even so much as a sign of caution.

Nicole could not understand this. A murder had happened at this location a mere days before. Where was the police tape? Where were the cops, milling about, intent on keeping a nosey public out of the crime scene?

Then she realized the police would most likely not do anything to block the entrance. It was a tourist attraction, after all. Most of the action she has seen on TV was in the clearing. That was where the real action had happened. That was where the police had probably set up camp.

But when she entered the temple clearing all she saw were four or five tourists milling about. No police. No police tape. No sign that a crime had been committed just days before at this very temple.

Worst of all, there was no sign that the police cared about the site as a crime scene, and nothing to show her where she should start her search for the clue that would set Michael free.

"What is wrong with these people!" Nicole yelled in frustration.

A Japanese couple nearby looked at her in surprise. When they realized she was alone, that there was no one there for her to talk to, they quickly headed for the exit.

"That's right! Move away from the crazy woman!" Nicole yelled, after the retreating couple.

Nicole was not particularly proud of her next action. When the couple looked at her again, probably to judge if they should run or if it was safe to continue walking, she stuck out her tongue. Which, of course, did make them break into a run.

Other tourists in the area noticed the exchange and quickly moved on.

"Harumph!" Nicole grunted.

She straightened her shoulders and looked around. Although she knew that sticking out her tongue was a particularly immature thing to do, it had made her feel surprisingly better. Since Michael's arrest, she had felt helpless, weak, and rather useless. Scaring the tourists so they scattered like beetles gave her a sense of power. She liked the feeling.

One of the tourists peeked around the corner of the temple. Nicole quickly yelled, "Boo!"

The tourist jerked his head back and Nicole could hear the pounding of his footsteps running away. It was a satisfying sound, a sound that made her smile. It was not a feeling she had ever had before. Never in her life had she been thought of as big, bad, or scary.

Nicole fidgeted her shoulders about, as if trying on the feeling. She nodded and smiled. It was rather nice being the intimidating one.

Big, bad Nicole had a job to do, and those tourists needed to leave her alone so she could do it. She scanned the clearing for a likely place to start. Now that she knew the police had been too lazy to secure the crime scene, she was sure they had also been too lazy to do a thorough search for clues. It was up to her.

"They missed something, I know they did," she muttered, as she moved aside a few leaves to look inside a bush before twisting around to peer up into the treetops. But she found nothing.

She continued the search for minutes, then hours. The first hour was the toughest, that was when she was still trying to preserve the integrity of the crime scene. Then she realized that if the police did not consider it a crime scene, why should she?

From that point on Nicole was hyper-focused on her task. A casual onlooker might think she was manic. At least, that was what happened with the tourists who wandered into the clearing over the next few hours. No matter the size of the group, as soon as they noticed Nicole scrambling around in the dirt like a crazy person, they made themselves scarce rather quickly.

No one wanted to deal with a crazy lady on vacation, and Nicole certainly looked like a few of her cogs had slipped their gears. Her fingernails were caked in mud, her clothes were painted with smears of dirt, and the welt that had formed across her cheek was only the latest in a series of scratches and cuts that now decorated her body.

But Nicole did not care how she looked or what the tourists thought of her. She was on a mission to find a clue that would free her husband, and that was all that mattered.

This was unfortunate, because among the people that Nicole failed to notice was a dangerous man who was on the crazy spectrum himself. He strolled into the clearing after Nicole had been searching for several hours and noticed her right away. But instead of scampering away in fright, like the twenty or so tourists who had strolled into the clearing with him, he took a different avenue. The scowl that had been on his face when he arrived turned into interest, and he retreated into a thicket of nearby bushes to stare at her.

He saw Nicole not as a crazy woman who might act irrationally, but as a vulnerable one who had lost track of her surroundings. She was the perfect prey, and he had every intention of stalking her.

Nicole, unaware she had gained an audience, continued her frantic search. But no matter how hard she searched it was to no avail. She found nothing.

Sore as she was from bending, stretching, and twisting as she climbed trees, plowed through bushes, and dug up the jungle floor, Nicole was even more exhausted. But she had no intention of stopping. Instead, she decided to take a break by revisiting a previously searched area. At the bottom of the temple were plenty of potential hiding places for clues, and all of them could be searched without crawling on her hands and knees over roots and stones.

She leapt to her feet and bolted for the temple. The sooner she found that elusive clue the sooner she could return to her hotel room and get some rest. But exhaustion made her clumsy, and her single-minded focus made her stupid. She had only taken a few quick steps before she tripped over a low bush and slammed to the ground.

Pain shot through her hands and stomach, both of which had taken the brunt of the fall, bringing her to her senses. What was she doing? Did she think she was some sort of bloodhound?

She dragged herself to her feet, one achy muscle at a time, and limped to a nearby stone that was conveniently flat. As she awkwardly lowered herself onto it the likelihood that she would be unable to rescue Michael overwhelmed her. Disheartened, she drew her knees to her chest, wrapped her arms around her bruised legs, and began to quietly cry.

"What am I going to do?" she whispered to her bruised and bloody knees. But they, being a non-verbal part of her body, did not answer. She slammed her fist onto the stone in frustration, which only made matters worse as it added several new scrapes and bruises to the already impressive list of wounds she had acquired while scrambling through the underbrush.

But her external wounds mattered less to her than the ant that was crawling across her shoe. The real wound was in her soul, and that wound ripped wider each time she failed Michael. No scrape, scratch, or bruise would ever compare.

She did what any self-respecting young woman would do. She had a wallow fest. She allowed all those feelings of self-disgust and failure to wash over her like a wave of despair and drown her in sorrow.

Meanwhile, her creepy audience continued to watch with interest. After several minutes of being entertained by her anguish, he was one of the broken who enjoyed watching others in pain, it made him feel big, he scanned the area to see who was around. A twisted smile sprouted on his face as he realized there were no tourists in sight.

An innocent might wonder at the man's intent, thinking he was simply curious about the crazy woman or was concerned.

Until he pulled a machete out of its sheath and smirked. Now, it was painfully clear that his intentions were purely evil. He was a predator. And Nicole, the crazy woman currently wallowing in self-pity, was to be his prey.

"I can't do this alone," Nicole groaned into her knees, "I can't. I just can't!"

Quietly as a snake the man slithered closer. Step by step, inch by inch, until he was a mere five feet from the unsuspecting Nicole. Almost in striking distance.

He raised a foot to take another step closer but was stopped by the sudden appearance of a full-bodied apparition of a woman.

It was the Stone Woman, and she had materialized in the five-foot gap between Nicole and her stalker. Eyes blazing a bright red, she dared him to take even a single step nearer.

The man, having grown up in the area, knew of the ghost's reputation. He had often heard stories of sightings of the ghost of Xunatunich, and of the deaths that happened shortly thereafter.

Whether the ghost was a harbinger of death or simply a messenger who gave warning, he wanted no part of it. In his hurry to backpedal away from the ghost he tripped over a low bush and crashed to the ground. Nicole jerked her head up in time to see the terrified man scramble to his feet and flee into the jungle, flailing a machete about like it was a plastic bat instead of the potentially deadly weapon it was.

Nicole, startled, frantically wiped away the flood that continued to stream from her tear ducts. It took longer than it should have, probably because tourists rarely wear sleeves in the tropics and arms are not efficient absorber of tears.

After several moments of struggle, she was finally able to clear the watery mess from her eyes and bring them into focus.

She almost wished she could blur them again. Because there, standing directly in front of her, was the Stone Woman. The ghost of Xunatunich.

Seeing the ghost again was frightening, and disturbing. But the real shock came from the look of pity on the ghostly face.

Why did the Stone Woman pity Nicole? How could a dead woman pity a live one?

Nicole, not prepared to dive into the brain work that would be required to solve that conundrum, scrambled to her feet and backed away.

Unfortunately, the jungle was made up of flora of all shapes and sizes, and she had only moved a few feet before she tripped and landed on her rear. When she looked up the Stone Woman had vanished.

CHAPTER 11

That night, tired, frustrated, and more freaked out than she would ever admit, Nicole returned to the police station for visiting hours. She knew Michael would be disappointed by her lack of progress, but that did not matter. She needed to reconnect with him. His strength would give her strength. His innate cheeriness would banish the doldrums that threatened to overcome her. His good energy would give her the push she desperately needed to keep going.

And then there was that strange apparition she had seen again. Everything was the same as the first time, both times she had been on her rear in the clearing looking up at the ghost, but this time there was a twist. It had almost seemed like—

Nicole shivered. Best if she refrained from thinking about the ghost's expression until she had a chance to talk to Michael about it. Together they could work out what that look had meant.

One of the younger, not-at-all-menacing policemen was manning the counter that evening, so Nicole smiled as she approached to sign in. But when she reached for a pen, the man, whose name badge said Officer Flowers, pulled the pen cup away and shook his head.

"No visitors."

Nicole stared at the policeman, who, after taking away the pens, returned to his crossword puzzle. She watched as he mouthed the word 'banquet'. When he closed his eyes to figure out how to spell the word, she quickly grabbed a pen and began to sign the book. But before she could get more than an N written the pen was snatched out of her hand.

"No visitors!"

Officer Flowers dropped the pen back into the cup and shoved the entire cup of pens into a drawer behind the counter. As he slammed the drawer closed, he picked up his pencil and pointedly turned his attention back to his crossword puzzle. He even twisted around a bit so that his back was partially toward Nicole in case she was too dense to get the message.

"Wait," Nicole pleaded, a sure sign she was too dense, "you have to let me see him. Please!"

"I can't. He isn't here," Officer Flowers stated bluntly.

Brusqueness was not the norm for Officer Flowers, but the day had been long and boring. Besides, he was hungry, and tired. The last thing he wanted to do was deal with an inconsiderate woman who wouldn't listen.

Nicole blinked multiple times as she attempted to process the policeman's words. It had sounded like he thought Michael was gone. Gone? Michael wasn't gone. He was in his cell, just through those doors. The police officer was confused. He must be thinking of the wrong man.

Then panic hit. What if Michael was gone? What if they had moved him to a worse prison, where she couldn't see him? What if—?

"That's impossible," Nicole squeaked. She tamped down the panic and continued. "You're thinking of the wrong man. My husband's name is Michael Quinn, and he was brought in four days ago."

"I know who he is. He's gone."

"Gone? Where?"

Officer Flowers sighed. Obviously, this woman had no intention of letting him finish his crossword.

As the newest member of the police department, he had been relegated to desk duty, the least desirable and most boring assignment in the department. At one point, he had become so bored he had thought of quitting the police force and seeking another career, until, in a flash of brilliance, he realized he could fill the dead time with his passion, crossword puzzles.

It had been a life saver. He was able to complete several puzzles a day, and was on track to win an international, crossword puzzle contest, if annoying people would stop nattering at him so he could focus.

He had answered the woman's question. She should go home and leave him alone. Was that too much to ask?

He raised his head to give a stern reprimand to the American. Unfortunately, he made the mistake of looking her straight in the eyes.

Those eyes! They were just like his sister's eyes. His sister had once fallen into a well and been stuck there for two days. The panic in her eyes. The despair. It was exactly like the American's eyes. And —

Compassion — he was often plagued with the stuff and worked hard to hide that flaw from his coworkers — welled up and flooded every cell of his body. He had no choice, he had to help this woman.

Not because he liked Americans, though he did harbor a secret fondness for many parts of their culture, but because she reminded him of his sister. A sister who had had that very look in her eyes, and who had become so terrified of the world that it had taken two full years to convince her to take more than a few steps outside their family home.

After a quick look around the room to make sure no one was paying attention, Officer Flowers leaned over the counter and whispered, "He's gone."

Nicole flinched as if she'd been slapped and turned to stare at Officer Flowers. He nodded to reassure her, only to witness her eyes fill with tears.

He turned away. In his need to help he had only made matters worse. Now she —

Nicole reached across the counter and gently laid a hand on Officer Flower's arm.

"Please," she whispered quietly, "I can't deal with this. May I please see my husband?"

Officer Flowers stared into those eyes that were so much like his sister's and caved to his warmhearted nature. After a quick scan of the patrol room, he again leaned in to whisper to the distrait woman.

"Okay," Officer Flowers began, "I'm not supposed to tell you this. Last night —"

A throat being cleared directly behind Officer Flowers caused him to twirl around in fear. A well-founded fear, it turned out, since Chief Valente had somehow managed to appear out of thin air.

"Chief."

It took a lot of effort, but Officer Flowers managed to look respectful rather than guilty as he stepped away from the counter.

Which, in retrospect, made sense. He had joined the force three months ago, and in those three months, he had had more opportunities to practice the art of deception than was comfortable. The first lesson he learned was that the chief demanded absolute respect at all times and in all places. Anything less resulted in the type of disciplinary action that left bruises.

The second lesson Flowers learned was that the chief was lighter on his feet than he appeared. It had been made painfully clear to him, very painfully, that bulky men, like the chief, could suddenly appear in the least expected places.

It was the chief's own brand of keeping his men on their toes. They never knew when or where to expect the chief, he often materialized out of nowhere without warning.

Chief Valente looked from Nicole to Officer Flowers, and Officer Flowers barely managed to restrain a sigh of relief when the chief's steely glare shifted back to the American. As Chief Valente swaggered the two feet to the counter Nicole froze in fear.

"Is this...," Chief Valente gave Nicole the once over, then continued, "person giving you trouble?"

Nicole gulped. If disgust were a poison Nicole would be twitching in the last throes of death on the floor about now.

"Because if she is," the chief used his thumb to casually point to the door that led to the cells, "we can have her take her husband's place."

A doe in the headlights had nothing on Nicole as she took a quick step away from the counter. The last thing she wanted to do was aggravate this man. She had heard about him. If she were to also get locked up, it would be over. No matter who came looking for them, no matter how many lawyers her parents hired, she and Michael would disappear into the cells forever, never to be seen or heard from again.

"Flowers!" Chief Valente growled. "I asked a question. Is she giving you trouble?"

"No, sir!" Officer Flowers answered. "She only wants information about her husband."

"Does she now? And what did you tell her?"

"Nothing, sir!"

Chief Valente raised a brow at Officer Flowers, who flinched.

"I mean, I told her exactly what you said to say."

Again, the brow was raised, and this time Officer Flowers' face blanched.

"I told her that her husband is not here," Officer Flowers pleaded. "I told her nothing else. I swear."

The fear in the young officer's voice startled Nicole. He was too cowed by the chief to help her. They were probably all too cowed. Which meant that the only person in this police station who could help was the chief himself. She had to find a way to appeal to his better nature.

Nicole took a deep breath, squared her shoulders, and turned to address the squatty, little man who held so much power in the police department.

No, revise that. Based on what she had discovered while searching for a lawyer, this man held too much power over the entire town.

"Excuse me, sir," she kept her voice polite and courteous, "can you tell me about my husband, please?"

Chief Valente turned to sneer Nicole's way and slowly moved his eyes from the top of her head to the tip of her toes, then back again.

Being looked at with that much disdain made Nicole's insides quiver, but she knew it was vital she held it together and stood her ground. This was for Michael.

Nicole endured a full minute of contempt before Chief Valente grunted and turned away. She was relieved to no longer be a victim of those eyes, until she looked at his face.

He had no intention of answering her question!

She rushed to the counter and threw her arms across it, pleading to the chief.

"Please," Nicole begged. "I have to know what happened to my husband. You have to tell me."

The only response she got was another grunt. Chief Valente did not even expend the energy it would take to turn and look her way.

"Tell me!" Nicole wailed.

At that, the chief shook his head and turned to look at Nicole, disgust written loud and large on his face.

"Same old story," he sneered angrily. "You Americans think you can go where you want, do what you want. Well, your husband paid the price for his arrogance."

Nicole blanched white and froze. The words 'paid the price' sounded like something bad had happened to Michael. Really bad.

She gulped down the fear that threatened to overwhelm her. Then she leaned heavily on the counter and pushed herself into an upright position.

"What," Nicole squeaked. She cleared her throat and began again. "What do you mean? What price?"

Officer Flowers, who was watching this interaction, felt sorry for the young woman. She was not being unreasonable. All she wanted was to find out information about her husband. Any wife would do the same, no matter what country they were from. The chief could make things easier by telling her—

"Tell her!" the chief growled.

"Sir?" Officer Flowers' eyes flew to his boss, terrified that his mind had just been read. But the chief was still sneering at the American and was not paying the least bit of attention to the young cop. Thankfully, he had not seen that tell-tale look of pity.

"I said," Chief Valente's voice was as smooth as silk as he transferred the sneer to his subordinate, letting the younger man know with a look that his weak moment of pity had been noted. "Tell her why she can't see her husband. After all, she IS an American, whatever she wants, she gets."

Nicole's hope-filled, doe eyes turned to Officer Flowers, who suddenly got a bad case of the fidgets.

This was another one of Chief Valente's many tests. Officer Flowers knew it was a test, but his mind twisted in knots trying to figure out what kind of test it was. The chief obviously wanted him to tell this poor woman about her husband. Buy why? What was the purpose? Was he supposed to—?

Chief Valente released his gaze from Officer Flowers, and the young man's brain untangled enough that he could speak.

"He's in hospital," Officer Flowers blurted. He immediately felt proud of himself. He had only had to clear his throat two times before he spoke. Proof positive that he was finally learning how to control his fear of the chief.

"A hospital?" Nicole swayed and would have fallen if the counter had not been there to provide support. Chief Valente smirked at her reaction. Officer Flowers, after a quick look at his boss to make sure the boss's eyes were pointed in the right direction, allowed himself a quick cringe of concern.

"Tell her the rest," Chief Valente grunted.

"He was stabbed." Officer Flowers did not relish having to give this news. "By one of the other inmates. He used to work for Dr. Morgan. The man your husband killed. He—"

"My husband did not kill anyone!" Nicole yelled. She took a breath to calm her frayed nerves and continued more calmly. "Will he be okay? Which hospital was he taken to? I want to see him."

"Again, with the wants," Chief Valente scoffed. "Americans!"

He gave Nicole a sneering but quick once-over and flapped his hand dismissively in her direction.

"Come back tomorrow."

Two huge tears broke free of the pond that had formed in Nicole's eyes and danced down her cheek. With a heavy plop, they hit the counter.

Nicole's parents had taught her that if she cared for something deep enough, cared enough to persevere when the going got unimaginably tough, she could win. But Nicole had never had the opportunity to try out that philosophy for herself. She had always been protected. There had always been someone near who could ease her way, so she had never had a reason to try, really try, to push through an obstacle. Certainly not an obstacle as tough as this man.

But this was for Michael. Her husband. The love of her life. The man she planned to raise a family with, to grow old with, to…to…do whatever old people did who had spent a lifetime together as a couple.

"Michael," she whispered.

"What did you say?" Chief Valente growled, his eyes narrowing threateningly. He truly had not heard what she said and suspected that she had cursed at him.

But word had not been a curse, it had been a promise. Armed by her love of Michael, the chief's threatening look had no effect on Nicole. She shoved a steel rod down her back and wiped the tears from her face.

"I can't wait until tomorrow. I must see my husband now," Nicole's voice was surprisingly calm and resolute.

Chief Valente's eyebrow rose at this firm demand.

"Please?" Nicole's voice cracked a bit as she tried to keep the pleasantry from becoming a plea. She lifted her head high and pulled her shoulders back, for she had realized Chief Valente was the type of man who was emboldened by any sign of weakness.

Officer Flowers, who had watched the entire encounter, stared at the puddle of tears on the counter, horrified by this sign of pain. Chief Valente glanced from the puddle to his underling, then at the stubborn face of the American who stood straight and tall before him. He sighed and rolled his eyes.

"Fine," he said, with a shrug that made Officer Flowers stare, open mouthed, in surprise. "Follow me."

Chief Valente turned to Officer Flowers.

"Close your mouth and clean up that mess," he barked, as he pointed at the pool of tears decorating the countertop. Officer Flowers immediately snapped his mouth closed and grabbed a rag from under the counter.

The chief gazed thoughtfully at Nicole for several seconds, then nodded as he came to a decision. He led her down a hallway to a 10 X 10 office that had Mayan artifacts of all shapes and sizes cluttering every surface. He pointed to a seat for Nicole, while he took his place behind the desk.

As Chief Valente relaxed back into his chair, he put his feet up on the only clear spot on his desk and he picked up a phone.

"Let me call the hospital," he said, as he dialed.

Nicole, watching anxiously, reminded herself that she needed to remain stoic. But she felt far from stoic. She was frightened, frustrated, and more than a little angry. But she was determined to hide those emotions since Chief Valente seemed to be the type of person who responded better to strength.

Which was why she was also careful to hide her hands under her handbag. If the chief couldn't see her hands, she was free to twist them into knots that matched the knots in her heart.

"I see," the chief said, into the phone. "Can he have visitors?"

As the chief listened to the response, he shot a glance at Nicole.

"Good." He gave a firm nod to the phone. He cut his eyes again quickly to Nicole and back away. "I'll take care of it."

He hung up the phone and turned to address Nicole.

"They say he'll be fine. You can see him."

An odd whooshing sound filled the room, and it was several seconds before Nicole realized it came from her. She had been holding her breath as she waited for news of Michael. When her shoulders had slumped in relief, it had opened a valve that let all the pent-up air out. Very, very slowly.

She finally reached the end of the long, loud breath. Then, with a gasp for new air, she jerked herself upright and leaned forward.

"When?" she squeaked, too excited to control any part of her voice. "Can I go today?"

"I think the hospital will allow it."

Chief Valente was looking at her rather oddly, but Nicole was too caught up in the thought of seeing Michael to notice.

"Can you write down the directions?" Nicole patted her pockets and dug through her purse in search of a pen and paper. "I get lost kind of easy."

Chief Valente snorted in disgust but grabbed a piece of paper to write down the directions. While he penned a complicated list of twists and turns, a mist formed behind him. As Nicole watched in horror, the mist solidified into the Stone Woman.

Nicole jumped out of her chair, shocked. This was the third time she had seen the ghost.

Unfortunately, when she jumped to her feet she slammed into a bookcase. On that bookcase was a foot-tall statue of a Mayan woman. The statue teetered, then fell to the floor with a loud crash. As the shattered pieces scattered across the office floor the Stone Woman ghost disappeared as quickly and mysteriously as she had appeared.

At the sound of the crash Chief Valente's head jerked up. He threw down his pen, and moving at the speed of a much younger, thinner man, he was around the desk and staring at the broken pieces before the pen had time to clatter to the ground.

"I'm sorry," Nicole bit her lip. "I'll buy you another one."

The chief gingerly picked up a quarter-inch piece of modeled clay and stared at it.

"Don't worry. I've seen dozens of statues just like it. They sell them all over the place."

Nicole was embarrassed by her clumsiness and wanted to assure the chief she would make things right. But when the chief rose to his full height and leaned toward her menacingly, she realized he was furious.

"You'll pay for this."

"I know," Nicole gulped. "I said I would. I'll replace it as soon as I see Michael—"

"Replace it!" Chief Valente roared, his face redder than a juiced beet. "You can't replace it, you foolish girl."

That was when Nicole realized that the artists who drew old cartoons had not been using quite as much imagination as she had originally thought. The chief had already turned red, and now he seemed to fill with steam while sweat poured from his pores.

It would have been fascinating if it wasn't so scary. But the man looked like a bomb ready to explode. She felt a sudden, desperate need to get as far away from him as she could.

Nicole looked behind her, to see if there was a safe escape route in that direction, but she was blocked by a bookcase. Which, like every other surface in the office, was packed with the chief's knickknacks.

The man obviously had a collecting addiction. She looked over her shoulder at the bookcase. She had seen hundreds of collections such as this being sold by vendors. Cheap knockoffs of the real thing. Worthless and easily replaceable.

Unless...there was only one reason she could think of that explained why her breaking the statue infuriated the chief.

"I'm sorry. I get it. The statue must have sentimental value."

"Sentimental value!" The chief's eyes bulged at the suggestion. "That statue was priceless. A one-of-a-kind treasure."

"But," Nicole's forehead crinkled in confusion, "I've seen vendors—"

"No!" The chief was now so angry that even he recognized that he needed to calm down. He took a deep breath, returned to his seat behind his desk, and motioned for Nicole to sit. Then, after a few more calming breaths, he continued in a much calmer voice.

"The statue was authentic. All these artifacts are authentic. You cannot buy replacements."

Nicole looked from Chief Valente's angry face to the artifacts that littered his office. If these artifacts were indeed irreplaceable, why were they being stored in the chief's office? Wasn't that rather irresponsible of him?

She snuck a peek at his face and was relieved to see he now appeared to be more disturbed than angry. She decided to not mention that in reality, he was to blame for the statue's destruction. If he had stored the statue in a safe location, not on a bookshelf in his cramped office, she would never have bumped into it.

"I'm sorry," she said kindly. "It was an accident. I'll clean it up."

"Clean it up!" the chief growled, his anger resurfacing with a vengeance. "You mean throw it away. You Americans always want to throw away my heritage like yesterday's garbage. Americans are arrogant."

Nicole had had the worst week of her entire life and was tired of the chief's anti-American attitude. She jumped out of her chair ready to give him a piece of her mind, but her arm grazed another statue and knocked it from its perch. This time, fortunately, she caught the statue before it hit the floor. She carefully restored it to its original position and slowly moved away from the other breakable artifacts.

"Trying to destroy another one?"

Nicole tried to hide the flood of anger that bubbled up at the chief's snarky comment. But it was difficult. No matter what she did, no matter how hard she tried, the man was determined to find fault.

She would tell him exactly what she thought of him. He was despicable. An arrogant blowhard who...

She stopped short the rest of the insult as she realized she needed this man on her side. Without his help, she was unlikely to find where Michael had been moved.

She took a deep breath and gulped down her pride. She was not exactly known for her diplomatic ability, but both of her parents were rather good at it. Surely, she had picked up a trick or two over the years.

Mimicking her parents when they were about to deal with a difficult neighbor, she conjured up her biggest smile and plastered it on her face.

"Chief Valente, I think we've gotten off on the wrong foot."

Her parents would have been proud of her. She kept that smile on her face even though Chief Valente glared at her like she was a howler monkey that had broken into his house and was swinging on his light fixtures.

The two stayed like this for several minutes. Nicole thought she was succeeding when she saw a crack in the chief's glare, but he was only changing positions. Now, he had his arms crossed tightly across his chest to block her offer of friendship as he gave her a scowl that could sink a ship.

Okay, maybe she wasn't good at diplomacy.

"In for a penny, in for a pound, as my grandmother would say," Nicole muttered, when it hit her that it would take more than a smile and a few kind words to break through this man's barrier.

"What was that?" Chief Valente asked suspiciously.

Nicole brightened her smile even more. A smile, even a fake one, never hurt in a negotiation. At least, that's what her parents always told her.

"Just an old saying."

She patted the chair next to her.

"Come sit here."

Chief Valente looked at her like she had grown a horn on top of her head and was beginning to sprout hooves.

"Please?"

Nicole was careful to keep her voice calm, but not too friendly. Her parents had warned her about people who viewed niceness as weakness. They often attacked at the first sign of vulnerability. She was pretty sure Chief Valente was one of these people. She needed to show respect, but in a way that made her look strong.

"Can we sit a moment and talk?" She again patted the chair.

For the first time since she had met him Chief Valente was unsure of himself. He even uncrossed his arms a bit, which in body language meant he was unbending.

"I'm sorry I broke your statue."

Immediately, Chief Valente re-crossed his arms.

"Very sorry. I know you probably think I don't care."

The chief growled.

"But I do."

Nicole tilted her head and gave the chief the sincerest look she could muster.

"It was an accident. Honestly. I would never purposefully destroy artifacts."

The chief's scowl was a fraction less intense, which encouraged Nicole to continue.

"I respect you, and your country, really, I do."

A glimmer of confusion broke through the wall of glare the chief had built.

"Please, Chief Valente," Nicole continued, as she again patted the chair invitingly. "I have an idea, but I can't tell you while you're glowering over me like that."

As probably could be predicted Chief Valente's glower intensified at the mention of glowering, but Nicole was not worried. She had seen her mother handle people every bit as stubborn as the chief more times than she could count. As long as she continued to mimic her mother's negotiating tactics, everything should be okay. So, she gave the chief one of her mom's warmest smiles. The chief, not immune to her mother's smile even if it was a secondhand imitation, uncrossed his arms and slowly dragged himself around the desk to sit beside Nicole.

"Okay," the befuddled man grunted, "I'm listening."

Nicole, who had become comfortable in the role she had chosen for herself, felt she no longer needed to channel her mother. She wiggled a bit in her chair, settling in.

"So," Nicole gave a conspiratorial, we're-on-the-same-team look to Chief Valente, "I bet you rescued all these artifacts and they're headed to a museum, right?"

Chief Valente's face was totally devoid of emotion as he stiffly replied, "Right. Good guess."

"And there was probably an inventory done and you will be held responsible for the loss of the statue."

Nicole felt proud of herself, both for figuring out what the chief was worried about and for making a friend. She could tell by the speculative gleam in the chief's eye that he was sizing her up for friendship material.

"I will be blamed," the chief cautiously agreed, with a nod.

"What if I tell you I know," Nicole pointed to herself, "someone who can help you," she pointed at the chief, "find another one of those? So, you won't get into trouble?" She ended her little performance by pointing at a statue.

"I'm listening," the chief guardedly replied. And Nicole was pleased to see he actually was listening.

"It's Michael!" Nicole blurted. "Michael can help!"

"Your husband?"

Nicole nodded excitedly.

"The man I arrested for murder a week ago?"

"Four days. But yes, the man you mistakenly arrested for murder. He's very good at finding artifacts, like that statue."

Chief Valente got up and stood over the broken statue for several moments, staring. Then he nudged one of the bigger pieces with the toe of his boot.

"You think Michael can find more like this?"

Chief Valente gave his full attention to Nicole, as if to measure her answer.

"Probably better," she replied, with a proud smile. "He's an exceptionally good archaeologist."

Chief Valente paced the room for a couple of turns, then abruptly returned to sit at his desk. He studied Nicole for several seconds before he leaned back in his chair and formed a steeple with his fingers.

"He will help me?"

"Why not?" Nicole scoffed. "You have to understand, archaeology is his life! He loves finding new artifacts for museums."

"Yes." The chief's eyes became hooded and unreadable. "Museums."

Chief Valente leaned forward.

"I'll take you to the hospital myself," he declared.

"Really?" Nicole gasped. This was better than anything she could have hoped.

Chief Valente picked up a statue from his desk and inspected it from all sides.

"Michael is about to become my new favorite archaeologist."

Nicole, never good at reading undercurrents, smiled sweetly at the man who held the safety and well-being of her husband in the palm of his hand.

CHAPTER 12

The crunch of wheels as the car weaved down the gravel dirt road deep in the jungle was loud, so loud it nearly drowned out the howler monkeys. Which was saying something, because the howler monkeys in this section of the jungle were particularly vocal. Whether they were in an uproar because of the interlopers, or they were always this boisterous, was unclear.

In the car, two sets of white knuckles revealed that neither Chief Valente, nor Nicole, were comfortable. Nicole sat in the passenger seat with her hands clasped tightly to the dashboard. While the chief, who was driving, had both hands glued firmly to the steering wheel. He was obviously determined that nothing was going to knock them loose, not bumps, not potholes, not even one of the many skids across the loose gravel.

"We're going the right way, right?"

Nicole had kept silent as long as she could. She had remained silent as they drove over rickety bridges. Silent as they left the last tiny village in their dust. Silent as they drove deeper, and deeper into the dense jungle.

"I mean," she continued with a gulp, "we haven't seen anyone for miles."

"The shortest way to the hospital is this road. Don't you think I know where I'm going?"

The chief shot her a glare that made her gulp a second time. It reminded her a bit of the look her father would give her when they took family vacations and she asked if they were there yet, only this look appeared to have been taking steroids.

"Yes?" Nicole hazarded a guess.

It was a weak answer, said without conviction, but it was enough to satisfy the chief.

"Then shut up and let me drive," he growled. But the growl was not particularly angry. It seemed more like something the man did naturally.

Nicole spotted a colorful bird out her window. As she loosened her grip on the dashboard to turn to see it better, the car went into a particularly big pothole, banging Nicole's head on the roof. She glanced at Chief Valente sheepishly as she rubbed her head.

"I just wanted to see—"

"This isn't a tour bus. I told you to hold on. With both hands."

Nicole nodded and put both hands firmly on the dashboard. And just in time, too. They went over another unbelievably huge pothole, and it was only her grip on the dashboard that kept her head from slamming into the roof. Again.

After several more minutes of driving in silence, human silence at least, the howler monkeys were as vociferous as ever, Nicole turned her head enough to study the chief's profile.

He must have felt her eyes on him because he asked, "What?"

"Chief Valente, do you believe in ghosts?"

Whatever the chief expected Nicole to say, this was not it. He squinted at her a split second before he replied, "If you follow the ghost you'll jump in the water."

"What?" a confused Nicole asked. "What water?"

"It's a saying," Valente explained. "It means you have to be careful about who you trust."

Nicole thought about the saying for several minutes. So many minutes, in fact, that the chief's mind had already drifted to bigger and better things.

"I wondered because I heard a story about a ghost at one of the temples yesterday."

"What?"

"A ghost, that's supposed to haunt the ruins. It's said—"

"Superstitious nonsense," Chief Valente scoffed. "Only fools and idiots believe in ghosts."

Having no good argument to counter the chief's proclamation, Nicole sat silently, hands gripping the dashboard as if her life depended on it. Which it probably did.

A flash of light in the rearview mirror caught Nicole's eye. She twisted around to find the Stone Woman glowing brightly in the backseat.

Nicole screamed, but not a normal scream. This was a scream of true terror. The scream of a woman at her wit's end who wanted nothing more than for her parents in the States to hear her cry for help and come to her rescue.

It startled the chief and made him lose control of the car. They hit a crater-sized pothole, skidded several feet, then careened into a tree.

They sat for approximately five seconds in relative silence—the chief shocked by the accident but not worried since he believed the car was still drivable—until copious amounts of smoke began to billow from the engine.

"What is wrong with you!" Chief Valente yelled. "Don't you know better than to scream like that?"

Nicole shot a look into the backseat. The Stone Woman was gone. Not that it mattered. The chief would never believe she had been there since he did not believe in ghosts.

But he would require an explanation for that scream. One that she needed to supply. After a short search through her memories, she decided to rely on an old, tried-and-true excuse. One that she had used many times in her childhood.

"I'm sorry," she apologized. "I saw a spider?"

Chief Valente rolled his eyes as he slammed his fist onto the steering wheel.

"She comes to the jungle and she is afraid of spiders."

Chief Valente scowled at Nicole. He wanted to yell. He wanted to punch something. He wanted to—

The hopefulness that shone on Nicole's face broke through his consciousness and he sighed. He did not understand this American woman. It made him uncomfortable, that he did not understand. She confused him.

"Sorry?" Nicole shrugged.

Chief Valente grunted, and Nicole realized that was probably the best response she could expect. She sat quietly while he climbed out of the car to inspect the damage. Then she took the time to wipe the sweat from her brow and steady her heartbeat before following him.

Smoke poured from the crumpled hood of the wrecked car. But while this upset the humans, it amused the howler monkeys overhead to no end. They gleefully crisscrossed the trees above the crash site, laughing hysterically at the sight of humans in trouble.

Chief Valente's lips pursed in disgust as his eyes shifted from the damaged car to Nicole. He opened his mouth as if to say something, looked speculatively from Nicole to his watch, then snapped his mouth closed again.

Nicole noticed none of this. Feeling sorry for herself, she was fully engaged in the time-honored pastime of shoulder scrunching and head drooping.

"Because of its mouth, the fish got caught."

"What?" Nicole's head jerked up at the odd words. What was this about fish? Had the chief decided to go fishing?

"Stay here." Chief Valente slapped his hand on the roof of the car. "I'll go for help."

"Really? You want me to stay by myself, in the dark, in the middle of the jungle?"

"Stay in the car," Chief Valente ordered. "You'll be safe enough."

"Safe enough?"

Nicole shivered as she eyed first the crumpled car then the surrounding jungle. There was not one thing in her surroundings that looked safe to her.

"You're kidding, right?"

The chief reached through the driver's side window and grabbed a gun from beside the seat.

"So, tell me, little girl," he scoffed, as he holstered the gun and did an inventory of his pockets, "how many times have you traveled through the jungle? At night?"

"Once. The night we went to the temple. The guide took us—"

"I go alone."

Nicole heard, and was forced to accept, the finality in his voice. This man intended to leave her alone in the jungle. She opened her mouth to protest, but the chief raised a hand to silence her arguments. He took a step toward her as he pointed at the jungle.

"First, it is dark in there, very dark. The trees are too thick for the moon to get through."

He swung his arms around as if to illustrate his point. Nicole looked overhead, and there was, indeed a gap in the trees over the road.

"And then there are the jaguars, hiding in those trees," he wiggled his fingers, "and spiders. Lots of spiders. And roots that trip you, and vines that wrap around your throat."

He paused to pantomime a struggle with an invisible vine wrapped around his throat.

"But some vines aren't vines. They're snakes."

He wrapped his arms around his torso and mimed a creature squeezing tight.

"Snakes that want to squeeze the life out of you so they can eat you for dinner."

Nicole shivered at the thought, but she was not ready to give up.

"I want to go with you," she argued. "If we stick to the road, we can miss all that nasty stuff, right?"

"It would take too long," the chief negated, with a shake of his head. "The road twists and turns constantly. If I cut straight through the jungle, I'll be there in just a few hours."

"I want to go with you," Nicole demanded, and to prove she was serious she crossed her arms stubbornly.

"Same old story, the spoiled gringa thinks she can have whatever she wants. Well, Miss Pampered American, you are not coming."

"I can't stay here by myself!"

"You screamed. That's why we crashed."

Nicole hung her head in shame. She had, indeed, caused the crash and she knew it.

"You," Valente pointed at her accusingly, "have no say in the matter. I will move much faster by myself."

"But—"

"Enough talk. Stay in the car. You'll be okay."

"But—"

"Car!" Chief Valente yelled, as he pointed at the car and scowled. Nicole stepped back, startled by his vehemence.

The chief checked his watch again, then retrieved a flashlight and two water bottles from the trunk. He tossed one water bottle to Nicole and motioned for her to get into the car. Cowed, she climbed in.

Eye rolls and head shakes seemed to be all Nicole was going to get out of Chief Valente as he walked away. Until he gave her one final parting shot.

"I'd roll up the windows, if I were you," he suggested, "unless you want to be snake chow."

Nicole's eyes widened with fear as she frantically rolled up the windows. Snakes! She could not deal with snakes. No, no snakes.

Nicole huddled down in the seat as far as she could without losing sight of the dancing flashlight that moved further and further into the distance.

The smoke had ceased billowing from the hood and the monkeys, having lost interest in the odd humans who had disrupted the peace of their territory, seemed to be in the intermission phase of their concert. There was only the random howl of a particularly noisy monkey to remind Nicole she was probably surrounded by the little beasts.

"If I go to sleep, morning will come faster," Nicole muttered, as she curled into a ball and squeezed her eyes tight.

"Morning will come," she said firmly, deriving comfort from the sound of her own voice. "I can sleep the night away."

One eye crept open at the unexpected sound of scratching in the backseat. Then both eyes, and her mouth, popped open wide as she realized the Stone Woman was in the backseat, staring at her.

"Why do you keep following me? What do you want?" Nicole yelled.

She clawed frantically at the door handle. Her hands, slick with sweat, lost their grip multiple times, until she was finally able to get the door open and scramble out of the car. Panting in terror, she backed away, never taking her eyes from the backseat.

Which was lit by the Stone Woman's glow.

Frantic, Nicole looked around for any safe haven. In the distance, almost out of sight, was a miniature beam of light bouncing in the distance. It was all she could see of Chief Valente's flashlight.

She bent down to take a quick peek into the backseat and tripped over her own feet. The ghost, the one called the Stone Woman, was glowing steadily in the backseat as if it was the most natural thing in the world.

Nicole looked from the chief's dancing light to the car. As if in response, the ghost's light intensified, and pulsated.

That was enough for Nicole.

"Chief Valente!" she yelled, her eyes still firmly on the car. "I'm coming with you."

Nicole backed away quite a few steps before she felt safe enough to turn and bolt toward the jungle. Unfortunately, in the meantime, Chief Valente's light had continued to move further into the jungle and now seemed to blink out of existence every few seconds.

"Wait," she yelled, "or I might lose you!"

Frantic, she picked up speed as she ran into the jungle, intent on rendezvousing with the light. But the light was very far away and was quickly moving further. In her panic to catch up with it she forgot to watch her feet, tripped over a large root, and plummeted to the jungle floor. When she scrambled to her feet again the light was gone. Nicole stood very still as she scanned her surroundings. There, in the distance, was a light. It looked more like a distant star than a flashlight, but she headed that way anyway.

A hanging vine brushed across her shoulder, startling a scream out of her. Her scream startled a monkey, which howled in irritation, startling Nicole even more. Flustered and afraid, Nicole began to run. Her foot snagged on dense underbrush and before she what was happening, she was on the jungle floor again.

Brushing herself off she jumped to her feet. She looked to her right, to her left, behind her, then forward. No matter which direction she looked, she could find no sign of the light.

"Chief Valente!" she yelled.

She twirled around multiple times, searching for any sign of the light. There was none.

"No matter," she said, "I know I was heading in this direction, toward that big log."

She moved toward a fallen log, only to realize there was another fallen log, in another direction. Then another, in a third direction. She looked around and realized the jungle floor was littered with fallen logs, all nearly identical to the untrained eye, particularly in the dark.

"Oh, no!" Nicole muttered, as she sunk down on the nearest log. "Now what am I going to do?"

CHAPTER 13

A few hours later, an exhausted Nicole was dirty, disheveled, and asleep, huddled in the trunk of a hollow tree.

A jaguar, lithe and graceful, stopped abruptly to sniff the air. He smelled an unusual scent nearby. A whiff of fear and anxiety. The aroma of prey.

The big cat turned toward Nicole's hiding place. Before he could take so much as a single step the Stone Woman appeared to block his way. She stood silently, no movement from her face or body. But even jaguars keep their distance from ghosts, and this jaguar knew there was plenty of prey elsewhere in the jungle. He quietly veered away from the ghost and vanished into the night.

Several hours later, inside the hollow tree, Nicole twitched, then stretched out an arm. The ghost faded away as Nicole slowly opened her eyes to look around groggily. When she recognized the first streaks of dawn, she yawned and climbed out of the tree.

All was quiet in the early dawn. If Nicole had been jungle-savvy she likely would have checked around her sleeping site and noticed the large paw prints a mere few feet away.

But Nicole knew little about the inhabitants of the jungle, so she remained blissfully ignorant of her close brush with the jaguar.

Or that she owed her safety to the Stone Woman, who had quietly stood guard over her during the night.

* * *

After several more hours of tramping through the jungle, Nicole felt like a pro. Gone was the squeamish girl who jumped at the slightest noise and screamed at the sight of bugs.

Not that she liked those things—she most assuredly did not. But she had already jumped and screamed enough for a lifetime. All those flaps and squeals did nothing, absolutely nothing, except use more energy than she had to spare.

A heavy vine trailed down from a high branch directly in Nicole's path. Without a second thought, Nicole slapped it out of the way and pushed forward. She came to a clearing and paused to catch her breath. The hand she used to brush a strand of hair out of her face had broken her fall on the jungle floor numerous times and was less than pristine. But Nicole did not care that she left a streak of dirt on her face. Her goal was to find her way out of the jungle, or at least to a place that would be safe to rest for a bit.

As she stood, exposed in the middle of the clearing, a large animal growled menacingly in the distance. Nicole shivered but held her ground, until another growl, this one much closer, sent her scrambling to find something she could use as a weapon. She found a sapling and wrestled with it a bit until she managed to snap off a stick with spear-like proportions. Holding the makeshift spear gave her a feeling of strength. She was ready, reasonably ready at least, for any attacker.

"You'd better not mess with me today, Mr. Predator. This is one prey that will fight back," Nicole hissed loudly.

The scream of an animal in distress shattered the air.

"Good choice, Mr. Predator," a relieved Nicole whispered. "I wouldn't have been very tasty anyway."

Makeshift spear in hand, Nicole marched on.

Many hours later, as twilight set in, an exhausted Nicole trudged into yet another clearing. She was now so tired that the spear had become a walking stick. Mud covered the right half of her head. A vine trailed over her left shoulder.

A centipede dropped from an overhead tree onto her right shoulder.

"No hitchhikers!" she growled, as she brushed it off wearily.

One more step was all she took before another of those irritating roots that are invisible in the dark tripped her. She calmly rubbed a damaged elbow, then yawned.

"I've got to rest."

She looked around for a likely sleeping location and spotted a rock that gave her the height she needed to climb into the cradle-like branches of a tree. As she wedged herself into a nook she sighed.

A glow at the base of the tree startled her. To crane her neck to look down she had to twist around in a painful manner, but she managed to do it. There at the base of the tree was the Stone Woman, standing, glowing—and apparently guarding.

"You know," Nicole admitted, with a yawn, "I'm so tired I don't even care that you're here. All I want to do is sleep."

With that admission, she closed her eyes. But instead of drifting off to peaceful slumber her eyes filled with tears and sobs shook her body.

"Oh, Michael!" she whimpered. Tears continued to pour down her cheeks for several more minutes until, little by little, her sobs lessened. Soon, the only sounds heard were the normal jungle noises and the gentle snores of a distraught, young woman who slept the sleep of the exhausted.

A sliver of moonlight broke through the tree canopy and shone on the jade necklace Nicole wore. The resultant dance of lights was fit for a fairy festival.

CHAPTER 14

The jade necklace around the neck of Ix Tzutz Nik jerked and jumped as she bounded through the dense jungle. It was an erratic run, most likely explained by the small girl she pulled by one hand and the heavy basket she barely managed to clasp in the other. She paused just long enough to motion for two other children, preteen boys, to hurry.

As they ran, wind whipped the trees and the sky continued to pelt giant raindrops that drenched everything in sight.

It was hurricane weather.

A man was waiting for the woman and children at the edge of the jungle. He raced back to meet her, snatched the tiny girl from her arms, and motioned for everyone to hurry. The howling wind drowned out any other noise brave enough to make an appearance.

Ix Tzutz Nik struggled on. But the basket was awkward and heavy. It slipped from her hand. She dropped to her knees to scoop the items back inside. Her family, not noticing that she was no longer with them, raced onto a rickety rope bridge that spanned a deep cavern.

Frantic to catch up with her family, Ix Tzutz Nik tossed the last of the items into the basket and bolted, head down, to the bridge. Every ounce of energy she possessed was focused on reaching her family. Through the heavy rain, she could not see that her husband and children had reached the midway point of the bridge, but she had made this journey many times in the past and knew they must be there.

Just as she stepped onto the bridge a strong gust of wind picked her up and blew her several feet back, toward the jungle. She battled the wind to regain her feet. The gusts were strong, but she somehow managed to stand. Step by painful step, she struggled to the bridge, intent on rejoining her family.

But the bridge, and the people on it, had disappeared. Her family was gone.

CHAPTER 15

Nicole trudged through the jungle tired, dirty, and hungrier than she had ever thought was possible. Or maybe, trudged is too energetic of a word for the zombie-like way she put one foot in front of the other and pulled herself forward. Slogged might be more accurate.

But then again, it is not possible to even slog through the jungle if it decides to play a joke. Which it often does because the jungle is a mischievous beast.

The current joke the jungle chose to play on Nicole had to do with a vine. It was a particularly well-hidden vine, or maybe a lively one, because when it sprang up, right under her feet, it caught her off guard and nearly sent her tumbling headfirst into the biggest thorns she had ever seen. She only managed to avoid a world of pain by throwing herself sideways into a puddle of suspicious-looking mud.

As she struggled to her feet, panting as she brushed as much of the mud from her clothing as possible, she could hear the jungle giggle. At least, she thought it was the jungle. Something certainly had giggled, and it made sense it was the jungle since she was sure the jungle had enjoyed its little joke.

No matter. She took another look at the nasty thorns she had barely avoided and breathed a sigh of relief. She had been in a dismal fog for hours, scarcely aware of her surroundings. The threat of pain had shocked her out of that fog, and she realized the time for slogging or trudging, or whatever she had been doing, was over. She needed to add a bounce to her step. Not a bounce of happiness, of course. That would be asking too much. No, she needed a bounce of survival. Nicole needed to be on her toes, ready for whatever nasty surprise the jungle might choose to throw her way.

Fully back in the here and now, Nicole took stock of her surroundings. That's when she spotted a blackberry bush, a mere ten feet away, full of the most luscious-looking fruit she had ever seen. She charged at the bush, her stomach growling at the thought of those juicy berries, but before she had taken more than two steps an aggressive squeal stopped her short. She had no clue what creature belonged to that squeal, but she was sure it would be safer to find out before she took another step.

Slowly and carefully, she twisted to her left, but there were no creatures visible in that direction.

Turning the other way, she twisted around and immediately spotted the tiny snout of what looked like a pig poking through the blackberry bush. The snout sniffed loudly in her direction.

"Oh, what a cute little piggy!" Nicole gave a relieved sigh and managed a little smile. "Here piggy, want to be friends?"

Slowly, so as not to scare the little critter, she tiptoed toward the bush, eager to get a better look at the owner of that cute, little snout. She was feeling rather lonely, after her long trek through the jungle, and craved the sight of a friendly face. Any friendly face. Even that of a pig.

But Nicole had taken only a few timid steps when, immediately to her left, a monster-sized snout shoved its way through the bushes and morphed into the biggest, hairiest pig Nicole had ever seen. It snorted once, and there was nothing cute about this snort. This snort was menacing and frightening.

"Whoa there!" Nicole squealed, as she skipped away from the big pig.

She had not intended to squeal and meant no disrespect to the pig. It was simply one of those noises that sometimes escapes when a person is startled.

The pig, emboldened by Nicole's retreat, and possibly offended by the squeal, took several steps forward and grunted a further warning.

"Hold on, you big pig," Nicole warned, as her growling stomach reminded her of the need for food. "If you attack, I'll fight back."

She raised the homemade spear she had been using as a walking stick to show she meant business.

"You leave me alone, and I'll leave you alone. Deal?"

The pig, which was a peccary and not a pig at all, glared at her with mean eyes. Those eyes did not simply say she should stay away from the blackberries, they screamed that an end to Nicole's very existence was not out of the question.

Unfortunately, Nicole was beyond hungry and not thinking straight so she decided to risk it. She reached toward some tasty-looking berries that were a short arm's length away. She figured if she moved slow enough, and kept her distance from the pig, all would be good. After all, even a pig could spare a few berries for a starving woman lost in the jungle.

"I just want to grab a few of these blackberries," she explained, to the angry animal, hoping that he had more sympathy than showed in his eyes. "I haven't eaten in forever!"

But nature is nature, and a pig is a pig. Or peccary, in this case. This peccary was not of a sympathetic bent, and as soon as her hand touched a blackberry it stepped forward and gave a most aggressive snort.

Nicole's stomach responded with its own growl.

Nicole stared at the pig for several seconds, until her empty stomach forced her eyes back to the blackberries. There are times when the stomach outranks the brain. This was one of those times.

"You need to learn to share," she admonished, the pig, as she raised her spear threateningly. "There's enough here for both of us."

The bush rustled violently as forty snouts of varying sizes poked their way through. Nicole, startled by the sheer number of snouts, froze in shock.

She should have run. She should have taken one look at that army of snouts, turned her achy feet in the opposite direction, and hightailed it out of there.

But shock does funny things to people, like freezing them in their tracks. So, instead of booking it to safety, Nicole watched, frozen, while out of the bush pushed the biggest, meanest, hairiest pig imaginable. He must have weighed a hundred pounds, and he moved like he meant business.

His thoughts were not hard to read as he focused beady eyes on Nicole. How dare this puny, two-legged creature invade his territory? How dare it poach his berries? He would teach the creature a lesson. He would teach it who was in charge around here.

Frightened by the ferocity of the behemoth, Nicole swung her makeshift spear in the big pig's direction. But naive as she was in the ways of the jungle, she was no fool. The steps she took were away from the animal, not toward him.

"You are a big one," she muttered. "Why do you have to look so mean?"

The peccary advanced, his eyes on Nicole. And those eyes, though beady, glowed with menace.

"Okay. I get it. You have a big family to feed. I'll go. You stay here and enjoy your meal."

The peccary snorted fiercely. The ferocity of the noise startled Nicole and she stepped back quickly. Too quickly. Her foot snagged on a root and she tripped.

She was able to keep to her feet, barely. But she did it with an awkward wobble. Unfortunately, that wobble was enough to embolden the peccaries. Several of them crashed through the thick blackberry bushes to stampede toward Nicole. In less time than it took Nicole to blink in surprise, an avalanche of grunts and squeals overwhelmed her senses, and she could no longer string two thoughts together.

With her ability to reason out of commission, instinct took over. She knew she was in danger. She knew she needed to protect herself. Nicole did the only thing she could do—she threw her spear at the advancing horde. But she knew absolutely nothing about throwing a spear, so instead of finding a target, it fell harmlessly to the ground. Weaponless, she turned and ran for all she was worth, the horde of peccary in hot pursuit.

Luckily for Nicole, all the peccaries wanted to do was chase her away. After what felt like miles of clambering over underbrush and racing around trees—but was only a minute or so—most of the peccary felt they had accomplished their goal so they dropped out of the chase. They had proven their athletic prowess. They had ousted the trespasser and sent her scampering through the jungle. No need to expend more energy.

As Nicole scrambled into a clearing she tripped over a pile of rocks and landed face down in the dirt. She lay there, panting, for several seconds, until she had gathered enough strength to lift her head and look around. That run had included some of the scariest moments of her life. She was glad it was over.

Only, it was not over. She lifted her eyes to find she was not, as she had thought, alone. Directly in front of her, glaring at her with beady, hate-filled eyes, was that biggest, meanest pig of them all. She sucked in her breath, ready to scream for her life, when the creature gave a snort, turned, and trotted away.

Nicole breathed a huge sigh of relief, glad that the ordeal was over. She pushed off from the ground onto her knees. She put one foot on the ground, getting ready to stand up, when the click of a rifle directly behind her ear froze her in place.

That's when Nicole looked around and realized she had stumbled into a military-style camp. Cautiously, it wouldn't do to startle whoever was big and bad enough to scare off the big pig, she twisted around to find a woman in her early thirties, dressed in camouflage, with a rifle pointed at Nicole's skull.

"Get up," the woman commanded. Nicole got up, and before she knew it, she was standing in the middle of a dirty tent that had two, metal, folding chairs and a cot as furniture. The woman tied Nicole's hands together in front of her body before shoving her onto the cot.

"Wait here," the woman barked.

Without another word, the woman left. Nicole took advantage of the time alone to look around for anything that might help her get out of this situation. But there was nothing, absolutely nothing, of use in that tent.

Not willing to give up so easily, she did what any right-minded woman tied up in a tent in the middle of the jungle would do. After a glance at the zippered entrance, she started chewing on her ropes.

Nicole had not made much headway when the entrance flap opened. She immediately dropped her hands into her lap. The last thing she wanted was for her captors to realize she had a plan to escape.

A man in camouflage walked in behind the woman. He was in his late fifties, and his friends called him Gregorio. But Nicole did not know this because she was not his friend.

"Here she is," the woman snarled, as she pointed her chin at Nicole.

Gregorio took one look at Nicole—her clothes were so ripped and dirty she looked like an extra on a post-apocalyptic movie set—and dismissed her.

"She looks worthless," he said, with a flap of his hand. "Kill her."

The woman raised her rifle to Nicole's head.

"Wait!" Nicole yelled, panicked to find herself looking down the long barrel of a big gun.

The woman paused, knowing it hurt nothing to listen to what her prisoner had to say. Nicole realized she needed to think quickly. She needed to give these people a reason to keep her alive. She needed—

"My parents are rich!" she blurted.

Gregorio placed a hand on the woman's arm and motioned for her to lower her rifle.

"What is this?" Gregorio asked with interest.

"My parents!" Nicole had thankfully hit on the most likely scenario that would save her life. Now she had to sell it. She was usually not very good at telling lies. But these were not usual times. She had to learn how to lie, and she had to learn fast. "They will pay a lot of money to get me back."

Gregorio looked less than impressed.

"I'm their only child." Nicole gave a silent apology to her sisters. Though she was sure they wouldn't mind being dismissed like this. It was, after all, for a good cause.

Gregorio and the woman moved off to the side to speak together quietly. Nicole watched closely, trying to decipher the multitude of hand gestures.

Based on body language, there was quite the argument going on.

"They own an entire block," she added loudly.

The two continued to argue as if they had not heard her.

"In New York City!" Nicole yelled, feeling the need to sweeten the pot for these two. "They've got oodles of money, simply oodles."

That got their attention. They stopped arguing and turned Nicole's way.

"They're filthy rich," Nicole continued. "Simply swimming in money!"

Gregorio took a step toward Nicole, but the woman grabbed his arm.

"Rudy won't like this!" she hissed.

"I'm tired of taking orders from Rudy!" Gregorio growled. He jerked his arm away from the woman's hand. "I say we ransom her, take the money, and get out."

The woman paused, and Nicole could almost see gears in her head shift and change direction.

"Do it for my grandchildren," Gregorio pleaded. "They deserve a better life than this."

The woman searched his face for several seconds, then nodded her agreement.

Gregorio stepped over to Nicole to sit next to her on the cot.

"Now, tell me how I can get in touch with your very rich parents," he ordered. "We get our money and you go home unharmed."

"It's a deal," Nicole agreed. Then she gave a few, slightly overdone, dry coughs. "But I need water. My throat is so dry I can barely talk."

Gregorio motioned to the woman, who left the tent in search of water.

"We'll start with your name," Gregorio declared.

"My name is—"

Nicole swayed and would have toppled over on the cot if Gregorio had not caught her by the arm.

"What is wrong?" he growled.

"I'm...dizzy," Nicole murmured, her words slurring slightly. "I haven't eaten for a while."

Gregorio grunted. He was perfectly willing to feed the woman if it helped her give him the information he needed. Rudy would not like this, asking ransom for an American. Going against Rudy's wishes was a huge risk. He needed to make it count.

Distracted by the thought of all the money he could get for this one American, he stomped to the tent opening, his back to Nicole.

It was the break Nicole needed. She jumped up, grabbed a chair, and, eyes scrunched closed, swung at Gregorio's head with all her might.

The chair connected with a resounding clunk and then clattered to the ground as Nicole let it go.

Gregorio crumpled where he stood.

Nicole ran to him and reached out a shaky hand to touch the side of his neck. She sighed with relief as she felt a steady pulse.

"Sorry," she whispered, "but it was you or me."

Trembling, she stepped over Gregorio and peeked outside. The coast was clear. She silently slipped through the opening and escaped into the jungle.

Only this time, there was no thought of walking. And since her hands were still tied together her balance was off and she raced to escape, she often found herself on the jungle floor, struggling to get back on her feet.

She tried to bite off the ropes as she ran through the underbrush, but all she succeeded in doing was punching herself in the nose. Finally, scared and frustrated, she found a tree behind which she could hide as she focused all her attention on the ropes. Hands finally free, she sucked in a few deep breaths, then continued her journey.

CHAPTER 16

A primitive dirt road deep in the jungle wove its way through lush vegetation. It did not belong this deep in the jungle. It was an anachronism, an oddity. An alien from another planet would be forgiven for mistaking it for a natural phenomenon, so far from human activity the road seemed to be.

Nicole tripped through a patch of particularly dense brush and landed, on her hands and knees, on the packed dirt of the road. Surprised, she patted the dirt in several directions before her heart skipped a beat in elation as she realized what the road meant.

People. People who would rescue her. Save her. People with food, water, and probably a car. People who would take her out of this horrid jungle and back to civilization.

She scanned the road in each direction, not wasting the few seconds it would have taken to climb to her feet.

"I guess a car waiting for me would be too much to ask," she muttered. Then, because crawling all the way back to the hotel would be awkward and exceedingly slow, she took the time to climb to her feet.

Yes, walking was a much better option, she decided as she noticed the plethora of rocks mixed in with the dirt on the road. Those rocks would hurt her hands and knees, while her shoes provided protection for her feet.

"But which way?" she asked, aloud, as she looked to her right, her left, then back to her right again.

Right. She would go to the right. As in, this must be the right way.

With a decisive nod, she headed up the road but halted abruptly after only a few feet.

"No," she blurted, as she shook her head. She twirled around to face the opposite direction and headed back down the road. "It's this way."

But when she reached the point where she had fallen out of the jungle, her feet trudged to a stop.

"This doesn't feel right either," she muttered, as she bit her lip. Some decisions were excessively hard to make. Particularly decisions that could either lead her to safety, or deeper into the jungle.

The thought of going deeper into the jungle sent a shiver down her spine. Jungles were entirely too dangerous for her taste. And lonely. She needed people. Lots and lots of people.

Nicole stood with her feet planted firmly in place for several minutes as she whipped her head, first one way, then the other. She was so confused about the right thing to do that this might have continued for hours, which would have made her very dizzy, except it dawned on her that she had the perfect decision-making tool right in her pocket. Coins. She dug one out and tossed it high in the air.

"Heads to the left, tails to the right," she yelled at the coin.

When the coin landed it sent miniature clouds of dust at least a foot into the air. Nicole bolted to the coin's landing spot, flapped her hand around to clear the air, then squatted down to see the results. Then she smiled, grabbed the coin, and shoved it back into her pocket.

"Decision made!"

She did a military-style turn and saluted the road, so elated she was that she was about to be rescued. Unfortunately, her first step landed on quite a large rock, and since she was marching rather than walking, her foot slipped to the side, twisting her ankle. As she reached down to rub her throbbing ankle, she heard the distant whine of an engine.

Looking up, she spotted a plane. It rumbled loudly overhead, flying very low, obviously heading for a runway where it could land.

And the direction it was heading was opposite the one she had chosen to go.

"So much for the flip of the coin," Nicole grumbled. Then, because she was sick of her jungle trek, she did an about-face and limped quickly down the road.

But the plane, being a plane, moved quite a bit faster than an exhausted woman with a twisted ankle could limp. As it flew over the tree canopy it was quickly lost from sight, and Nicole feared the runway might still be many more miles away.

Panic set in, and Nicole got a sudden urge to find that plane and find it fast. She pushed aside the pain in her ankle to run full tilt down the dirt road. If she could find the runway, she would be saved. If—

She passed through a dense line of trees and suddenly found herself no longer on the dirt road, but on the smooth, black, tarmac of a runway. Shocked at the sudden change she stopped to look around and realized that she was in a small airport, complete with buildings and ground crew.

The plane's wheels touched down and skidded as brakes were applied. For some reason, it triggered another panic attack in Nicole, and she immediately began to chase the plane down the runway, limping and waving her arms like a mad woman.

"Hey! Anybody! Help me!" she yelled. "I'm an American. Help!"

The response she received to her plea for help was not at all what she had expected. Five men ran out of the nearest building, but instead of the friendly, welcoming uniforms worn by most airport workers, these men were dressed military-style, with camouflage uniforms and scary-looking rifles. Quicker than it took for Nicole's brain to register that something was wrong the men had her surrounded and were pointing rifles at her in a menacing fashion.

"I'm...American?"

Frankly, she wasn't sure what she should say. These men did not seem friendly, and she was afraid her being an American might hurt more than help.

One of the men motioned with his rifle for her to walk toward the buildings.

"That way?" she asked.

She tried to raise her hand to point, but the movement resulted in rifles being shoved into her face, so Nicole quickly lowered her hand and pointed her chin instead. In response she got a rifle jabbed into her back, which she took to mean, "Move."

Nicole limped toward the building, with her escorts so close she bumped shoulders with them multiple times. They led her to what looked to be a warehouse and, after two of the men had a short conversation, the other three rearranged piles of fifty-pound bags to create a cell. With the addition of a cot her prison was complete, and the next thing Nicole knew she was on the cot, with only a few shards of light that managed to sneak through gaps in the hastily constructed pseudo-wall to brighten her space.

The murmur of the men's voices and the slap of cards on a hard surface assured the captive that she was not alone.

Well, assured was the wrong word. The presence of those men did not mean safety to Nicole. She had never been in a situation that resembled this one, but her instincts told her she was in grave danger. The less attention she drew to herself, the better. These men were not her friends, and never would be.

"Might as well get some rest," she whispered, wanting to hear a friendly voice even if it was her own. She turned on her side and snuggled into a more comfortable position.

Before she could so much as close an eye, the murmur of voices from the other side of the wall became much louder and agitated. Two voices rose above the others in an argument.

Those two voices sounded vaguely familiar to Nicole, but she did not know either man well enough to recognize that the voices belonged to Gregorio and Chief Valente.

"I don't like it!" Gregorio yelled, then he regained his composure and lowered his voice. "I don't think it's a good idea."

"You don't have to like it, and I'm not paying you to think," Chief Valente growled. "You only have to take orders."

"But what if someone finds out it was me who killed Dr. Morgan? Everyone liked him."

Nicole popped up on the cot like a cork in water. Had she just heard what she thought she had heard?

"No one will ever find out," came the growling response. "I'll make sure of that."

"What about the American. Does he know?"

Now Nicole was even more interested. If there was an American involved, maybe she could convince—

"No," the growl was particularly fierce. "And don't tell him."

Before more could be said Nicole heard a door squeak open and slam closed, followed by a whispered, "Quiet. Let me handle this."

Nicole silently shifted to the edge of the cot, as close to the bags as she could get. She listened carefully as footsteps walked purposefully across the floor. They were assured footsteps, full of purpose. Nicole guessed they were the footsteps of the American. There was something about them that was familiar, so much so that the sound of them sparked joy in her heart and made her feel safe and protected.

"Let's go outside," a man's voice suggested.

"I was told you wanted to speak with me," an American said, from the other side of the wall.

At the sound of the American's voice, Nicole's vocal cords clamped down like a vise. She could no more speak than she could fly over the wall like Peter Pan.

That voice. It was Michael! He was here! Her husband was here! On the other side of this stupid, quickly constructed wall. How did he—?

A familiar sound broke through her musings as she realized her chance to call to her husband was quickly slipping away. Footsteps—she could clearly hear Michael's jaunty and self-assured set—were leaving.

Nicole opened her mouth to force a sound, any sound, past her paralyzed vocal cords. But it was no good. They were frozen solid.

Pausing, she wondered if she was mistaken. Michael had been stabbed and taken to a hospital. It was impossible for him to be here, at an airport in the middle of the jungle, walking his jaunty walk as if he had not a care in the world. Whoever that was, it could not be Michael.

She focused her attention on the jaunty footsteps and paled in shock. No, she was wrong. Without a doubt, that was Michael!

The door squeaked open and slammed closed. Suddenly, there was only silence.

"Michael?" she managed to whisper. But it was too late. Michael had left the building.

"Michael!" Nicole yelled, her vocal cords thawing quicker than a popsicle in July, "Michael, is that you?"

On the other side of the wall, someone banged their hand down on a hard surface. Then a gruff voice with an accent yelled, "Shut up over there! We're trying to play a game."

"Who was that man?" Nicole shouted, and in her frustration, she punched at the bags that made up the walls of her cell. "That was my husband, I know it was!"

"No!" her captor responded loudly. "Now, shut up or I'll shut you up."

Realizing that her captors were unpredictable and might follow through with their threat, Nicole slowly lay down on the cot and forced her body to be still.

But her mind continued to race, around and around her makeshift cell and around the airport. Because Nicole, though naive, was not naive enough to blindly trust whatever her captors decided to tell her.

She would think this through. After all, it might have been her imagination. She desperately wanted to see Michael, badly enough that her mind might conjure—

After a deep, calming breath, she forced her memory back to those few minutes when she heard the American, then heard his step.

"No!" Nicole whispered firmly. "That was Michael. I know it. But why was he here when he should be in a hospital?"

As confusing thoughts twisted and twirled around in her brain, the murmur of her captors' voices combined with her extreme exhaustion to lull her to sleep. Even the slap of cards was soothing.

In the relative safety of her makeshift cage, she slept the sleep of the weary.

CHAPTER 17

Several hours later, Nicole awoke to the sound of dolly wheels squeaking across the warehouse floor. As she lay quietly listening, the door creaked open, and the squeak of the wheels receded as the dolly was rolled out of the warehouse.

Into the silence that was left behind poured the merry chirp of birds.

Still more asleep than awake, Nicole was about to roll over to drift off again when a plane engine roared into life in the distance, and men, likely loading cargo onto a plane, began shouting to each other. She was almost able to ignore the shouts until one voice rose above the others.

"Where's my wife? I want to see her!"

The shout was loud, authoritative, and oh, so Michael.

Nicole sprang up like a jack-in-the-box, instantly fully awake.

"Michael," she whispered, her eyes aglow.

She jumped off the cot and immediately got to work inspecting the bag wall. She was ready for whatever that wall threw at her. She had, after all, just spent an entire night dreaming of every possible way she could get past it. In one dream, she even blew up the irritating monstrosity, though where she found the explosive was less than clear.

"It's just a bunch of bags. Surely, I can—"

The next few minutes were spent punching, tugging, and kicking every bag within reach, but unlike in her dream, they were surprisingly solid. No matter how hard she punched, pushed, or pulled, she could not get even a single bag to budge.

But she did, somehow, manage to get her foot stuck between two bags when she gave the wall a particularly vicious kick. And by the time she pried her foot loose she remembered her seventh dream of the night.

She stepped back several paces to study the tops of the bags. Yes, her dream was right. The gap at the top was plenty big for her to slide through.

What did it matter if she was afraid of heights? All she had to do to successfully scale the wall was resist the urge to look down.

"Let's do this," Nicole whispered enthusiastically, knowing she needed all the encouragement she could get.

And do this she did.

Not that it was easy. The first few times she jammed her foot between two bags she had all kinds of trouble getting it out again. No matter how hard her arms pulled, the only way she could retrieve the foot was if her other foot was planted firmly on the ground.

Not a valid climbing strategy.

After several attempts in which she experimented with different techniques, she finally found one that gave her enough support that she could climb, but not so much that it pinned her to the wall.

She quickly found that simply not looking down did little to solve the problem of her fear of heights. That had to be overcome by sheer willpower. When she was a mere foot off the ground her heart began to pound, her breath became shallow, and she feared vertigo was going to cause her to plummet to her death.

Somehow, she managed to push through it and continue to climb. It seemed that the desire to get over the wall was greater than her fear of heights. Before she knew it, she was at the top cautiously peering over.

"Well, this looks like a good sign," she muttered, when she found that she was alone and the door wide open.

Using muscles she had never, ever, ever in her life used before, she pulled herself all the way up until she was lying in relative safety on top of the row of bags. But that feeling of safety fled as she looked down to scope out the best landing spot. Who could feel safe while the room was bucking and shaking like a 7.9 earthquake?

Only, she knew it was not an earthquake. It was her old nemesis, fear of heights, rearing its ugly head at the most awkward moment.

"Oh, no you don't!" she growled, furious that she had so little control of her own brain. "I AM getting off this wall. And I AM doing it now."

She looked down at the floor and watched it buckle and roll like an ocean wave in a storm.

"Too far to jump," she decided, as she gulped and hugged the bags tightly, squeezing her eyes tightly closed to quell the queasy feeling in her stomach. Then, after a deep breath, she forced her eyes to open a slit, loosened her grasp, she resolved she would not let fear determine her fate.

"I'll just go down the way I came up."

Cautiously, she dangled a foot over the abyss. Then, gathering every random strand of courage she could find, she shoved her foot between two bags. But she was careful not to shove it in too far, she remembered the lessons she had learned earlier. After another deep breath, this one solely for extra courage, she slowly pushed her body off the top of the bags.

"Guess I'm committed now," she muttered. And she was. Now that she was on the free side of the wall, the shortest way to safety was straight down. Straight down she would go.

The rest was a matter of concentrating only on the next foothold, and then the next. Slowly and steading she progressed downward, until her foot hit the card table with a *thud*.

That *thud* sounded like heaven to Nicole, and the smile that blossomed on her face was probably brighter than it needed to be. Not that Nicole didn't deserve it. She had, after all, managed to overcome her fear of heights. Twice. First to scale the wall, then to climb down the other side.

Proud of her accomplishment, she jauntily dropped onto the table, then hopped to the floor. With only a small pause for one quick sigh of relief, she scampered to the door to peer out.

Men in camouflage with dollies were scrambling about in all directions as they loaded the big bags from the warehouse onto a cargo plane.

"Busy bees," she whispered, stretching her neck to its full extent to see better. "And I'm right in the middle of the hive."

Three men walked out of a building across the tarmac, heading for the plane. The men in front and to the rear both carried rifles. The man in the middle was Michael, and Nicole noticed that his hands were together in front of him, as if they were bound.

"Michael."

As Michael and his captors boarded the plane Nicole paused indecisively. She had found him. If she called out, he would hear her.

But so would his captors. It might put him in danger. What should she do?

"I have to do something, that's for sure, or I might never see him again."

She looked at the men loading the planes. All of them were armed. Every single one of them.

"So many guns."

Just then the men loaded the last of the bags from the dollies and headed for a warehouse twin to the one she was in on the other side of the tarmac.

Nicole's heart pounded as she realized now was the time for action. She squeezed her eyes closed as she mentally reached into her store of courage and grabbed a handful.

"You can do this, Nicole."

When she opened her eyes again, she gave an encouraging nod to herself, took a breath, and sprinted to a nearby building. After only a slight pause to make sure the coast was clear, she then jetted to the next building. Using short hops from place to place, she quickly reached a relatively safe spot a mere ten feet from the plane.

Nicole surveyed the area.

"Where are those invisibility cloaks when you need them?" she muttered.

Just then several men returned with more bags and Nicole had to inch around the corner of a building to avoid being seen. She held her breath as a man, whistling a merry tune, stopped to light a cigarette a few inches from her hiding place.

Finally, the last of the bags were loaded and the workers slammed the cargo door shut. As they walked away, Nicole had to do a bit more scrambling to keep out of sight, and in the process spotted a small door into the plane that had been left open.

Nicole craned her neck. If she tilted her head just right, she could see into the interior of the plane. Michael and the two men were in the front, away from the door. She bit her upper lip. She knew she needed to get on that plane. It petrified her, but it was what she needed to do.

"Wish me luck, Michael!"

It was more of a breath than a whisper. Nicole tensed her muscles, gave a little prayer, and shot across the open space and into the plane. The prayer must have worked, because, against all odds, she miraculously remained unseen.

Once inside she could see that the front and middle of the plane were relatively uncluttered. But the rear…the rear was another story. It bulged with piles of those same bags that had formed her prison.

Nicole crept along the floor, keeping low to make sure she would not be noticed. She found a likely hiding spot behind a pile of bags and wedged herself in. She was just in time, too, because as she pulled her foot out of sight one of the men slipped into the back of the plane from the cockpit to shut the door she had used to climb aboard. A few seconds earlier, and he would have seen her.

Fortunately, Nicole had had all the seconds she needed to tuck herself neatly away and he failed to see her. As the plane took off Nicole sighed in relief. And when the plane was fully in the air, she gathered her courage to peek her head around the pile of bags.

Michael! There he was, directly behind the pilot and copilot. She stared at his hands and realized they were not tied, as she had assumed. Nor could she spot a single rifle.

This required a bit of thinking. She shrunk back into her hiding spot to mull over the situation. Maybe things were not as dire as she had first thought. Could it be that Michael was not a prisoner? Had she been a prisoner? Was there any chance she had misunderstood the rifles shoved in her face and the makeshift prison cell? Might this whole mess be a simple misunderstanding?

Even though the three men in the cockpit had been talking since the plane took off, Nicole had been unable to hear what they were saying over the roar of the plane's engine. She decided her best bet, before she made any decisions about her next step, was to position herself so she could overhear the conversation.

Or, at least, that was her decision until she got a good look at the copilot. It was the very same man she had worked so hard to escape from earlier. The one his friends called Gregorio, but she only knew as the man who had wanted to kill her. The man she had hit on the back of the head with a chair.

She gulped. She could see the rather large bandage he sported under his hat. More proof that his identity, and her altercation with him, was not a product of her imagination.

Michael smiled at Gregorio, who was the copilot. Nicole realized her husband had no idea he was dealing with kidnappers and murderers. She had to warn him. The two of them had to get away from these men.

The conversation between the three men ended with a friendly laugh, and the pilot and Gregorio turned their focus back to the business of flying the plane. Nicole immediately rose to wave her arms about frantically, desperate to catch Michael's attention.

Gregorio turned to say something more to Michael. Nicole dropped back down behind the bags, barely in time. Gregorio, catching a glimpse of movement, probed the bags with his eyes. But he saw nothing. He shook his head in disgust—he likely thought the bump on his head had affected his eyesight—then spoke to Michael. After an exchange of a few more words, he again faced the front of the plane.

Nicole slowly and carefully peered out of her hiding place.

"Michael!" she hissed. "Hey, Michael!"

Nicole dove out of sight as Michael and Gregorio turned, in sync, toward her.

Frustrated that she could not get Michael's, and only Michael's, attention, Nicole inched around the bags to the other side of the plane.

"Michael!" she again hissed. "Hey, over here."

But Michael continued to sit quietly, oblivious to Nicole's presence.

Nicole crouched out of sight, frantic to come up with a way to get Michael's attention. Frustrated that no new ideas came to mind, she banged her fist against a bag. To her surprise, the pile wobbled. She gently pushed the pile a few more times, testing its stability.

The bags in her makeshift prison had been stacked in a way that made them virtually into cement blocks, sturdy and solid. The stacking here was loose and sloppy. There was no cohesion between the bags.

Nicole reached up to one of the top bags and shoved with all her strength. After several attempts, it tumbled over with a satisfying plop.

Nicole peeked around as Michael rose, only to be stopped by Gregorio. He seemed to be telling Michael to remain seated, not to worry about it.

But Nicole wanted Michael to worry about it. She wanted him to come to the back of the plane to check it out. So, she did the first thing that came to mind. She stood behind the pile and pushed with all her might. The pile swayed dangerously several times before it toppled over with a satisfying crash. Nicole dove behind a nearby pile before the men in the cockpit had time to react.

Breathing heavily from the exertion, Nicole pulled herself to her feet and carefully peeked around the bags. Good! Michael was rising from his seat.

Heart pounding in anticipation, Nicole took a few seconds to comb her fingers through her hair and bite her lips. She had not seen her husband in days, and even though she knew it was silly, she still wanted to look her best.

A huge smile spread across her face as the toe of a shoe moved into sight at the bottom of the bag.

But the smile vanished when around the pile walked Gregorio, a scowl on his face. Nicole stepped back from the angry man and straight onto another pair of toes.

CHAPTER 18

"Nicole? What are you doing here?"

At the sound of Michael's voice, Nicole spun around and landed in her husband's arms. She threw her arms around him and squeezed tight.

"Oh, Michael!" she said, into his chest. "I have so much to tell you! They said—"

Before she could tell her husband what they had said, Gregorio grabbed her arm, jerked her away from Michael, and marched her around the bags to the middle of the plane.

"It's okay, Gregorio," Michael explained, as he followed the irate man who was dragging his wife. "I know her."

"I do too," Gregorio countered, as he turned his scowl on Michael. "I do too!"

His face contorted with rage as he focused the full force of his anger on Nicole. He shoved her against the toppled bags, whipped out a gun, and thrust it in her face.

"Hey!" Michael bellowed. "What do you think you're doing?"

"Cleaning up a mess," Gregorio growled.

Michael grabbed Gregorio by the arm and pulled him away.

"Let her go!" he shouted. "This is my wife."

Gregorio shook off Michael's arm as he eyed him up and down.

"Then you're more of a fool than I thought," he sneered in reply.

Gregorio took a step toward Nicole, but Michael blocked him. Gregorio moved to the right, Michael followed suit. Gregorio jumped to the left, but Michael was a younger and quicker man, and again blocked him.

"Get out of my way," Gregorio growled. "You can't stop me, I will shoot her."

"What is wrong with you?" Michael roared. "I told you, she's my wife!"

"I don't care who she is," Gregorio snarled in return. "Nobody makes me look like an idiot and gets away with it."

Gregorio redoubled his effort to get to Nicole. Michael, determined to protect his wife, grabbed the gun. Gregorio countered by throwing himself at Michael and before either man had time to think through possible repercussions, they had begun to wrestle their way around the cabin. They even wrestled into the cockpit and slammed into the pilot. The plane tilted to the right as the pilot lost control, but luckily Michael and Gregorio took the fight back to the cargo hold, which gave the pilot a chance to right the plane.

"Keep fighting, Michael!" Nicole yelled, as she searched the back of the plane for anything she could use as a weapon. "I'll be right there to help."

Nicole grabbed a heavy flight manual, took aim at Gregorio, and threw it with all her might. But the heavy missile fell short.

She grabbed the next object she could find, which was a life preserver. She snatched it up and ran to slide it onto Gregorio's head, thinking she could use it to pull him off balance. But the struggling men suddenly switched positions and the life preserver landed around Michael's neck instead.

"Oops!" Nicole apologized. "Sorry."

Michael let go of Gregorio and ripped the preserver from around his neck. Gregorio took advantage of Michael's distraction to grab the gun and aim it at the young man.

"Michael, watch out!" Nicole screamed, terrified that her husband was about to be shot.

But Michael tossed the preserver out of the way and hit Gregorio's arm as the gun went off. The bullet missed Michael, but hit a bottle of oxygen in the cockpit, causing a fire to break out.

The pilot, suddenly confronted with flames lapping at his feet, struggled to maintain control of the plane. But he was finding it difficult to steer after the fire spread across the control panel and began to tickle his fingers with deadly flames.

Gregorio glared at Michael and Nicole, then at the flames.

"You idiot!" he yelled at Michael. He stopped fighting with Michael so he could pick up a fire extinguisher to try to put out the flames.

Michael grabbed Nicole's hands and pulled her to the back of the plane.

"Nicole, we have to get out of here."

"Michael!" Nicole ran her hands over her husband's face and chest. "Are you hurt?"

"Hurt?" Michael was offended. "Of course not. That guy is half my size and twice my age."

Michael shot a quick look at the front of the plane. Both the pilot and Gregorio were busy trying to put out flames and save the plane.

"But the stab wound?" Nicole continued her search for a wound. "At the jail, they told me you had been stabbed."

"Oh, that." Michael's face turned a deep, painful red.

"Yes, that. What happened?"

"It was nothing. Only a flesh wound," Michael dismissed his stab wound with a flap of his hand. "We can talk about it later."

Michael squinted toward the front. Gregorio was getting the flames under control.

"Look, Nicole," he grabbed his wife by the shoulders and stared deep into her eyes. "These guys are dangerous. We need to be out of here before they get that fire under control."

There was a loud pop from the cockpit followed by an explosion. Nicole looked worriedly toward the front of the plane. She was not at all sure Gregorio and the pilot would be able to get the flames under control.

"You don't think they'd fall for the old 'I can get you
lots of ransom' again, do you?"

"The old what?" Michael asked.

Nicole looked at his confused face, then at the flames
dancing around the cockpit. The explanation would take
too long. It could wait for later.

"Never mind," she said.

"Help me look," Michael pulled her behind the bags
and began to search the area.

"For what?"

"For parachutes. I saw some being loaded on."

Nicole watched in horror as Michael opened cabinets
and boxes until he finally found the parachutes. He put
one on himself and handed the other to Nicole to put on.

Nicole shook her head.

"I'll take my chances here," she declared, her eyes
wide in fear. "You go ahead."

Michael grabbed the parachute from her hands and
put it on her. As he snapped one of the harnesses closed,
Nicole grabbed his hand.

"Michael, I can't," Nicole shook her head violently.
"This is a lot higher than a temple and I couldn't even
climb the temple."

"If you stay, they'll shoot you."

Nicole blinked like a butterfly preparing for liftoff,
then nodded. She fastened her other harness while
Michael checked both parachutes to make sure
everything was secure. Nicole again grabbed his hands.

"Michael, why are you here?"

Michael looked Nicole in the eye and grinned
broadly.

"To rescue you, of course," he said. "Chief Valente told me you'd been kidnapped."

"But—"

A loud explosion from the front of the plane was followed by a change in the plane's movements as it began to rock erratically.

"Later." Michael inched around to open the plane door. "We've got to go."

Wind whipped through the cabin and fanned the flames Gregorio was working so hard to put out. The fire crackled merrily.

Nicole inched around the bags and hugged them tight, keeping as far from the open door as possible.

"Michael," she began when, catching sight of the empty space on the other side of the doorway, words failed her.

"Close your eyes. We'll do it together," Michael coaxed her. "Once we're out, count to three and pull the cord."

When Nicole's grip on the bags didn't lessen, Michael cast around and noticed a helmet on the other side of the plane.

"I have something that will help!" he shouted, as he jetted across the plane to grab the helmet.

The breeze from the open door alerted Gregorio to Michael's intention to jump, and the thought of Nicole escaping again infuriated him. Snatching up his gun, the angry man aimed at Nicole, determined to put an end to this particularly, pesky irritation.

Nicole, waiting near the open door, was an easy target for Gregorio. And with her eyes closed, she had no chance to realize that she was in danger.

But Michael did. With no thought of anything but his wife, he dove across the plane and pushed Nicole out the open door at the same moment the gun fired. The bullet missed Nicole but hit Michael in the leg. He fell to the floor in pain.

The flames, emboldened by the continued rush of oxygen flowing in the open door, spread from the cockpit to the rear of the plane.

Nicole missed all of this. After she felt Michael shove her out of the plane and the weightlessness of the open air, she waited the required three seconds to pull the cord. Other than the sudden jerk as her chute opened, it was rather pleasant to float peacefully down, eyes still closed.

"Michael, this is great!" she yelled, to her husband.

After a few more seconds of floating, she smiled.

"It isn't anywhere near as scary as I thought it would be!"

Several more seconds went by. It finally dawned on Nicole that although her husband should have responded, he had not.

She opened her eyes to find that Michael was nowhere in sight.

But the plane, the plane was fully visible, in the distance, completely enshrouded in flames.

"Michael!" Nicole cried, as she twisted frantically to try to catch sight of her husband.

"Michael! Where are you?"

The plane began to nosedive.

"Michael!" Nicole screamed, sure that he must be floating safely out of sight, somewhere behind her.

But her scream went unanswered and there was no sign of another parachute. The plane crashed into the jungle and exploded into even bigger flames.

Nicole sobbed hysterically as she floated gently toward the ground.

CHAPTER 19

A cool breeze brushed Nicole's cheeks and nudged her out of the blessed unconsciousness that had cocooned her for several hours.

"Michael where are we?" she called lazily, still mostly asleep.

And why shouldn't she be? It was her honeymoon, after all. And what was a honeymoon but a very specific type of vacation? Everyone knew vacations were for resting, relaxing, and sleeping late—

As if a switch had been flipped, her ears were abruptly attacked by a veritable cacophony of noises. Monkeys, frogs, crickets—

"The jungle," Nicole groaned, disgusted by the assault on her ears. "We must be back in the jungle."

A loud growl cut through the nighttime chatter of the jungle inhabitants, causing instant silence. Even Nicole, in her half-asleep state, held her breath. She couldn't help herself, since the growl had been disturbingly close. She gingerly opened one eye, fearful that she would find a big cat crouched in front of her, ready to pounce.

She sighed in relief when she saw only darkness. Complete, and utter darkness.

But where was she? Since her eyes were worthless in the thick darkness, she decided to put her hands to use. It only took a few seconds of exploring her surroundings to realize she was attached to a parachute and suspended in the air.

"Well, this is interesting," she muttered. She raised her voice a bit to yell to her husband, "Michael, I can't see anything. Where—?"

The memory of the plane dropping out of the sky, in flames, with Michael still on it, hit her like the proverbial ton of bricks. There was no more Michael. He was gone. He was—

"No!" Nicole wailed, as she dove so deep into an ocean of despair that she nearly drowned in grief. She sobbed uncontrollably for a full five seconds before another growl, this one even closer, shocked her quiet.

She stifled her sobs—not an easy thing to do while guilt and anguish warred for top place in her heart—and tightened her jaw. As quietly as humanly possible, she swallowed her tears and sucked in a slow, calming breath. Then, because she absolutely needed to know how high in the air she was hanging, she kicked her feet toward the ground.

But the kicks did nothing but make her bounce about like a puppet controlled by a three-year-old puppeteer. No matter how far down she reached she could find no ground beneath her, only air, air—and more air.

"Hey, cat! Make a little noise, why don't you? I think I'd feel better if I know where you are."

But the cat, being a magnificent predator, remained silent.

"Now what do I do?" Nicole grumbled.

As if in answer to her question, the moon peeked from behind a cloud and shot a ray of light through the branches and past her parachute, to shine a spotlight directly on a bright, yellow snake that was gliding its merry way in her direction along the branch directly above her.

"Snake!" Nicole yelled, as she caught sight of the slithering varmint. "It's a snake!"

She wiggled and twisted frantically as she tried to get out of the harness. When that proved useless, she ran her hands along the harness. There had to be a release mechanism, she knew there must. Safety regulations would require a quick way—

The snake hissed menacingly as it flicked its forked tongue at her, warning her to be still.

Nicole, terrified of snakes, froze in fear. But only for a moment. As soon as the serpent began to slither again in her direction, she thawed like a popsicle in the Sahara.

Especially when it licked its lips. Nothing makes a girl want to find the mechanism to release her from a hanging parachute than a hungry snake licking its lips.

Finally, she found the button, and after taking a deep breath, pressed it.

Nothing happened.

"No, no, no. Come on, work, you stupid button!" she yelled, as she frantically stabbed at the release with her thumb.

She shot a quick look at the dreaded snake, which was now so close she could probably see herself in its beady, little eyes. If she were stupid enough to look it in the eyes. Which she certainly was not. She watched *The Jungle Book* as a kid. She knew snakes hypnotized their prey. Uh-uh. Not her!

"Release!" she demanded, as she stopped stabbing it with her thumb and began to slam it with her fist. "Release! Come on!"

Without warning she got her wish. With a definitive *click*, the latch detached, and Nicole plummeted thirty feet to the ground.

Fortunately, Nicole was in luck. Instead of splatting onto hard ground, she splashed into a river. As she sputtered and spattered to the surface a low, guttural growl to her left caught her attention.

"Oh, no you don't!" she roared into the darkness, more angry than afraid. "I didn't escape that snake to be your midnight snack!"

The response she got sounded to her suspiciously like a frustrated snarl.

"Go do your shopping elsewhere. This grocery store is closed."

She turned to the right and swam to the shore opposite from where she had heard the big cat. As she dragged her exhausted body out of the water she was racked by shivers.

"I don't think I like the jungle very much," she muttered, through chattering teeth.

She wrung as much water as she could from her clothing, but it was of little use. She was wet through and through. Shivering in the cold, night air, she stumbled through the jungle underbrush, on her way to she-knew-not-where.

After nearly thirty minutes of stumbling over a plethora of invisible obstacles Nicole needed to catch her breath, so she found a handy tree against which to lean. But the tree was mossy and her hand wet, and before she knew what was happening, she had slipped sideways, her hand falling into a hollow space in the trunk of the tree.

Moonlight shining through the trees showed her that the hollow was uninhabited and dry. Exhausted both emotionally and physically, she climbed inside to relax against the warm bark.

"I love you, Michael," she whispered.

Then she fell into a deep sleep. So well hidden was she that no one passing would ever have known she was there, unless, as now, the moonlight hit at the right angle, causing the jade gemstone of the necklace around her neck to glow softly.

Chapter 20

The jade necklace glowed softly in the moonlight. Ix Tzutz Nik, tucked safely inside a hollow tree, sighed in her sleep as she turned to a more comfortable position. This shifted the necklace just enough that it was out of the light and no longer a beacon for the predators that prowled the nighttime jungle.

Not that Ix Tzutz Nik gave any thought to predators, or a desire to protect herself from them. She had chosen to sleep in the hollow tree, not for protection, but because she had stumbled across it after hours of wandering aimlessly through the jungle. She was tattered, torn, and more exhausted than should be humanly possible. That the tree would be a warm place to sleep had been her only consideration.

She slept deeply, but not dreamlessly. The horrible moment when she had lost her family replayed again, and again, all night long.

If only she had ignored the basket and stuck with her family. She would have been on the bridge with them. They would have been together when—

The growl of a jaguar, dangerously close, woke her. Instinctively alert and frightened, she scrambled out of the hollow only to find, a few feet directly in front of her, a powerful jaguar with its kill.

The jaguar growled loudly at her, as if to say, "this is mine!"

Ix Tzutz Nik, ruled by an instinctual need to survive, backed away from the big cat slowly and carefully. When her instincts deemed she was a sufficient distance away from the predator, they told her to run, so run she did. But her running was erratic, as nothing could stop the tears that streamed down her face.

Distressed, but compelled by a deep-seated need to save herself, Ix Tzutz Nik splashed across a stream as she ran for her life. Finally, wobbly with exhaustion, she tripped over a root and hit the ground. Too tired to rise, she wearily raised her head and there, above the tree line, was a familiar temple. She laid her head on top of her arms and sobbed hysterically.

Chapter 21

It was pure luck that Nicole managed to catch herself when she tripped over yet another root strewn across the ground. Had she not been able to keep to her feet, her trajectory would have landed her face first in a thorn bush the size of Minnesota. There would have been pain. Lots, and lots, of pain.

Exhausted, hungry, and as close to defeat as a person can be without truly being defeated, she straightened her back. Using more willpower than she knew she had, she forced her right foot to disconnect from the ground and move forward a step. Then she did the same for her left. And again, for her right. Over and over, step by step. Because unless she wanted to disappear into the jungle forever, it was imperative that she trudge on.

By this time, the jungle noises had become normal to her. So normal, in fact, that she almost failed to notice, mixed in with the ever-present bird and howler monkey noises, the sound of children's laughter.

Almost.

A snippet of high-pitched joy wafted past her ear, short-circuiting the zombie-like need to put one foot in front of the other that had kept her moving for hours. Her brain, which had been deadened by the drudgery of an unending hike, switched on as she stopped to listen.

But the snippet was a mere wisp, and like most wisps, it fluttered away into nothingness.

Disappointed, Nicole sighed as she allowed her brain to switch off again. The trance-like state was the only defense mechanism she had left. It kept her moving, but more importantly, it kept her sane.

Nicole shoved her way through a particularly thick set of bushes and kept moving. She was too out of it to notice that the ground beneath her feet had been cleared of roots, rocks, and low-hanging vines that might trip her up.

Clear and vibrant, the irrepressible laughter of children filled the air as a ball bounced a few feet from Nicole before hitting her on the head with a resounding thump.

The ball caused no pain but did manage to dislodge a burst of hysterical laughter that Nicole had tamped down hours earlier when she had fallen face-first into who-knows-what-kind-of-animal's poo. She allowed herself half a minute or so to let the laughter run its course. Then she grabbed the ball and ran like a quarterback toward the happy sound of children playing.

She shot out of the jungle into a small village made up of a few rudimentary roads and several shacks. In an open field at the edge of the tiny town, Belizean children had gathered to kick around several balls, most likely playing a game of their own design. Nicole tossed the ball back to them and turned her sights to the village.

She honed in on the first adult she spotted. It was a woman with a broom who appeared to be intent on rearranging the dirt in her front yard. With the woman as her goal, Nicole put her head down and made a beeline. So intent was she on reaching the woman that Nicole did not notice the other adults she passed. But they noticed her. Every one of them stopped what they were doing to stare at the crazy woman who was limping through their town covered in jungle gunk.

"Can you help me?" Nicole called, to the woman as she approached. But the woman ignored her and continued to sweep.

"Do you speak English?" Nicole yelled, in that extra-loud voice people so often use when they think someone cannot understand a language. "I need help. There's been a plane crash in the jungle."

As luck would have it, Nicole had chosen the only person in the entire village who was incapable of answering her question. Not only was the woman unable to understand English, but she was deaf as well.

But she could see perfectly well. As Nicole took another step forward the movement caught the woman's eye and she looked up. Startled to find a stranger covered in muck heading her way, the woman tilted her head and stared.

"Please!" Nicole pleaded. She practically ran the last few feet so she could grab the woman's arm. "Is there anyone who can help?"

As Nicole's hand fastened onto the woman's arm, the villager's face flooded with panic. She was a well-respected member of the village and could not understand why this strange woman was grabbing her this way.

Nicole should have recognized the look of panic on the woman's face. She should have let go of the poor woman's arm and gone in search of someone else who could help her.

But Nicole's brain had ceased working properly hours ago. Besides, she was frantic. So instead of letting go, she pulled on the woman's arm as she continued to plead.

"Please help me! My husband was on that plane. I need to find him."

The woman's eyes grew larger and larger as she struggled to pull away. Nicole did not notice. This villager, wearing her clean clothing and holding a broom, represented civilization. Civilization meant safety. Nicole had no intention of letting safety slip out of her grasp.

The village woman was about ready to faint when a girl of about ten rushed over to intervene. The child pointed toward a dilapidated building in the center of the village.

"Thank you," Nicole responded, as she smiled at the girl. Then, without a further thought for the woman she had just been accidentally torturing, she released her grasp and ran to the building. A knock on the door brought an elderly woman, who ushered Nicole inside.

Several hours, numerous explanations, and a gruelingly long car ride later, Nicole found herself at a table in the San Ignacio police station. After bringing her a cup of coffee, Policeman Flowers pulled out a chair and sat across from her.

"We are very sorry about your husband, Mrs. Quinn," the kind officer assured Nicole.

Unfortunately, after all she had been through, kindness was too much for Nicole. A floodgate of tears opened and before long there was a small lake on the table. Officer Flowers quickly retrieved a box of tissue, which he placed in front of Nicole.

"I'm sorry," Officer Flowers continued, as he resumed his seat. "We found the plane, but there's nothing left for you to take home. Only the shell of the plane remained intact. Everything inside was burned beyond recognition."

Nicole's face blanched white as she imagined Michael trapped in the burning plane. Instantly, her sobs grew too loud for Officer Flowers' sensitive ears. He grabbed a fresh tissue from the box to hand to her, and when that did not help, he reached across the table to awkwardly pat her shoulder.

Still, even with Officer Flowers' kind ministrations, it took several minutes for Nicole to regain enough control that she could take the sobs down a notch or two.

"Couldn't he have jumped?" she finally managed to ask. "Like me?"

Officer Flowers looked at the grieving woman with pity. No matter how gently he tried to say what he needed to say, he could not make this easier for her. It was best to pull the bandage off quickly. Get all the pain out of the way at once, so the healing could begin.

"No chance," he declared bluntly. "We searched the jungle for miles around. We found no sign of your husband."

"But what if—?"

"He went down with the plane, ma'am."

"But—"

"Accept it."

Officer Flowers knew it was his duty to convince this grieving woman that her husband had died in the plane crash. It was the only way she could move on and go back to America.

He was focused on the task at hand and failed to notice the man and woman, both suspiciously clean-cut, who entered the station. Not that it mattered, because after a quick question to the patrolman behind the counter, the pair made a beeline to where the young police officer was awkwardly consoling the bereaved widow.

"Mrs. Quinn?"

At the sound of new American voices, Officer Flowers twisted around so fast he nearly pulled a muscle in his neck. He was offended that these new people, whoever they were, felt they had a right to interfere with a police officer doing his duty.

"You are?" he challenged. His voice had lost any sign of kindness.

"Cassidy Diaz and Andrew Larkin," the woman replied. "We're conducting an investigation into the plane crash."

"You're Americans?" Nicole looked up when she heard familiar accents. She grabbed another tissue and tried to mop up her face.

"We are from the American embassy," the man called Andrew Larkin explained, with a nod. Without asking permission, Andrew and Cassidy took seats at the table. This further insulted Officer Flowers, causing him to sit back in his chair so he could cross his arms in front of his chest.

This interested Nicole enough to close the floodgates to the river of tears, but it also confused her.

"The embassy?" Nicole's eyebrows shot nearly to her hairline. Then, in the next instant, the brows dropped down to sit close atop her eyes as she asked suspiciously. "I was told you guys just stayed put and gave advice."

"Normally we do." Diaz smiled pleasantly, as she explained. "We are on a little, fact-finding mission. There are things we don't understand about the crash, things you might be able to clear up."

"You could have asked me to come to the embassy," Nicole challenged.

"We could have," Ms. Diaz agreed, "But we knew you'd be upset. We didn't want to inconvenience you, so we decided to come to you."

"What exactly are you investigating?"

"Your husband—," Cassidy began, but when she paused to order her thoughts Nicole took it to mean they were investigating Michael. When the widow's eyes widened in shock, Andrew Larkin noticed and broke in.

"Any time an American citizen dies on foreign soil, there's an investigation," he explained. "We've been tasked to write the report."

Cassidy turned to the young police officer and respectfully asked, "Can she go now? I'd like to get her somewhere more comfortable."

"Certainly," Officer Flowers agreed, flattered by the respect in the woman's voice. "You could take her back to her hotel."

"And she can return home—?"

"Whenever she wants." Officer Flowers shrugged dismissively. "We have no reason to hold her."

Cassidy raised an eyebrow to her partner and received what must have been a telepathic answer. She gave a nod.

"In that case," she said, as she rose to her feet, "I think our conversation would be better accomplished at the hotel."

"Agreed." Andrew also rose and turned to Nicole. "Would you like us to drive you there, Mrs. Quinn?"

Nicole stared at the three, compassionate faces turned her way. The two emissaries from the embassy were obviously the nurturing sort. Officer Flowers, having forgotten he should be offended that the embassy had sent interlopers to butt in, had again allowed his natural compassion full rein.

It was almost enough to make her cry again.

But crying took a good bit of energy. More than she had left after her trek through the jungle. She simply nodded her agreement, and the three Americans left the station together.

Nicole's first chore was to pack her belongings. Then, unfortunately, she had to pack Michael's. After she recuperated from the bout of sobbing that brought on, she called her mother.

Breaking the news to her mother was an ordeal all its own. After Nicole managed to deal with the spate of blubbering shock that poured from the phone, she did the first truly adult thing of her life.

"No, Mom," she decreed, when her mother offered to call Michael's parents, "they don't know yet and don't you tell them. It's my responsibility."

Nicole listened with as much patience as she could muster to the tearful plea that Michael's parents deserved to be told immediately, but she remained firm.

"Michael is," she paused, just long enough to gulp before she continued, "Michael WAS my husband. His parents deserve to be told in person. By me."

Nicole listened for several more seconds, but the flow of words from her mother only made her sadder.

"I know, Mom. But I can't talk about that right now. I just need to come home."

Before her mother could continue, she took a deep breath and blurted, "Will you go with me?"

The response, so loud Nicole had to pull the phone away from her ear, brought a watery smile to the new widow's face. When the noise level lessened somewhat, she put the phone back to her ear.

"Thanks, Mom. I need to go now. Love you."

Nicole hung up the phone and tossed it onto the bed. Then, catching sight of Michael's suitcase, she ran her hand across it lovingly.

"One, stupid, little suitcase," she whispered, "that's all I have left of him."

Grief stabbed her heart, causing her to lash out at the unsuspecting suitcase. She slammed it with her fist.

"We were supposed to grow old together!"

She continued to slam the suitcase, only stopping when her palm bled.

"We were supposed to have adventures together!"

Cradling the injured hand, she threw herself onto the bed and curled into a fetal position.

"We were supposed to have a whole life together," she sobbed. "Together!"

Then the sobs turned into wails and Nicole cried herself to sleep.

Chapter 22

The following morning found Nicole at the entrance of the airport with those two nice embassy representatives, Cassidy and Andrew. Not only had they taken care of her plane ticket back to Seattle and hotel bill, but they had even given her a ride to the airport.

"I'll get a dolly for the bags," Andrew proclaimed, as he unloaded suitcases from the trunk.

"Are you sure you don't want us to go in with you?" Cassidy kindly asked Nicole. "We can make things easier."

"I don't want things to be easier," Nicole replied, "and I want to be alone."

Cassidy nodded to show she understood and would comply.

"We want you to know the embassy is very sorry about the loss of your husband. We put you in first class."

Nicole opened her mouth to deny that the extra comfort was necessary but was stopped by Cassidy.

"It'll give you a little more privacy. The least we could do."

Nicole shrugged, nodded her thanks, and marched into the airport, dragging her luggage on a dolly behind her.

As Nicole trudged across the airport on her way to the customs line, a pathway magically opened before her. It was as if sadness exuded from every pore of her body, creating a forcefield around the grieving woman that no one could penetrate. And once she reached the customs line, while she still had to inch along like all the rest of the international travelers, everyone continued to give her space.

Which proves that even if misery does like company, no one wants to be that company.

Fellow travelers on either side of Nicole instinctively created as much distance as possible from the ground zero of misery. When she took a step forward, those further along shoved, crowded, and stepped on toes to keep outside her bubble of sadness. Those behind her waited a ridiculous amount of time before they 'noticed' that a gap had formed in the line.

It was quite like a slinky that had had its middle stretched out of shape. It worked, but its movement was unnatural and wonky.

But not everyone took notice of Nicole's grief. Whether by natural ability, or a wall that had taken years to build, there were those who neither noticed, nor cared, about the feelings of the people they encountered.

The customs officer was such a person. When presented with Nicole's smiling face on her passport, he compared it to the tear-streaked face in front of him, smiled, and asked, "Do you have anything to declare?"

The waves of sadness that flowed from Nicole as she shook her head could have sunk a ship. Tears streaming, the grieving woman dug through her purse to find a fresh tissue to dam the river that refused to stay behind her lashes.

"In that case," the customs officer laughed merrily, immune to the drama of tears, "I hope you enjoyed your time in Belize and will come again soon."

Nicole took the passport the jovial man handed her and silently moved on. Tears blurred her eyes to about 20/200, so she was oblivious that she had left a line of tissues fluttering like white flags of surrender in her wake across the airport.

As she boarded the plane a stewardess approached her with a smile bright enough to light up the gloomiest bog.

"Good morning!" the stewardess chirped merrily. "Anything I can get you? Pillow, drink, snack?"

"No, thanks," Nicole mumbled in reply.

"Enjoy the flight. You'll be back home in no time!"

The stewardess went about her business, unaware that in the battle between light and gloom, her battle-hardened smile, crafted through years of working with the irritable and the irrational, had won the day.

Nicole nodded sadly, buckled her seat belt with a resounding click, and closed her eyes.

As a single tear rolled down her cheek her seatmate, a middle-aged woman who had a daughter about Nicole's age, was suddenly reminded that that daughter had recently been through a bad breakup. She pulled out a tissue and surrendered to the dark side.

* * *

The contagion of pain continued to spread the next day when Nicole and her mother visited Michael's parents to give them the sad news. It was every bit as hard as Nicole had thought it would be. As Nicole watched, Michael's parents grieved—his dad in a daze and his mom sobbing hysterically with her son's picture clasped to her breast. Only then did Nicole realize she was not the only one who had suffered a tragic loss.

She sprang from the couch where she had been sitting with her mother to wrap her arms around her in-laws. They were family and would cry as a family.

* * *

Tears might be shed and hearts broken, but life goes on. When college classes resumed in the fall, Nicole opted to attend. She had already spent too many lonely days in the apartment that had been leased as the newlywed's first home together. More time would do nothing to lessen her pain.

Besides, the sooner she began her career as an artist the better. She had emotions galore bubbling up inside, waiting to burst out on the canvas. She would put them to good use.

Only, when classes started, she found she had a problem. Instead of the pain giving her a reason to paint, it drained her. Even picking up a paintbrush was a chore.

One day, a few weeks into the quarter, Nicole was in Professor Scott's class. Professor Scott was her favorite, the very professor who had inspired her to pursue a career as an artist.

The twenty students in the classroom, each with a clear view of the dais at the front of the room, had been tasked to translate a three-dimensional model into streaks of paint on a flat surface.

The professor, as good professors often do, walked around the class, stopping every so often to give advice or comment. Nicole was neither surprised nor insulted when the professor stopped at her painting to inspect it.

"Nicole," the kind professor asked, after she looked from the canvas to the model, "how are you holding up?"

"I'm fine," Nicole answered, as she added a bit of blue to a corner.

"You know," the professor continued, stepping back to take an overview look at the huge canvas, "it's only been a month. No one would think less of you if you took more time before you resumed your studies."

Nicole continued painting, as if she had not heard her teacher's words. She purposefully added a few strokes of green to the center.

"Nicole, do you hear me?" the professor prodded gently.

"I don't need time," Nicole replied gruffly, never taking her eyes from her work. "I'd rather paint."

As she reached over to add yet another dab of paint to the canvas Professor Scott gently caught her hand.

"Nicole, you're not ready."

"What?" Nicole asked in surprise. "Why would you say that?"

The professor dropped Nicole's hand and headed to a storage room. There she retrieved three paintings of various sizes. After lining them up next to Nicole's current painting she gently guided Nicole to a spot where she could view all four paintings at the same time.

"Look at them, Nicole. Really look."

Nicole stared at the paintings blankly for several moments. Then her face crumpled into tears.

"They're Michael," Nicole whispered, as she covered her face with her hands. "How did I not notice?"

"Take the rest of the quarter off. Give yourself time to heal," the professor urged.

"But I thought painting would help me heal," Nicole moaned. "I thought—"

"It will," the professor reassured her, "when you're ready."

Nicole nodded and began to gather her paintings. The professor reached out a hand to stop her.

"I'll take care of that. Go home. Mourn your husband. Heal."

Nicole stared into the kind eyes of her professor for several seconds before she nodded and left. The professor sighed and moved Nicole's paintings to the storage room for safe keeping.

CHAPTER 23

A few days later Nicole embraced a self-prescribed healing routine which included a daily visit to at least one of Michael's favorite places. Third on the list was Gasworks Park, Michael's favorite location for picnics and kite flying.

Not that Nicole planned to do any of the more popular activities, such as kite flying or lunch eating. No, the most she could hope for was a meandering trudge around the park with the occasional pause to smell a flower or two.

She had totally discounted the human element. Her meander stalled to a halt every time she spotted a young man with Michael's build, a couple holding hands, or, the most mesmerizing of all, children.

She thoroughly freaked out a young mother when she gave her a very sad, very haunted smile. But she could not help herself. The baby was wearing a tiny fedora that was an exact replica of the one Michael had loved to wear. It nearly broke her heart.

Nicole's eyes remained glued to the child as she wistfully thought of the children she and Michael would have had. Should have had.

Tears filled her eyes and blurred her vision for several seconds. Long enough for her to miss the suspicious look the young woman threw her way. The grieving widow had no clue she was the cause when the young mother quickly strapped her fedora-wearing baby into a stroller and headed to the other side of the park.

Nicole wiped tears from her eyes and gave a watery smile to the pair as she watched them move away. This disturbed the young mother, who became even more concerned as the strange woman continued to watch her baby. Deciding it would be better to go home and feed her child early rather than risk him being snatched by a crazy woman, the worried mother changed direction and headed straight for her car.

Later that day, while the young mother was cleaning smeared banana from the wall, the image of the crazy woman's smile came back to haunt her. She still could not pinpoint what about the smile disturbed her, but she suddenly had an uncontrollable desire to hug her child.

Back at Gasworks, Nicole had resumed her search for healing. It was a slow process, and Nicole could see herself haunting Michael's favorite places for years, until a movement in the distance caught her eye. She was nearly startled out of her grief when she recognized the unusual figure in a nearby grove of trees. It was the Stone Woman.

"She followed me here?" Nicole whispered in shock.

The next several minutes consisted of Nicole staring at the Stone Woman, while the Stone Woman stared at her. Meanwhile, all around her, recreation proceeded as normal. Dog owners walked their dogs. Parents played with their children. Friends exchanged dreams about the future and chatted about mundane happenings in their daily life.

Nicole should have wondered why no one else was surprised the see a ghost in the park. But quite frankly, she had forgotten that there was anyone else in the park. Her focus was locked on the ghost that had followed her home all the way from Belize.

Then a ball, thrown by a toddler, hit her legs before landing with a thump at her feet.

Strange as it may seem, Nicole's eyes were drawn away from the otherworldly presence of the ghost by that multicolored toy. Mundane as it was, the plastic ball refused to be ignored.

Grabbing the ball, Nicole smiled as she brushed off several grains of sand and gently tossed it back to the child. Without missing a beat, the child grinned mischievously, grabbed a shovel, and preceded to bury the ball in the sand.

That made Nicole smile. Then she remembered the Stone Woman and scanned the grove of trees for her, but the ghost was gone.

The next day Nicole was scheduled to work. The retail job she had gotten several years ago was so familiar to her she could perform her duties without having to think. While people around her shopped for clothes, Nicole retreated to her own little world as she folded a pile of shirts destined for a display rack.

She finished stacking the shirts and moved robotically to the storeroom to retrieve more clothing that needed to be put out on the floor. But as she grabbed a pile of jeans and turned toward the doorway, the Stone Woman appeared, blocking her path.

"What do you want?" she yelled, fear causing her voice to be more belligerent than she intended.

But the Stone Woman gave no answer. She simply stood in the doorway, silent and semi-transparent.

"Why are you here?" Nicole yelled.

The Stone Woman disappeared as another one of her coworkers stepped into the storeroom, obviously offended.

"To tell you that the manager wants you to hurry up with those jeans. Aren't you the touchy one!"

"Oh, sorry." Nicole cringed as she realized her coworker had assumed that she was the target of all that aggression. "I didn't mean—"

"What? To bite my head off? Well, you did. And I don't appreciate it one bit."

Nicole squeezed her eyes closed, which caused a tear, one of many that had taken to hanging out in the corners of her eyes, to roll down her cheek.

"Jeesh! Are you crying again? You've turned into a real waterworks, you know."

"I'm not crying!" Nicole angrily wiped away the offending tear. "My eyes just got watery from dust. This storeroom is a mess."

The coworker looked around the storeroom, which was indeed rather dusty. She nodded.

"Then what about those jeans?" The coworker raised a brow as she tamped down any remaining anger she felt. "If you're not going to get them, I'll have to—"

"I've got them right here," Nicole huffed, as she raised the pile of jeans in her arms and shoved her way past her coworker to the store floor.

"Fine," the coworker muttered, as she looked back at the storeroom. Then under her breath, she added, "But I'm not cleaning this storeroom."

That was the last of the Stone Woman for that day, but not for the days that followed.

The next few days, it seemed that wherever Nicole went, so went the Stone Woman.

Even shopping with friends at her favorite downtown store, a place she assumed would be safe, filled, as it was, with crowds of people.

But the Stone Woman followed her even there. No one else noticed the semi-transparent woman who gazed at Nicole with the saddest eyes imaginable. Her friend even walked right past the ghost to give a donation to a street musician who was playing the violin just outside the door. Nicole rushed through the glass entrance doors, intent on facing her fears. But the Stone Woman had vanished.

Nicole had breathed a sigh of relief when the ghost disappeared. Though she had gathered the nerve to face the ghost, she did not want to confront the woman.

That night Nicole watched a movie on her couch, tears streaming down her face as she gave in to her overwhelming loss. The flood of tears made her eyes too blurry to see Cinderella with her Prince, but that did not bother Nicole. She had seen the movie at least a thousand times as a child and had it memorized.

What the grieving woman did not realize, and could not see, was that she was not grieving alone. Sitting on the arm of the couch, wispy and silent, was the Stone Woman.

And so, it continued. The Stone Woman appeared to Nicole several times a day, sometimes noticed, sometimes not.

But even when she did not see the ghost, Nicole always felt her. The ghost's grief slowly and gradually became mixed with Nicole's, giving Nicole an extra heavy burden to bear.

As time went on, instead of Nicole learning to live with her grief, she became more and more overwhelmed by it.

Nicole's mother noticed Nicole sliding deeper into grief and planned an outing for Nicole that she hoped would brighten her child's outlook on life.

Nicole had always loved museums. Knowing this, the grieving widow's mother grabbed Nicole's sister, Jessica, and off the three women went to absorb a little culture.

As Nicole, her mom, and Jessica paid their admission fees to the smiling cashier Nicole felt a slight lessening of pain.

"Thanks for suggesting this, Mom. It's just what I need."

"I'm worried about you, sweetie," her mother replied, as she guided her daughters toward the first exhibit. "Ever since you came back from Belize you've been...a little depressed."

"It's not called depression, Mom." The snarky tones and eye rolls were leftovers from Nicole's teenage years and typically resurfaced in times of stress. "It's called grief."

Mother and daughter glanced at each other—daughter, in this case, meant Jessica as Nicole was currently stuck in a teenage-inspired sneer—as if they were asking the other if it was time to execute the plan. Nicole caught the look and went on instant alert.

"Nicole." Jessica bit her lip as her eyes darted to her mother. When she got the nod, she continued. "I wanted to ask you something."

"Shoot," Nicole said cautiously, fully aware she had been set up.

"I was thinking about what you told me the other day, about that ghost you saw."

Nicole intercepted another look that passed between her mother and sister. What were these two up to?

When her mom gave a second nod of approval, Nicole steeled herself. Whatever Jessica planned to ask had to be a real doozy. This belief became even stronger when, as her sister stepped closer, her mother stepped away a few paces and stared, seemingly enthralled, at an artifact enclosed in a glass case. It was her mom's 'on guard' mode, one she only used when what was about to be said needed to be kept private.

"Do you still see it?" Jessica whispered.

"You mean, like now?" Nicole whispered back.

"No, silly," Jessica gave up whispering to speak in a normal voice. "I mean, have you seen it since you got back home?"

Nicole scrutinized Jessica closely, which made her sister fidget nervously.

"Why?"

Jessica bit her lip and shot a look at her mother, who mouthed encouragement.

"Jessica, why?" Nicole demanded, and this time a small flake of the anger that had been just below the surface since Michael died slipped out.

"I've been doing a little research about ghosts, that's all."

"Right." Nicole grimaced as she rolled her eyes. "Research about ghosts. Uh-huh. Sounds good. What did you find? That people who see ghosts need psychological help?"

If Nicole had even a smidgen of doubt that her mother was a part of this conversation, it was obliterated when she swooped in to gently place a hand on Nicole's arm.

"Sweetie, your sister isn't trying to make fun of you, or hurt you," the woman who spent years keeping the peace in their home said, "she wants to help."

"How, by getting me locked up somewhere?" Nicole turned to her mother in despair. "I can hear it now, you'll tell all your friends how your daughter lost her mind when she lost her husband."

"Nicole!" her horrified mother scolded.

Nicole pulled away from both mother and sister and practically sprinted to the other side of the room. It was lucky that the museum was nearly empty because her eyes were too blurred by tears for her to be able to see where she was going. If anyone had gotten in her way, she most likely would have mowed them down like spring grass.

As it was, she somehow managed to find a display, which she spent the next few minutes pretending to be fascinated with as a deluge of tears turned her face into a swamp of grief.

Nicole's back was to her mother and sister, so at first, they thought Nicole only wanted a few moments alone to get over her anger. But when a gasping sob flew across the room to tattle about Nicole's true feelings, both women promptly rushed to Nicole's side.

"Leave me alone!" Nicole wailed, before either woman had a chance to lay a consoling hand on her shoulder.

"Nicole, you misunderstand," Jessica pleaded. "We believe you."

Nicole turned misery-filled eyes on her mother and sister.

"Honestly," Jessica continued. "We don't think you're crazy at all."

"Really?"

Hope glowed on Nicole's face as she took the tissue offered by her mom and used it to wipe up as much of the swamp as she could from her face.

"You don't think I made the whole thing up?"

"No, sweetie," her mom's smile was gentle and loving, "we don't! Not at all."

"Thank you!" Nicole wrapped one arm around her mom and the other around her sister and squeezed tight.

"But it sounds so crazy. How can you believe me?"

Nicole's mom exchanged yet another look with her sister, then smiled.

"You're my daughter, Nicole," she explained softly. "Of course, I believe you."

"Okay, chalk one up for motherly love," Nicole giggled, then turned to her sister. "What about you? What makes you so sure I haven't gone totally cuckoo?"

"One, you're my sister. I love you. And trust you," Jessica replied, with a grin.

But when she stopped and said nothing else, Nicole was forced to ask, "Okay. Is there a two?"

"Yep," Jessica answered mischievously, "a good one."

Instead of telling her sister what that good one was, she grinned the same grin she used when they were growing up. The one that meant she knew something that Nicole did not.

Nicole detested that grin. It had tormented her in her childhood and made her distrust her own budding thought processes more times than she would care to admit. To regain what little self-esteem she still possessed, she put her hands on her hips in the traditional Superman style and raised an eyebrow at her always mischievous, sometimes irritating sister.

This power stance should bring Jessica down a peg or two, Nicole thought. Make her rethink the advisability of that childish grin.

Unfortunately for Nicole, Jessica was not built that way. Instead of being intimidated, the mischievous girl was vastly amused. Maybe it was because she had always thought power stances were silly. Maybe because growing up, she had always been the intimidator. Either way, the result was that Jessica's grin, instead of dimming, grew brighter than ever.

Worse still, she giggled.

It was the giggle that caused Nicole to concede defeat. Just as she had always done.

"Fine, I'll bite," Nicole grumbled. "What is it?"

"It's standing right there," Jessica snickered, as she pointed across the room.

Nicole looked where Jessica was pointing to find the Stone Woman, watching, her eyes exuding a sadness greater than any human should be forced to bear.

Nicole whipped around to her sister and grabbed the girl's arms like a drowning swimmer grabs a life raft.

"You see her?" she asked, her voice barely above a whisper.

"We both do," her mom interjected. "How could we miss her? She's been following you around for weeks."

"I know."

Nicole tilted her head and blinked rapidly for at least a full minute. It was a mannerism she had started as a youngster, a mannerism that never failed to amuse her sister. Jessica turned slightly to hide her smile.

"No one said anything," Nicole mused. "I thought—"

"Said anything! What were we supposed to say, 'Hey Nicole, you've got a ghost for a shadow?'" Jessica quipped. "It's a bit too creepy, you know."

Nicole rolled her eyes at her sister. Jessica rolled her eyes right back. Their mom handled the situation by doing what she always did when she suspected one of her children was upset—and how could Nicole not be upset when on top of losing Michael she was also being haunted by the ghost of a strange woman—she wrapped her motherly arms around the wounded daughter and squeezed tight.

The warmth of her mother's loving embrace worked its magic immediately. Nicole instantly felt stress leave her body and hope take its place.

"What does she want, Nicole? Why does she follow you?"

"I don't know, Mom," Nicole answered. She allowed herself a long, slow sigh and felt another level of stress leave her body. "She won't talk to me."

"You've got to do something to get rid of her, sweetie," the worried mother explained. "It's not healthy having a ghost follow you around all day."

The comment was so true, yet so ridiculous, that Nicole could not help but smile.

"You're so good at stating the obvious, Mom," Nicole tittered, as she squeezed her mother tight. "I think that's what I love about you most!"

"I would think it would be because she puts up with your nonsense!" Jessica snorted.

"Jessica! Your sister—"

"Nicole!" Jessica ignored what was likely the start of a reprimand from her mother to pull Nicole out of the hug and twirl her around. "What are you going to do about her?"

Nicole's gaze shifted from her sister to the ghost as she contemplated her choices. She had no idea how a person would go about getting rid of a ghost. She had never believed in ghosts. Had not thought of them except as a possible costume for Halloween. And since she had no interest in ghosts, she had avoided movies and books that had ghosts as their focus.

Her knowledge of ghosts, and how to deal with them, was sparse.

Still, she had a gut feeling that the first thing she needed to do was figure out why the dead woman had begun following her in the first place. As far as she could see there was no connection between them—

Nicole smiled gently as a memory intruded into her thoughts. It was of the day Michael had given her the necklace she still wore around her neck. She could almost feel the touch of his hands, and the feel of his kiss.

As she thought of Michael, Nicole gently laid her hand on the necklace. The Stone Woman glowed brighter, and her smile seemed a tiny bit less sad.

Nicole stared at the ghost. Then she held the necklace away from her body so she could see it. After looking from the necklace to the ghost several times, she realized the ghost was standing in front of a graphic of a Mayan woman, wearing a necklace very like Nicole's.

It made sense. That ghostly glow in response to Nicole touching the necklace had given her the clue she needed to understand. She believed she knew why she was being haunted.

"I'm going back," Nicole blurted out without warning. It sounded more like the final words of a long argument rather than the beginning of an explanation.

"Back?" Jessica asked, not sure if Nicole meant she was going back to the last room of artifacts, back to her apartment, or back to their parents' house.

"Yes, I've decided. I'm going back to Belize." Nicole laid her hand over the pendant of the necklace and gave a rather enigmatic smile. "I'm taking her home."

Something about that smile frightened Nicole's mother and sister. It was not an expression they typically associated with Nicole. It was secretive, mysterious, and implied an independence that was foreign to Nicole's nature.

Nicole's mother looked for the ghost, but she was gone. But instead of the ghost's absence reassuring her, it planted a seed in her brain that quickly sprouted into a terrible thought. And when Jessica saw the look of horror on her mother's face, the same thought became planted in her head, too.

Nicole had been possessed by the ghost!

Fortunately, before either woman had time to fall too deep into that particular rabbit hole, Nicole noticed the looks on their faces and decided to explain.

"I have to take her back," she gently told her mother, as she took the older woman's now trembling hands. "I don't have a choice."

"Of course, you have a choice. Fight it. Why don't you—?"

"Mom, I have to do this."

"Why? You can—"

"What? Live with the ghost for the rest of my life?"

"No, Nicole, that's not what I meant. We can find help. We can—"

"I'm going to Belize, Mom."

"Nicole! Don't let her take you!"

"No one's trying to take me, Mom. I need—"

"Can't you see you're being controlled, Nicole? If she gets you back in Belize, she'll never let you go. We'll lose you. Oh, Nicole—"

"Mom," Nicole reassured her, "I'm not staying in Belize."

"Nicole you can't—"

This continued for several more minutes, each side restating their argument multiple times. Finally, when Jessica was tired of watching, she stepped between the combatants and grabbed Nicole by the hands.

Turning her sister until they were eye-to-eye, she stared closely into what she hoped was the very depths of her sibling's soul. They stayed that way for quite a few moments, until Jessica dropped Nicole's hands and shrugged.

"That's Nicole, through and through," she said with finality to her mother. "No ghost there."

Then she turned to give a puzzled look to her sister.

"I don't get it," Jessica shook her head. "Why don't you just get some ghost buster type of person to get rid of her? Why do you have to go back to Belize?"

"Necklace," Nicole explained, as she gently placed her palm over the jade stone.

Both her sister and mother stared at her blankly. Which was fair, since as explanations went, Nicole's one-word explanation explained very little.

"Michael was told this necklace was a fake, so he didn't examine it. He assumed they'd want an arm and a leg for the real thing."

"So?"

"I think this necklace belonged to the ghost. Before she was a ghost."

The two women looked at Nicole blankly. She pointed to an illustration of a Mayan woman wearing a jade necklace.

"She wants her necklace back."

Jessica and her mother did not look in the least bit convinced, but Nicole wasn't worried. Because during that awkward conversation with her mother, only part of her brain had been focused on the argument. The other part had been busy coming up with a plan.

She bought her ticket to Belize that very night, and miracle of miracles, there was a cheap fare available for the very next day. She packed a suitcase, laid her passport on top, and climbed into bed.

CHAPTER 24

That night Nicole had the best sleep she had gotten since Michael's death. Whether it was because she finally had a goal, or because she was simply too tired to lay awake bemoaning her loss like she normally did, she awoke refreshed after a dreamless night.

More importantly, when she opened her eyes and looked around her apartment, there was no ghostly figure watching her every move.

Not that the Stone Woman had deserted her. Once she got to the airport and had cleared customs, she spotted her ghostly friend near the door. Nicole unconsciously reached up to touch her necklace, but before her hand made contact a man late for his flight slammed a suitcase into her legs and nearly knocked her off her feet. The glare she sent the oblivious man went unnoticed, as he had already moved on. She watched for a moment as he ran over the toes of an elderly man sitting in a chair, separated a toddler from his mother—which resulted in a wail of fear on the toddler's part—and crashed into a woman as she took a sip from a steaming cup of coffee.

The woman managed to avoid a scalding spill, but only barely, as the human bulldozer plowed his way across the airport, blind to the path of devastation he left in his wake.

Nicole shook her head in disgust as she glanced toward the Stone Woman, who had once again disappeared.

After that, Nicole did what every other traveler around her did. She kept a sharp lookout for more bulldozers as she waited for her flight to be called, took her seat after she boarded the plane, and continued on her journey.

Nicole's plan was simple. Figure out where the necklace came from and put it back. That should satisfy the ghost.

But the plan was given a hiatus when, the moment her feet touched Belizean soil, she was overwhelmed by a grief so deep and wide that it rendered her unable to function properly.

She needed closure, and she needed it fast.

The best way to find that closure, she realized, was to get as much information about the crash as she could unearth. She needed to understand how her husband died. Where he died. And perhaps most importantly, why he died.

Her first stop, she decided, would be the embassy. That man and woman who had interviewed her had seemed to be competent people. Surely by now they had finished their investigation and knew all the who's, where's, and why's of the crash. They could help her fill in the blanks.

But when she arrived at the American Embassy, she hesitated. As she stood staring up at the cold stones of the building, she inadvertently blocked the sidewalk being used by Belizean passersby and vendors going about their daily business.

She wanted to go in. She needed to go in. But she simply could not make herself take that first step.

"What is wrong with you?" she muttered under her breath. "Move!"

She slapped the back of her leg with her hand, thinking she could spur it forward. But the leg remained where it was. It had no intention of moving.

"Come on, get going," she growled, through gritted teeth, "go inside."

This continued for several more minutes, with Nicole muttering while she slapped, pinched, and punched different parts of her body to encourage them to follow her commands.

Those whose paths took them past the embassy found themselves giving plenty of elbow room to the strange woman who had planted herself in the middle of their walkway. She was facing a wall, so who did she think she was talking to? Why did she keep punching her own legs and slapping her own face? Was she harmless, or was she a danger?

Not a single person wanted to get close enough to find out, so each of them individually decided to make a wide berth around the odd creature. If she was harmless, it never hurt to give a person enough space to work through their issues. If she was dangerous…well, it was wise to keep a good distance away from those who were mentally unstable.

Like this kook.

Nicole was oblivious to the worries of the people around her. Just as oblivious as that human bulldozer who had nearly bowled her over in the airport earlier in the day. The only difference was that the airport dude had run into and over several people, while Nicole's feet were glued firmly to the ground. The bulldozer in the airport had been set to full throttle—she was stuck in neutral.

Nicole, the bulldozer, spent quite a bit of time trying to get out of neutral and back in gear, until the right wheel in her head turned, which clicked a cog into place, which dropped a lever, which raised a panel. And just like that, she knew why her body refused to go through those doors.

It was all about Michael, or Michael's death, to be exact.

Or to be even more exact, it was about a little glimmer of hope that Michael had survived the crash and was still alive. That glimmer lived behind the panel, and unbeknownst to her, her brain would do anything to protect it.

It was a very important little glimmer.

The problem with going to the embassy was that they might have solid proof that Michael was gone. That he was never coming back. That the hope that lived behind a panel, deep in her brain, was false hope.

She could not risk it. That glimmer was the most important thing she had left in her life. If she lost it, it would be like losing her husband all over again.

Oh, Michael!

She stood in front of the Embassy, staring at the cold stones of the building for a full ten minutes. She was so deep into her own thoughts that she almost jumped a mile when a hand touched her shoulder.

"Are you okay, miss," a concerned voice asked, in her ear.

Nicole twirled around so fast she almost slammed into a vendor who had set up shop practically on her heels. As it was, she had to grab hold of the girl's arms to keep from toppling over onto the ground. The owner of the voice was a girl of about twelve or thirteen.

"Are you an American?" the girl asked excitedly. "Because you look like an American, and you're standing outside the American Embassy."

Nicole turned her focus to the girl. Her English was very good, but something about the way she said her words made Nicole think she had not learned it in the States. But before Nicole could so much as open her mouth to respond, the girl continued.

"I've always wanted to go to America, but the closest I've ever gotten is this Embassy. Both of my parents are dead. I live with my aunt. She works here, but she doesn't like it if I hang around. Says it could get her into trouble. Most of the people that work in there are from here, not there. So, are you?"

"Am I...what?" Nicole asked, confused by the abundant flow of words.

"Are you an American?"

"Ah," Nicole realized that whether she was an American or not was the question of the day, "yes I am."

"You're so lucky! What's it like? Is it like on the television, with people chasing each other through the street with guns all the time?"

"Not that I've seen," Nicole replied, trying to hide her smile.

"Have you ever seen a car chase?"

"Sorry, no." Nicole smiled at the girl. "Where I live it's just a normal place with neighbors, and family, and a job—"

"Sounds great," the girl interrupted, with a sigh. Then she looked through the glass of the door and shouted, "Gotta go!" Before Nicole knew what was happening the girl had hightailed it down the street and out of sight.

Nicole stood there, blinking in surprise. Then the door swung open and a woman who was a thirty-year-old version of the girl poked her head out.

"Was she bothering you?" the woman asked suspiciously, clearly not happy with the girl.

"Oh, no, I asked if this was the American Embassy, and she was telling me it was," Nicole quickly fabricated, hoping to keep the girl out of trouble.

"Humph," the woman seemed to not believe Nicole, which was both insulting and embarrassing.

"So, the girl is right? This is the American Embassy?"

In response, the woman pointed to the large plaque with the words AMERICAN EMBASSY installed in unavoidable glory by the door.

"Ah," Nicole bit her lip, "I didn't see that."

"Coming in?" the woman asked, as she shifted her weight to better hold the door open.

Nicole realized she had no choice but to go inside. If she refused it would be an admission of guilt. Nicole would be proved to be a liar. The girl would be in trouble with her aunt.

Not comfortable with any of her choices, Nicole straightened her shoulders and marched past the woman and straight to the reception desk.

It was no surprise that after the woman followed her inside, she walked past her to take a seat at the desk.

"Fantastic!" Nicole worked hard to infuse her voice with the proper amount of satisfaction. "You must be the person I need to speak to."

"About...?" the woman asked.

"Well—"

The receptionist's face was stiff and red with anger, a sure sign Nicole needed to scramble to get herself out of this mess without getting the child into trouble.

Michael would have been able to do it. Easily. He was a smooth-talking, people person who exuded charm. But since he wasn't here—Nicole had to tamp down a sudden, almost overwhelming desire to curl up on the floor in a fetal position and cry—she would have to use whatever tricks she had learned from her husband. As an American archaeologist who focused on Mayan ruins, he often found it necessary to smooth bruised feelings or butter up local bureaucrats. He had developed a technique. All Nicole had to do was emulate that technique.

She threw a glance at the woman's nametag. Michael always said that calling people by their names made them into friends, and therefore more likely to help. Nicole leaned in, as if to share a secret with her best friend.

Nicole had seen Michael melt the coldest of people with this tactic many times. She hoped it would work as well for her. But then again, Michael had a natural charm that caused most people to instantly like him, an attribute Nicole could only pretend to possess.

"Maria, is it?" Nicole chortled in her best imitation of Michael's good humor.

Maria nodded, and she looked more suspicious than friendly.

"Nice to meet you Maria, my name is Nicole." Nicole reached out a hand like she had seen Michael do. After a slight hesitation, Maria shook it.

"Well, Maria, I'm looking for a couple of your employees. They told me their names were Larkin and Diaz."

Nicole did her best to smile like Maria was her best friend, but she suspected the smile looked fake. Her suspicions were correct.

"Never heard of them," Maria replied, and Nicole noticed that the smile on the receptionist's face appeared to be made of a hard, non-pliant material, like plastic.

"Wait! Let me check!" Nicole squeaked in panic. She frantically dug through her purse to find the paper with the embassy employees' names on it, which she pulled out and read it.

"Larkin and Diaz. Yep, that's what they told me." Nicole turned the paper so Maria could read it for herself. "See?"

"No," Maria took a quick look at the paper before shaking her head adamantly. "No Larkin. No Diaz."

Nicole bit her bottom lip as the gears of her brain whirled wildly. She had assumed the two would be easy to find. She had imagined herself walking in, asking to see them, and getting closure.

And even though her brain still desperately needed to protect that oh-so-important glimmer of hope, it irritated her that the receptionist wanted to keep Larkin and Diaz from her.

Nicole took a deep, calming breath to pull herself together. This was a hitch in her plan, just a teeny, little hitch. There was never only one way to do anything. If this woman refused to help her, she would find someone who would.

When in doubt, ask for a supervisor.

"No problem." Nicole masked her face with a confident smile and speared the woman, Maria, with her eyes. "Just let me see whoever is in charge of writing up the death reports."

"The what?" Maria's statue-like mask slipped a bit, she was so surprised by the request.

"Death reports."

"What are 'death reports'?"

"You know," Nicole struggled to keep her voice friendly and stress-free, "you guys have to write a report whenever an American dies in Belize. I want to talk to the person in charge of those reports. Whoever who runs the department."

"No one is in charge of," Maria used air quotes for the next two words and the tone of her voice stopped just short of a jeer, "'death reports'."

Nicole stared at the woman for several seconds as she blinked like a butterfly caught in a downdraft. This made no sense.

"Well then," Nicole finally countered, "who writes the reports?"

"No reports," Maria stated firmly. "The Embassy doesn't do reports like that."

Nicole's forehead crinkled as she struggled to make sense of the woman's words. Larkin and Diaz had clearly stated that they were from the Embassy. They had made all the arrangements for her return home, even paid for her ticket.

This woman was wrong. She had to be.

"Okay then," Nicole challenged. "If the embassy doesn't write death reports, exactly what does the embassy do? Tell me that!"

"I have pamphlet. Take it." Maria reached into her desk, grabbed a pamphlet and shoved it at Nicole. "Read the pamphlet, then we'll talk."

"But—"

"Read it! Then come back," Maria commanded, and to make sure Nicole knew this was a dismissal, she pointed to the exit.

Nicole, flustered, frustrated, and confused, grabbed the pamphlet and headed out the door.

CHAPTER 25

As her feet hit the sidewalk outside the embassy, the glimmer of hope that lived behind the panel in Nicole's brain dimmed almost out of existence. It was only then that she realized she had expected to find the report writers and have them tell her that Michael was alive, well, and ready to return home.

Looking at her hand, she decided she might as well look through the flimsy pamphlet. It only took a few seconds, and it told her absolutely nothing. She was about to go back inside to do battle with Maria, the receptionist, when her way was blocked by a young man wearing a suit that made him look like he had just stepped out of the 1950s.

"Hey, did I hear you say someone you know died here in Belize?" the man squeaked excitedly.

Nicole looked the man over. How insensitive did a person need to be to ask a question like that?

"Who," Nicole stressed the first and last words, "are you?"

"Name's Joe. I'm a here to do a story about corruption in Belize."

The man named Joe looked more like a puppy waiting to be petted than anything else. Then he shifted his weight to the balls of his feet as he waited for the verbal ball to be thrown his way. If he had let his tongue hang out a bit Nicole probably would have instinctively reached over to pat his head, the resemblance to a puppy was so uncanny.

This man could not be dangerous, could he? Should she talk to him?

Nicole bit her lip as she looked up and down the street. Here in the middle of town, a mere two feet away from the embassy, the streets were packed with people. If there was anywhere she should feel safe to have a chat with this man, it was here.

Still, the report writers had not been who they said they were. It would not hurt to be a little cautious.

"Do you have proof you are who you say you are?" Nicole asked.

"Sure, sure." Joe patted pocket after pocket until he found the right one. "I've got my press badge right here."

He pulled an identification badge out of an inner pocket and handed it to Nicole. While Nicole compared the picture to the real man, he pasted a fake smile on his face which was an exact match to the plastic smile on the badge.

"Well, it looks okay to me." Nicole sighed. She had scrutinized every detail, but frankly, had no clue what a press pass should look like. "But for all I know, this could be forged."

"It could. I happen to know these badges are easy to fake," Joe replied, with a good-natured grin.

Nicole studied him suspiciously. Was this an admission he was a fraud?

"But it's not a fake," he continued, his grin still ear-to-ear. "It's the real deal."

"Way to build confidence," Nicole grumbled, as she handed the badge back to the beaming man.

"So," Joe quizzed, as he lost no time putting away the badge and grabbing his notebook and pen, "who died?"

Joe shrugged as Nicole's startled face clued him in that he may have been too blunt. But he had not been hired for his empathy, though he had been accused of lacking subtlety quite a few times.

"Sorry to be blunt, but I've got a story to write—see."

Nicole squinted her eyes as she studied the young reporter.

"I think I do see," she said slowly as the pieces of the puzzle clicked together in her brain. The old-timey speech pattern, the 1950s suit—this young man was emulating reporters from movies he had seen. He had probably decided to become a reporter at a young age and has been studying for the part of star reporter most of his life.

Nicole smiled kindly at the young man, and that smile nearly destroyed him. It was not at all the smile a cut-throat reporter expected to see on the face of someone he was interviewing. There was no fear, no sign that he was pushing the bounds of intimidation.

Instead, isn't that cute, was the message this smile sent. As if this woman was an adult humoring an imaginative child.

Joe took a step back in confusion. He needed time to regain his composure, so he cleared his throat to buy himself a few seconds. Then he put pencil to pad, schooled his face for seriousness, and continued.

"So, who was it?"

"My husband." The sadness in Nicole's voice should have at the very least put a dent in the young reporter's heart, but he was too busy being a cut-throat reporter to notice. "A little over a month ago."

"Sorry for your loss," Joe replied robotically.

His boss had recently lectured him on the danger of lacking empathy, so he had worked on his people skills. He had trained himself to say the right things at the right time, but they were only words to him. The emotion attached to those words was lost on him.

"You said some people from the embassy were asking questions?"

"Yes," Nicole replied, as she straightened her back and pulled herself together. Breaking into tears on the streets of Belize would help no one. "Right after it happened. They visited me at my hotel and asked a lot of questions."

"I believe you said their names were Diaz and Larkin?"

"That's right."

"A man and a woman?"

Nicole scrunched her eyes at Joe suspiciously. Surely, she had not mentioned the fact that the report-writing team had been a man and a woman. She thought back over her conversation with Maria the receptionist. No. She had not said one word about the sexes of the duo.

A woman exited the embassy and paused to look at the two curiously. Joe smiled at the woman, who suddenly seemed a little confused. Joe kept his gaze on her until, uncomfortable, she moved off down the street, turning to look back at the two suspiciously every couple of feet.

Something about the whole exchange made Nicole self-conscious, and she was relieved when the woman finally turned the corner and walked out of sight.

"Look, Joe, right?" Nicole turned to Joe.

"That's right," Joe said, his eyes still focused on the spot where the woman had turned the corner.

"You want a story?" Nicole lifted her chin. "I've got a story."

Joe's attention was instantly sucked back to Nicole. He perked up like a puppy who smelled his favorite treat.

"We can exchange information, at my hotel." Nicole gave a single, firm nod. But when Joe lost that puppy dog look and leaned toward her, she took a step back as she raised her palm. "In the restaurant."

"Lead the way," Joe chuckled, with a philosophical shrug.

Which was exactly what Nicole did. Without another word, Nicole turned on her heel and lead him down the street and across town—straight to the pristine restaurant located at her hotel that catered to American tourists.

It was too late for lunch and too early for dinner, so Nicole and Joe were the only two people in the restaurant. Except for the waiter, of course, who waited patiently for their order as they took their seats.

Nicole took a quick look at the menu and handed it back to the waiter. "I would like a side order of french fries and a coke, please," she said.

"Water for me," Joe the reporter said, with a smile for the waiter. As the waiter headed for the kitchen he explained to Nicole, "No expense account."

The two were now alone in the dining area of the restaurant. Since it was still a couple of hours until the dinner rush no one had turned on the music and the murmur of voices, laughter, and clanking dishes could be clearly heard coming from the kitchen.

"Okay," Nicole pinned the reporter with her eyes, "what is this story you're doing?"

"Right," Joe reached into his pocket and pulled out a picture of Chief Valente in casual clothing. He handed the picture to Nicole. "Recognize him?"

"Sure," Nicole responded, with a shrug, "that's Chief Valente."

"Chief? Chief of what?"

"Chief of Police, of course."

"Man, oh man!" Joe slapped his palm on the table and grinned. "This is gonna be great."

"What—?" Nicole began, but decided to hold her questions since the waiter had suddenly reappeared with Joe's glass of water.

Joe grabbed the water and gulped about half of it down. Nicole thanked the waiter for the water, and watched until he had returned to the kitchen before she continued. When the door clicked closed, she swung around to Joe.

"Why do you have that picture of Chief Valente?" Nicole asked suspiciously. "And what about the other two, Larkin and Diaz. What about them?"

"CIA," Joe blurted, too pleased with himself to take the time to think through how much of his story he should share.

"CIA? What do you mean CIA?"

"That's who Larkin and Diaz are," the young man answered, as he snickered with glee at the thought of the story he planned to break. "Oh, my boss is going to love this!"

Then he lost himself in dreams of fame, glory, and promotions.

"Joe! Focus!" Nicole snapped her fingers in front of the reporter's face. He turned his attention back to his table mate.

"The CIA are trying to uncover a drug trade ring that is funneling drugs into the States," the reporter explained.

"They told me they were from the embassy," Nicole grumbled. She hated it when people lied to her. It made her feel dirty, as if she were the one lying. "Are you sure about this?"

"Sure, I'm sure. I have very reliable sources. Very reliable."

Nicole studied him for several seconds, searching for any sign that he was joking or lying, but could find none.

"Okay, so they're CIA," she said, resigning herself to this new truth. "Why are they talking to me? I don't have anything to do with the drug trade."

The waiter appeared with Nicole's fries and coke, and after setting them on the table he retreated to a small table on the far side of the restaurant to fold napkins.

"Maybe," Joe paused to inhale a lungful of heady, deep-fried potato aroma, never taking his eyes from the fries, "you know something they want to know."

"They were asking me about a plane I was on with my husband. Do you think they thought the plane was being used by drug runners?"

"Probably," Joe replied, but he was having trouble focusing on Nicole's questions. He was too distracted by the tantalizing smell of the fries. "Umm, can I have a fry?"

Nicole raised an eyebrow.

"Please?"

"Why didn't you get your own?" Nicole asked. She hated it when her friends pretended to not be hungry, then cadged her food. And this guy wasn't even a friend.

"Just one?"

Nicole noticed the young man genuinely looked hungry, and it gave her an idea. She could use the fries as a bargaining tool.

"Okay, you can have one," Nicole agreed, schooling her voice to the most diplomatic tone she could manage. "But only if you tell me why you are carrying around a picture of Chief Valente."

Joe grabbed several fries and shoved them into his mouth. His eyes closed as he chewed, relishing the taste. Nicole wondered when he had last eaten.

"The picture?" Nicole prompted.

"Another fry?"

Nicole shoved the plate an inch closer to Joe.

"The man in the picture is Rudy Valente, the leader of a gang that mixes running drugs with illicit antiquities. I've heard it's very lucrative."

"That can't be right," Nicole argued. "He's the chief of police!"

"Well, I didn't know that, until you told me. I got his name and picture from one of my contacts. They never mentioned he was a cop."

Nicole stared into the distance. Joe took advantage of Nicole's distraction to grab another handful of fries and shove them into his mouth.

"Did you say his first name is Rudy?" Nicole asked.

"Yep," Joe answered, and since Nicole was still distracted, he snuck another couple of fries off the plate and popped them into his mouth. "And boy does he hate Americans. He blames Americans for everything that has gone wrong in his life from his bad education to his ingrown toenail. He hates us with a passion."

Nicole rubbed her forehead. Joe ate a few more fries.

"This can't be a coincidence," Nicole muttered.

"What?" Joe asked, still more focused on the fries than Nicole's words.

"That name, Rudy. I heard it while I was being held hostage. And that the CIA think drug runners owned the plane that went down with my husband."

Joe paused, the latest handful of fries he had snuck off Nicole's plate hanging in mid-air.

"Hostage? They held you hostage, and you actually lived to talk about it?"

Nicole nodded as she bit her lower lip. Then she looked Joe straight in the eyes and said, "Joe, I've got a deal for you."

"What kind of deal?"

"Tell me everything you know about Chief Valente."

"No deal. I can't reveal my sources, see."

"You watch too many old movies," Nicole scoffed. "I couldn't care less about knowing who your sources are, I just want the facts."

Joe shoved more fries into his mouth and chewed thoughtfully. Then, obviously coming to a decision, he narrowed his eyes and raised a brow. Nicole assumed this must be his negotiating face.

"What do I get?" he countered, sounding suspiciously like a weedy crook from a film noir, crime, mystery movie.

"I'll do my own digging and tell you everything I find."

Joe picked up Nicole's half-empty plate of fries and smiled. "Throw in the rest of these fries and it's a deal."

Nicole returned the smile as the two shook hands. It was good to feel she had a plan—and that she was not in this alone.

That night, in her hotel room, she made a list of all the ways she could gather information about Chief Valente. The list included hacking into his computer, breaking into his house, stealing his phone, talking to his neighbors, and following him around to see where he went. Following him seemed the least likely to get her into trouble, so she made a second list of all the shows she had watched where detectives followed the perps, and what she would need to do to do what they did.

She had never met a detective, so she had no real person on which to model her actions. But she had watched loads of police procedural shows. It was a favorite genre of her parents and somehow, she had also gotten hooked. And though she knew the TV shows and movies were pure fiction, they were all she had.

She sincerely hoped the creators of those detective shows had done their research. Otherwise…

The next day, Nicole installed herself in a sidewalk café across the street from the police station. After she had been there for several hours, she started to worry that the owners of the café would kick her out, until she noticed that she wasn't the only customer who had taken up residence. It quickly became clear that as long as she nursed her cup of coffee, and purchased a new one every so often, she was welcome.

Unfortunately, that meant she needed to drink a lot of coffee and would therefore need to visit a restroom every so often. Each time she left her post gave the chief an opportunity to slip away unobserved.

As a precaution, she drank like she imagined a sloth would drink, only taking a sip of the coffee about once every ten minutes or so.

She had reached the bottom of her fifth cup, and was contemplating the advisability of a sixth one, when Chief Valente stepped out of the police station and headed down the street. Nicole immediately tossed the money needed to pay her bill on the table and followed.

Nicole automatically shifted into her character of super-sleuth as soon as her feet hit the street. Maybe it was all the caffeine, or maybe it was because she was finally getting to do something, but she felt she was doing an excellent job of blending in.

Until Chief Valente stopped suddenly to look behind him. Nicole, frantic to avoid being seen, jumped into a doorway of a salon. A woman leaving the salon, who was caught up in her own thoughts and not paying attention, collided with Nicole. The two women bounced off each other and landed on their tail bones, with the bags and packages the woman had been carrying scattering all around them.

"I'm so sorry," Nicole exclaimed in horror.

The super sleuth quickly jumped to her feet to help the other woman—who was elderly and most likely from a Scandinavian country—to her feet. Then she gathered the woman's scattered items, arranged them into a semi-organized pile in the woman's arms, and apologized profusely.

Since the elderly woman appeared to be unharmed, Nicole made a speedy exit to get back to her spying. But apologizing and arranging the woman's packages had taken at least five minutes, an extremely long length of time for a sleuth to lose sight of the person she is tailing. The likelihood she would find Chief Valente again was slim. He might have walked down the street, gone into a building, driven away in a truck, or even jumped into a helicopter for all she knew. He could be anywhere.

Which was why she was shocked to the core when she turned a corner and there was the chief. He stood there bigger than life, chatting with a vendor like they were old friends, a mere two feet away from Nicole.

She jumped into another doorway and stood, her back plastered to a wall, her heart thumping to the beat of a hummingbird's wings. That was when she had the monumental realization that she was not cut out to be a spy. Or a detective. Or any other career that would require her to skulk around in the shadows.

Just when she had decided it was in her best interest to give up and slink back to her hotel, the sound of whistling moving away hit her ears. She managed to scrape up enough courage to peek her head out of the doorway to find a whistling Chief swaggering down the street away from her.

Encouraged by this piece of good luck she decided to continue to follow him. She regretted this decision many times in the next hour, as it turned into the most stressful mile Nicole had ever experienced. She spent more time hopping in and out of doorways than she spent walking. Finally, they came to what seemed to be the chief's destination, a small house on the outskirts of town.

The super sleuth hid behind a large tree at the edge of the yard as her target unlocked the front door. She was glad had taken that precaution because his eyes swept the yard before he stepped into the house.

"He didn't see me, did he?" Nicole whispered to herself.

She carefully peeked around the tree just in time to witness the door slamming closed, the chief nowhere in sight.

"Just being cautious, I guess!"

Nicole breathed a sigh of relief as she dove under some nearby bushes where she could hunker down and wait. It was dinner time. Quite likely the chief was in for the night. That would give her much-needed time to relax.

Nicole had snuggled into a more comfortable position and was ready for a long wait until she realized she had a problem.

"Darn that coffee!" she grumbled.

But she was determined to prove herself stronger than the gallon or so of coffee she had drunk that morning. No matter how uncomfortable it got, she had to stick it out. This would most likely be her only chance to tail Chief Valente. And if Joe was right and the chief was a criminal mastermind, surely his underlings would drop by for orders.

An hour later found her thoroughly regretting her decision. As she squirmed, trying to get into a more comfortable position, she realized it was no use. The coffee had won, she needed to head out and find a restroom.

She twisted around to grab her bag, which she had stashed under the bush, but froze instantly when she heard a sound she had only before heard on television. The click of a rifle.

Slowly she twisted back around and looked up. There was a smirking Chief Valente standing over her, a rifle pointed at her chest.

CHAPTER 26

"Sorry for the accommodations, Princess," Chief Valente sneered, as he manhandled a handcuffed Nicole into a cell.

The accommodations, as the chief called them, were old, slimy, dirty, and most certainly not located in the San Ignacio police station. Nicole glared at him as he slammed the door shut.

"You brought this on yourself, you know. For spying on me."

"Much good it did me," Nicole grumbled. "You never did anything interesting."

Chief Valente stared at Nicole—his face perfectly blank. But behind the blankness was an abundance of emotion, evidenced by the white marbles that grew on Valente's knuckles as he grasped the bars of his prisoner's cage. After several moments Valente managed to pull himself together to continue.

"Same old story," lectured the chief. "Americans think they can do anything they want."

He peeled his hands from the bars a few fingers at a time, readying to leave, but his anger acted like a magnet, and before he knew what he was doing he had again grabbed the bars and squeezed tight.

"Why were you spying on me?" he hissed, through the bars.

"You killed my husband," Nicole shot back.

Chief Valente let go of the bars as if they were white hot. He stepped back, honestly surprised.

"Your husband died in a plane crash," he sputtered, and the confusion on his face matched that of his voice.

"Ha! It was your plane," Nicole accused. "I found out—"

Chief Valente lunged at the bars as anger overtook him. There was nothing he hated more than someone who got in his way. Nicole had gotten in his way since the day he met her.

"What did you find out?" he growled, his knuckles again forming white marbles.

Nicole, suddenly frightened by the waves of palpable anger radiating in her direction, backed up until her legs hit the cot. She felt she needed to hide her fear from the police chief at any cost, so she somehow managed to nonchalantly plop herself onto the cot as if she had not a single care in the world. Or at least, she hoped that was what it looked like.

"Nothing," she answered casually.

It was a good thing the chief did not know Nicole well, or he might have recognized that forced indifference for what it was—a last-ditch effort to hide a truth she did not want discovered. It was an old, tried-and-true device she had used often in her teenage years, until her parents cottoned onto it and were no longer fooled.

It had been years since she had tried the tactic. But based on the color of the marbles that were the chief's knuckles—they had darkened to a pinkish color, rather than pearly white—it was still a useful tactic to have in her toolbox.

"Talk," the chief growled, "or I'll stop being nice."

Nicole noticed that the growl had lost some of its grit, so she moved on to stage two of her tactic and crossed her arms as she pointedly looked away. It was imperative she keep the upper hand for as long as she could. The last thing she wanted was to show fear.

"So be it. I'm off to file a report."

Nicole's eyes flew to the chief. She would have preferred to ignore the man—it was obvious he was a bully and bullies were best ignored—but her life was in his hands. What was that about a report? Her eyes asked the question even if she was able to keep her mouth shut.

"A missing person's report," the crooked policeman said, when he saw he had her attention. And to make sure she understood, he gave her a smile that was pure evil.

Nicole's face lost all color as the message hit home, which made Chief Valente smirk in satisfaction. After a few moments of gloating, he turned and strutted out.

Left on her own, Nicole lay on her side as she tried to get a little rest. Before she knew it, her body, pulled by strings of instinct, had curled into a fetal position. That was how she was lying when, several minutes later, the lights went out and she was plunged into total darkness, without even a single star to shine a little hope on her.

The sobbing that followed would have been heartbreaking to an onlooker, especially if the onlooker could see through the darkness that Nicole was curled up in a tight, little ball on the cot. But there was no onlooker. Nicole was alone. And worse, she was the prisoner of a ruthless bully who detested everything about her.

Luckily for Nicole, tears drain a person's energy, so even though it was not exactly on her to-do list, she got a good night's sleep. Morning brought renewed hope, a clearer head, and a plan of how she should deal with her captor.

She had already checked every square inch of the cell for a way out and had resorted to pacing by the time Chief Valente returned with a plate of food. Nicole ran to meet him at the cell door to try to make a connection with him.

"Look, I was rude," she apologized promptly. "I'm sorry I spied on you."

But instead of accepting her apology, or even acknowledging her existence, Chief Valente ignored her. He was much better at stage two of Nicole's tactic than Nicole was.

Maybe it was one of those person in-power versus not-in-power things.

He put the plate of food on the floor, slid it through a slit, and walked away several paces, his back to her.

"You can't keep me here forever!" Nicole yelled, her voice cracking as panic overwhelmed her. "My family will come looking for me!"

"Your family is grieving. You were lost in the jungle." Her kidnapper turned his head so she could see his smug smile. "Presumed dead."

Nicole froze as a picture of her parents' distraught faces flooded her mind. They would be heartbroken! Her dad would suffer in silence, and her mother would inevitably blame herself, saying—

"Of course," Chief Valente said, as he twirled around to face her, "the lost can be found."

He speared Nicole with eyes that had not a single smidgen of softness or warmth.

"If the lost knows when to talk and when to keep her mouth shut. Think about it."

With those words he strutted out, clanging the door shut behind him.

Alone again, Nicole grabbed the plate and retreated to the cot to eat. It had been a full twenty-four hours since her last meal. She was famished.

But one look at the contents of the plate killed her appetite.

"Disgusting!" Nicole muttered, as she stared in disgust at the brown and black mass on the plate.

Nicole stood up, ready to throw the plate across the cell, when she realized that was probably exactly what Chief Valente expected her to do. He had called her a princess and a pampered American. He expected her to act like a spoiled brat.

She would prove him wrong! She would eat this poor excuse for food, every bite of it.

As long as this was actual food, her body would use it to keep up her strength. She needed strength to escape. Because she would escape. Hopefully sooner, rather than later.

Nicole took the plate to the cot to look it over. She recognized corn and rice in the dish, but the rest was a mystery to her.

She took a sniff of the food. Beans. The brown mushy stuff was beans. There was also some sort of spice that was unfamiliar to her, but she would not let that stop her. Using her fingers—

the chief had neglected to give her any utensils—she took a tentative first bite.

The food hit her tongue and activated her taste buds, causing her stomach to growl in anticipation. Twenty-four hours was a long time to have an empty belly. Before she knew what she was doing, she had scarfed down every morsel and was licking the last traces of the beans from an otherwise empty plate.

Chief Valente, who was watching from the other room, was disappointed. He had purposely chosen a local dish he assumed would make the pampered American princess turn up her nose in disgust. He did not want her to eat, he wanted her hungry. And tired. And uncomfortable. He wanted to punish this woman who dared to follow him in his own town. Punish her good. He had thought the food would—

A wicked smile slowly grew across his face as an idea sprung from a special well in his brain from which a whole plethora of evil ideas flowed. He took one more peek at his prisoner.

"That will do it!" he snickered. "Let her try to stay calm. Just let her!"

With that he left, still snickering to himself.

Many hours later, when the first light of dawn began to paint slashes of gold across the morning sky, an emotionally distressed Nicole slept deeply on the cot. While the food had dulled the worst of her hunger pains, it had also allowed her to think. What had followed was a deep, intense, need to cry. With a strength of will she had not known she possessed she had managed to keep the floodgates closed until darkness consumed her cell. She would not put it past Chief Valente to have a hidden camera pointed her way. The last thing she wanted to do was give him the satisfaction of her tears.

Unheard by Nicole, who was deep in a glorious dream in which she and Michael had opened a coffee shop together, the door of her cell squeaked open several inches to allow a box to be scraped across the floor as it was shoved inside.

Nicole had just turned to smile at her wonderful husband as he bagged a fresh scone for a customer, when the door of the coffee shop opened, and a strong wind made tendrils of her hair dance across her face. It tickled, but something was wrong. She brushed her hand across her face to control the wisps of hair that refused to behave.

Suddenly, a veritable hurricane blew into the coffee shop and every item in the shop began to fly about chaotically. Before Nicole knew what was happening,

Michael was sucked away by the hurricane, and she was left to defend herself from a flock of hostile aprons.

In her dream, she flailed her arms about to keep the aprons at bay. So intense were the feelings of danger that her arms began to flail about on her cot, until one particularly erratic swing caused her to hit her own face with her fist. She opened groggy eyes to find she was not surrounded by aprons, but spiders.

Spiders! On her arms, on the cot—even crawling on her face!

"Get them off me! Get them off! I hate spiders!" Nicole yelled, as she bounded up from the cot and frantically jumped around, trying to shake the crawly creatures from her body.

Chief Valente's laughter could be heard from another room. Proof that he had, indeed, installed a camera to spy on her.

That vile laughter from the other room worked as a virtual slap to Nicole's face, snapping her out of her frenzy. She was determined not to give her kidnapper the satisfaction of having bested her, and that determination must have been stronger than her fear of spiders, because she straightened her shoulders and calmly brushed off every part of her body that she could reach with her hands. Then, when she was free of the creepy crawlies, she picked up the mattress and shook it vigorously.

"You're not going to break me that easy!" she yelled defiantly, as she calmly sat on the cot to pull her knees up tight. "I'm tougher than you think."

The laughter died and there was a disappointed silence. She maintained that pose, statue like, until she heard the outer door slam closed. She waited a few extra minutes to make sure the chief had actually left, then she lay her head on her knees and wrapped her arms around her head. Two large tears formed at the corners of her eyes, but she brushed them away ruthlessly before they could fall.

"I won't let you break me," she whispered defiantly, her eyes squeezed tight, "for Michael."

She stayed like that for hours as the spiders escaped to freedom through a tiny window high in the old stone wall. Like Nicole, they too had no desire to stay in the dank cell.

It took until midday for all the creepy crawlies to desert her, and when she was once again alone in her prison, she began the painful process of unfurling herself. It seemed her muscles had become accustomed to this new position and wanted to stay that way. The worst was her right leg. When she tried to stretch it out, she realized it was locked in position. It took more than ten minutes for her to massage the muscles of the leg until they softened. Only then could she straighten it. When she was finally fully unfurled, she lay flat on her back on the cot to wait for whatever might come next.

Later that day Chief Valente entered with a slice of pizza in one hand and a small pizza box in the other. Nicole's stomach growled when the smell of pizza wafted her way, so it was a hopeful Nicole who rose from the cot to take the box from him. Maybe, Nicole reasoned, he was regretting his actions. Maybe his plan was to soften her up so she would not press charges.

"Did you sleep well, Princess?" the chief asked in what certainly sounded like a sincere voice, "I've heard that these old cells aren't all that comfortable."

"I slept like a baby, thanks."

"Anything you want to tell me?" the chief asked, with a raise of his brow. "Like a name, maybe?"

"Nope," Nicole replied firmly, "I'm good."

Nicole licked her lips, which were dry and cracked.

"May I have some water, please?"

"Certainly," Chief Valente replied, with a smile, and he reached around back to pull out a small water bottle, most likely from his back pocket. He reached through the bars to set the bottle on the floor.

"Enjoy your meal," he said. "It's all you'll get today."

Nicole, not trusting her captor because of a strange vibe she felt from him, blinked twice, held her breath, and slowly opened the lid of the box. Chief Valente watched closely from the open doorway. As soon as the lid was opened just a crack, cockroaches swarmed out of the box and fell to the floor. Nicole, who was more disgusted than surprised, frisbeed the box as far from her as she could in the small cell.

Chief Valente laughed sadistically, taking joy from Nicole's discomfort in a true bully style. Then, still chortling, he slammed the door behind him, leaving Nicole alone with her new friends.

"Bet he was a charming child," she muttered, at the closed door.

Shivering uncontrollably, she snatched up the box and managed to shove it through the bars of the window. Then, still shaking, she chased down the cockroaches, one by one, and tossed them after the box, out the window.

"And don't come back!" she yelled, to the last cockroach as it disappeared through the small opening.

Spotting the water bottle, she ran to it and picked it up, only to find that it was empty. She unscrewed the lid to make sure, but there was not a single drop of water inside. She tossed the plastic bottle away in disgust.

Shaky, and who wouldn't be in her position, she returned to her cot and wrapped her arms around her knees. Even if her leg did seize again, forming herself into a human pill bug made her feel safer.

After several seconds her whole body began to shake as sobs struggled to break through. But Nicole was having none of that. She stiffened her shoulders and back, successfully closing the floodgates that threatened to overwhelm her. But unbeknownst to her, a few stubborn tears escaped their watery prison to slowly run down the cheeks of her determined and angry face.

CHAPTER 27

The chief's next form of torture became glaringly obvious when he kept his distance for the next two days. Or at least Nicole thought it was two days. Since her imprisonment, she had only been given one plate of nasty food to eat, and for the first time in her life, she knew what it meant to be truly hungry. What she discovered was that her brain did not work at all well without food and her frequent naps, sometimes awakening in the dark, sometimes during the day, made it hard to keep track of time.

All she knew for sure was that she was hungry. And thirsty. Her kidnapper must have assumed she was part camel because he had yet to give her even a drop of water. Luckily, she had discovered that her cell was blessed with a leaky roof, and every time it rained, and it seemed to rain daily, a puddle formed in an indent in the floor. The taste was rather disgusting, but Nicole had reached a level of thirst that made being picky seem ridiculous. The puddle got rid of the worst of her thirst, and that was the important thing. She was still thirsty, but she was alive.

The moon must have been waxing, because when Nicole was startled awake by the squeak that meant the outer door was being opened, she could see moonlight shining through the tiny cell window. She immediately jerked into an upright position and wrapped her arms around her knees.

"What now?" Nicole muttered, dreading whatever the chief had in store for her next.

There was the sound of metal scraping against metal, then two dark figures appeared in the cell doorway.

"Great! He's got company," Nicole muttered, under her breath. She frantically ran her hands over the surface of the cot, searching for something, anything, she could use to protect herself, but there was nothing. She balled her hands into fists and jumped to her feet, ready for a fight.

"Mrs. Quinn?" a male voice, it sounded American, asked.

Nicole, surprised, lowered her fists.

"Mrs. Quinn," another American voice continued, and this one was female, "it's us, Larkin and Diaz. We've come to get you out of here."

"Are you CIA?" Nicole blurted, strangely flattered by the thought that she was important enough to warrant CIA intervention. "You were sent to rescue me?"

There was enough moonlight shining in that Nicole could see that a glance was exchanged between Larkin and Diaz.

"I'm not sure how you knew we are CIA," Diaz answered, "and we weren't exactly sent, but yes, we are here to rescue you."

"If you'll come with us, we'll take you to a place of safety," Larkin continued.

Nicole nodded and gladly followed the two CIA agents out of the jail. It was with a great deal of satisfaction that she slammed the door shut with a loud CLANG as she left.

Once outside, Nicole climbed into the back seat of a sedan as Larkin took the wheel. Diaz, in the passenger seat, pointed to a few water bottles and granola bars that had been tossed into the back seat. Nicole did not need a second invitation. She dug in and was hungry and thirsty enough that it tasted like the best food and drink on the planet.

The worst of her hunger and thirst was quenched before they had even pulled into the road, and Nicole was feeling pretty darn good about her prospects until the downpour started. It slowed them down quite a bit since dirt roads turn quickly into mud roads, and mud does not supply enough traction for safe driving.

But Nicole was not worried, she was in the hands of trained, CIA agents. She was safe. She was on her way back to civilization. All was right with the world.

A clap of thunder masked the sound of the bullet that flew past Nicole's ear, but it did nothing to hide the shattering of the rear window. Before she could figure out what was happening a barrage of bullets flew into the car, a tire blew, and the car skidded to a halt by the side of the road.

Larkin and Diaz quickly climbed out of the car and used it as a shield while they drew their guns. Nicole found herself alone inside, so she copied something she had seen on television and rolled out of the backseat. She had never been around flying bullets before in her life. They were much more intimidating than she had imagined.

The bullets continued to fly as the three Americans huddled beside the car. Larkin inched forward to examine the flat tire. It was shredded and was not going to be taking them anywhere. Not yet beaten, Larkin crab-walked to the trunk, used his key fob to open it, and took a quick peek inside. Then he crab-walked back to the two women.

"No spare. We need to find better cover."

"Can you see where they are?" Diaz asked, as she lay flat on her back to kick off the car mirror, which she then used to look around while staying protected behind the car.

"All I know is the shots started out behind us. But how they're coming from over there." He pointed to the other side of the car.

"I don't see anyone," Diaz said, as she continued to use the mirror to scan the area. "Maybe we could—"

The mirror shattered. She dropped the single piece that was big enough to hold and shook her hand in pain.

"Well, that smarts. Time for better cover."

"Agreed," Larkin said. Which was funny, since finding better cover was his idea in the first place.

"There are some large rocks over there," he continued, as he pointed to a hill several yards away. "Better cover and less likely we'll get surrounded."

Diaz turned to Nicole. "You ready?"

"Do I have a choice?" Nicole replied, for all the world as if they were talking about choosing a table in a crowded diner.

Diaz shook her head as she hid a smile. Larkin looked around for several seconds, then signaled the time was good. The three of them ran together as fast as they possibly could to the rocks.

Diaz and Larkin, guns at the ready, positioned themselves strategically behind a couple of large boulders as they tried to get a good view of the shooters. Nicole, unsure what role she should take, was thankful that at least the rain had finally ended. She took a moment to look around and was shocked to see the Stone Woman about ten feet away.

"You!" she whispered.

The Stone Woman turned and walked toward a particularly large boulder, away from all the action. Nicole followed cautiously. When the Stone Woman reached the boulder, she kept going, through an opening and out of sight.

"Looks like she wants me to go inside," Nicole muttered. "But what about—?"

At that moment, Larkin and Diaz raced up to Nicole.

"We're in trouble!" Diaz blurted. "There are a lot more of them than we thought, and they're close. We've got to hide."

"Would a cave help?" Nicole asked, as she pointed to the opening behind the boulder.

Without another word, Larkin grabbed Nicole's arm and pulled her inside. Diaz followed closely behind.

The cave was dark, wet, and barely tall enough for them to walk upright. But at least they weren't being shot at, and when they heard voices outside it made sense to move deeper inside. Quickly and quietly the three felt their way toward the back of the cave where they discovered several tunnels. They chose the narrowest one and headed down it as they heard what sounded like an entire army reach the mouth of the cave.

When they came to a spot where there was again a choice of tunnels Larkin signaled for Nicole and Diaz to stay put as he headed back to the entrance to check things out. After a few moments, he scuttled back to them, quick and quiet.

"What—?" Nicole began, but Larkin quickly covered her mouth with his hand. When he saw from her eyes that she understood the need for silence he released her and signaled for them to follow him deeper into the tunnel system, which proved to be extensive.

They traveled for several minutes in complete silence, until the scuffling sounds of their followers were no longer audible. Then Diaz grabbed Larkin's arm and pulled him to a stop.

"Tell me," she ordered.

"They've followed us in," he reported. "There are at least ten of them, maybe more, all with rifles."

Diaz took a moment to process this information before she asked, "Think we can wait them out?"

Before Larkin had time to answer Nicole stepped between the two CIA agents.

"Don't even try to leave me out of this," she whispered, hands on hips.

Larkin and Diaz glanced at Nicole like she was a quaint, little butterfly that had landed on a nearby flower. Interesting, but not worth much attention.

Determined to have her voice heard she continued, this time louder, "I have a say in this, too, you know."

Larkin cringed at the loudness of her voice, and after a quick, silent consultation with his partner the two agents nodded their agreement.

"Was Chief Valente there?" Nicole whispered.

"Yes," Larkin nodded. "He was giving orders to some of the men. And whispers carry. Just talk low."

"Do you think they'll come all the way back here?" Nicole asked, keeping her voice low as requested. She looked behind them in the tunnel, hoping her eyes had acclimated enough that she could recognize the shadowy shape of a person if she saw one.

"You can bet on it," Diaz grimaced. "They won't like it that we rescued you."

"Then I vote we find another way out," Nicole declared boldly. "I've heard that many of these caves have multiple entrances. Maybe we'll get lucky."

Diaz nodded her agreement. But Larkin's face said he did not believe in luck. Or the existence of another entrance.

"Look, we have three choices," Nicole said, in effect taking charge. "We find another way out, shoot our way out, or wait for them to catch up with us."

Larkin and Diaz exchanged a look.

"Me," Nicole continued, "me, I prefer to look for a way out. I don't have a gun, or know how to shoot, and I've been Chief Valente's prisoner once."

Nicole shivered at the memory of her time as the chief's prisoner.

"I could do without doing that again."

Larkin studied Nicole for several moments before he blurted, "You're braver than you look, you know."

"Thanks, I think," Nicole returned, squinting as she tried to see the expression on Larkin's face. But it was too dark.

"And smarter too."

Nicole scowled at Larkin as the three moved deeper into the cave. She had a suspicion that he had just joked with her. But what kind of man joked while being chased by drug runners through a dark cave?

Nicole stumbled a step as she realized that that was exactly what Michael would have done. Used humor to lessen the tension. She had seen him do it time and time again.

It shocked her to think someone in the CIA could have a sense of humor like Michael's. Heck, it shocked her that anyone, anywhere, could be in any way like Michael.

It was something she would need to think about. But later. Right now, she needed to keep her focus on finding another way out.

Larkin reached into his pocket and pulled out a small flashlight. He showed it to Diaz, who nodded her agreement. He flicked it on and led the way deeper into the tunnels, Nicole in the middle, and Diaz taking the flank position.

Thirty minutes or so later Nicole realized she was not the only one who was tired. After about the fifth time Larkin stumbled over a rock, she grabbed his arm.

"How about I lead for a while?"

Larkin hesitated for a split second, then nodded.

"Sure," he agreed. "I want to talk to Diaz for a bit, anyway."

Nicole grabbed the flashlight from his hand and took the lead. Larkin leaned against the wall until Diaz caught up, then fell in with her to begin a low conversation.

Somewhere in the distance, they could hear the murmur of voices and the sound of footsteps, a disturbing reminder that they were not alone in the caves.

Nicole came to a fork in the tunnels and stood for several seconds, indecisive. Then she closed her eyes and folded her hands together.

"Lord, please let me pick the right one," she prayed. After a quick sign of the cross, she veered left.

Larkin and Diaz were too caught up in their talk of strategy to pay attention to Nicole's prayer, or her decision. They simply followed her blindly.

The three continued for nearly an hour in this way, Nicole using her gut instincts to make choices, Larkin and Diaz too deep in a strategy session to pay attention to where she was leading them. Then, after a turn, they entered a large room with quite a few tunnels leading from it.

"Give me a minute," Nicole suggested. The agents, more tired than they wanted to admit, gratefully leaned against the wall to rest.

Nicole swept the flashlight around and noticed that a small tunnel to the left looked somehow different. She went to its entrance and shone the flashlight inside.

"Hey guys, look at this!" she called quietly.

Diaz and Larkin, alerted by the change in Nicole's tone, rushed over to see what she had found. Larkin grabbed the flashlight from Nicole's hand and shone it into the tunnel, then the two agents scrambled over each other to check out the stash of boxes and bags that filled the space.

Nicole, never a big fan of small spaces, stayed alone in the dark in the bigger part of the tunnel. She saw a movement out of the corner of her eye and turned to see the Stone Woman disappearing a few feet behind her.

Curious, she ran to where the ghost had disappeared and found a deep niche. Inside that niche was a pinpoint of light. As she stood, wondering what the source of that light could be, a gust of wind blew her hair and whipped it about her face.

She had not felt wind for several hours, so she moved inside the niche toward the pinpoint of light and found a tunnel leading off to the right. She followed that tunnel for several feet until she came to an opening out of the cave. Excited, Nicole stepped outside.

Morning had broken, and in the lovely, soft light of the sunrise, Nicole saw that she now stood at the top of a very high waterfall.

CHAPTER 28

Ix Tzutz Nik, bedraggled and sad, stood at the bottom of the towering temple and gazed up.

Without conscious thought, her hand moved upwards toward her necklace. As her fingers touched the cool stone she sighed. Then, after a pause to take a few deep breaths, she began to climb.

It only took her a few minutes to reach a ledge near the top, and once there went through a doorway into a small room, then through another into a bigger room. She removed a stone that she knew was loose and began to dig in the dirt with her hands. Several minutes later she sat back and nodded, satisfied by her work.

Then, with movements that seemed somehow ritualistic, she reached up and removed the necklace from around her neck. Lovingly, almost reverently, she placed the necklace in the crevice she had created and smoothed dirt over it. After replacing the stone, she smoothed the dirt near it until all evidence that it had been disturbed was gone.

With a sad smile, she returned to the ledge the way she had come and stood for a moment, gazing at the vista before her.

After one final thought of what she had lost, she straightened her shoulders, closed her eyes, and ran swiftly along the ledge until she reached the edge of the temple, where she plunged to her death.

Chapter 29

Uncomfortable to find her toes hanging over the edge of a decidedly tall waterfall, Nicole slowly and carefully put one foot behind the other as she backed away. When she reached a safe distance from the edge—one where she was no longer in danger of tumbling to her death in the frothy water below—she turned and ran back into the cave to find Larkin and Diaz. They had just returned to the main part of the tunnel and were in deep conversation, satisfied smiles decorating their faces.

"I found a way out!" she whispered excitedly.

"You also found the evidence we need to shut down the drug ring."

The smile Diaz gave Nicole as she pointed to the side tunnel was sincere and grateful.

But Nicole barely noticed. Her focus was on putting as much distance between herself and the goons with guns as possible. She had no intention of falling back into the hands of Chief Valente, and the first step to avoiding that was to get out of this cave. She grabbed both Larkin and Diaz by their arms and pulled.

"Come on!"

The agents must have been ready to leave because the resistance they put up was practically nonexistent. She pulled them through the niche and into the tunnel, then all the way to the entrance, or in this case, exit, to show them the opening that led to the waterfall.

Diaz motioned for Nicole to stand back as she poked her head through the opening and scanned around.

"There's no easy way down," she grimaced.

Larkin took a turn at the opening to look for potential ways to escape.

"We might be able to climb down," he mused. "If we can get a good handhold and the water doesn't wash us away—"

Before Larkin could do more theorizing, a man poked his head into the far end of their tunnel. Larkin pulled out his gun.

"We've got to jump," Diaz whispered.

"No!" Nicole's body tensed at that thought. "We're too high! Like, fifty feet too high!"

"We either jump," Diaz pinned Nicole with her eyes, "or have a shootout. And they have more guns."

Nicole's panicked face turned from Diaz to Larkin. Both had the most serious expressions she had yet seen on their faces. Which told her everything she needed to know.

So, she did the only thing she could do. She shut her mouth, closed her eyes, and shot through the opening at full speed. She didn't even stop running when her feet left the ledge, which made her look a bit like one of those cartoon characters who pedal through empty air when they suddenly find themselves no longer on solid ground.

Larkin and Diaz blinked in surprise, too shocked to react. But when Chief Valente's men began swarming the tunnel and a bullet smashed into the wall next to Larkin's ear, they quickly followed Nicole through the opening and over the edge.

Outside in the river, Nicole broke the surface of the water and sputtered, surprised that she had survived such a plunge. She trod water, not knowing what else to do, until Diaz and Larkin surfaced a few feet away.

Bullets peppered the water as the men at the mouth of the cave fifty feet above them gave an impressive display of firepower. Rather than continue to be used as target practice, the three dove underwater and swam downstream until they were out of bullet range, then they swam ashore.

When they finally climbed out of the water, they were waterlogged and exhausted.

Diaz dug into her pocket to pull out a sopping wet phone with a perfectly black screen. "Well, that's not going to help," she muttered, as she tossed it to the ground in disgust.

"But this will!" Larkin grinned like an eight-year-old performing a favorite magic trick as he lifted his pant leg to pull a phone wrapped in plastic from his left sock.

"Now look who's smarter than he looks!" Nicole joked.

Larkin's grin widened at the jib. Then his mind turned to the business of rescue. He knew they were only out of danger temporarily. They were still in the jungle being pursued by thugs with guns, thugs that knew this jungle much better than he and his partner ever could. So, he tightened his jaw with resolve and started dialing. Before long he had reinforcements on the way and the three knew they would soon be headed back to safety.

Later that night—after she had called her parents, taken a long shower, eaten a hot meal, and changed her clothes—Nicole took a trip to Xunatunich. As she gazed up at the temple, she paused, unsure if she was doing the right thing. Needing reassurance, her hand, of its own volition, reached for the necklace.

The Stone Woman, glowing gently, formed near the corner of the temple, and gazed at her sadly.

"I wish you could tell me if this was going to work," Nicole whispered to the ghost. She did not expect a response, and that was exactly what she got. No response.

"Well, here goes!" Nicole muttered, as she gathered her courage and climbed up a level. Then she climbed another.

The ledges were each a good two feet wide, but they seemed to be more like two inches to Nicole. Vertigo hit when she made the mistake of looking down. She was already a full story high! As the world swirled and shook, she grabbed hold of stones protruding from the wall and held tight. Wondering if her observer were still with her, she craned her neck to look for the Stone Woman. But the ghost was nowhere in sight.

"I hope this works," the resolute young woman muttered, as she shoved down the fear that was upsetting her stomach and climbed another level.

"I can do this," she told herself firmly. Reaching up to get a good handhold during the climb to the next level, she found that the Stone Woman was again with her. Only this time, she had appeared on a ledge several levels above.

"Oh," Nicole grumbled, as she tamped down the gush of panic that was trying to flood her chest, "I get it. You want me up there. Even higher."

Level by level Nicole continued to climb. Nervous sweat poured from every pore of her body as she focused all her attention on the task at hand. Every time she thought she was surely high enough, she would take a moment to look around and find the Stone Woman on the ledge directly above her.

Some people might wonder why she was pursuing the ghost. After all, common sense dictated that the living run as far from the restless dead as was humanly possible. But those people obviously were ignorant of the fact that she had already tried the fleeing tactic when she returned home to Seattle. It had worked about as well as running from a tick that had already implanted its head under her skin.

Just like a tick, the ghost had gotten under her skin. Even odder, the Stone Woman had become a friend. Nicole knew that just as the Stone Woman had helped her out of a few tight spots, it was now her turn to return the favor and help the ghost.

Besides, she had always wanted to overcome her fear of heights. Having the ghost with her spurred her on and encouraged her to keep climbing.

It was an odd sensation, knowing that she and the ghost were the only two beings on the temple. One dead, one alive, alone in the world, yet together.

What Nicole did not know was that she and the ghost were not alone. Every so often, a head would peek around a far corner to watch Nicole. The owner of the head was being very careful to remain hidden, but equally careful to keep pace with Nicole.

When Nicole was finally near the top she relaxed enough to look around.

"That was a mistake," she gulped, as she realized what a great height she had climbed. Flattening herself against the wall she squeezed her eyes tight. There she remained, forcing herself to take slow, even breaths, until the world stopped twirling like a merry-go-round on steroids, and she regained her balance. Slowly and cautiously, she opened her eyes to look around.

The Stone Woman was glowing several feet away, and this time she was on the same ledge as Nicole. Something about her face had changed. She somehow did not look quite as sad as before.

"Finally, no more climbing," Nicole muttered, but she smiled to let the dead woman know she was glad to see her.

The ghost pointed to a spot at the foot of the wall, then disappeared.

Nicole hugged the wall as she inched along the ledge to the spot the Stone Woman had indicated. At one point her foot slipped, causing her heart to do more flips than a gold-medal gymnast in the Olympics.

She paused for several minutes to give herself a stern talking-to about the importance of overcoming fear. And when she was done with that lecture, she took a moment to remind herself of mountain goats and rock climbers, both of which had no problem with inclines much steeper than this one.

"Goats, I understand," she grumbled, "but I can't believe there are humans who pin themselves to the side of a mountain on purpose. I mean, what are they thinking? What happened to keeping your feet on solid ground, or, if a higher floor can't be avoided, using an elevator? Why anyone would want to—"

Nicole's grumbles continued in this vein for quite a while as she slowly and carefully inched her way toward her goal. Somehow, complaining about other people's stupidity helped her shove aside her fears, and she only ceased muttering when she finally arrived at her destination.

"I hope this is it," she whispered, "I don't think I can take much more of this height."

She took a deep breath, pulled herself together, and yelled, "Hey, ghost lady. Is this where you want me to leave the necklace?"

But Nicole received no response.

"I'll take that as a yes."

Nicole squatted down to dig at the foot of the wall, until out of the corner of her eye she saw movement. Thinking it was her ghost friend telling her she was not at the right spot, she stood up and sighed. Then, pulling her shoulders back heroically, Nicole scuttled around the next corner and to practically fall into Rudy Valente's arms.

"Just who I was looking for," Valente growled.

He grabbed his victim by the wrists and twisted one of her arms behind her back. Then he did the unthinkable. He shoved her, forcing her to move closer to the edge.

It was a stupid move, shoving a woman who was deathly afraid of heights toward an excruciatingly tall drop-off. Sure, it made her brain shut down, but her instinct immediately took over. And it just so happened Nicole's instinct was to fight like a wildcat.

Of course, unlike a wildcat, Nicole had no claws. She did, however, have elbows, one of which was free. She used that free elbow to its best advantage and landed quite a few blows directly to Valente's nose.

Startled by this sudden onslaught from a woman he had thought of as weak and helpless, Rudy loosened his grip. Nicole jerked free and scrambled away, hugging the wall all the way. Her attacker snarled and wiped a stream of blood from his nose.

"You should have minded your own business," the furious man growled. "Now you have your hand in the tiger's mouth."

But Nicole was no quitter. She scuttled, crab-like, along the two-foot-wide ledge with Valente in close pursuit. When she came to a spot that seemed slightly less steep, she scrambled down a few levels.

Nicole twisted around to check her progress only to find that Valente was a mere arm's length away.

"I can do better than this," she muttered, and she threw caution to the wind to sprint along the narrow ledge, leaving the rotund Rudy Valente far behind.

"That's better," Nicole smiled. "Not that I can relax yet."

She climbed carefully down several more levels, then again began to run. She rounded first one corner, then another. Rudy Valente was nowhere in sight. Encouraged by her success Nicole slowed to a standstill, panting as she struggled to catch her breath. She had done it. She had gotten away.

Nicole heard a heavy thump behind her and twirled to find Rudy had dropped down from the ledge above.

"I know this temple like the back of my hand. You are on my turf," the evil man gloated. "No matter where you run, I will catch you."

He lunged at Nicole, but the young woman's agility saved the day. She slipped through his fingers and ran.

"You're trapped. My men are waiting at the bottom!" he yelled. "Give up!"

But Nicole had no intention of giving up. She knew she was younger and fitter than he was, all she had to do was wear him out. She scampered up a few levels, going in the opposite direction than she actually wanted to go. But Valente was relentless. He followed every move she made at his own pace, slow, steady, and unstoppable.

Nicole was young, but even the young have their limits. She tripped and fell to her knees, which gave Rudy Valente time to catch up with her. But as he reached for her, she managed to scramble to her feet and again get away.

"This is ridiculous," Valente yelled, after Nicole. "I had planned for you to slip and fall over the edge. But have it your own way, the report will say you were mugged by bandits."

Valente pulled out a gun and shot at Nicole. She ducked, and the bullet hit the stone of the temple with a resounding plunk.

"Missed me!" Nicole taunted, making Rudy's eyes bulge and his face turn red with rage.

"You should not call the alligator a big mouth until you've crossed the river," he warned, with a growl.

Nicole inched around a corner and scrambled down a level. She swiveled frantically to the right and then the left, then nodded to herself as she decided to head to the right. She was surprised to find that even though she was scared to death, there was a part of her that was enjoying itself.

No part of Rudy Valente was enjoying itself as he ponderously followed. There was a reason he usually let his minions do all the heavy lifting. He was horribly out of shape.

"I'll make a deal with you," he yelled, huffing like a locomotive climbing Mt. Everest. "Stop running and I'll let you live."

"Right!" Nicole yelled in response. "Like I'm going to trust you."

Nicole rounded another corner and paused to look around. Only this time she saw something on the next level that made her eyes gleam. She quickly scrambled down a level.

Valente rounded the corner, saw Nicole just below him, and took a shot. Nicole jumped through a small doorway in the side of the temple. The bullet slammed into stone, missing Nicole by inches.

The out-of-shape crook slowly climbed down to the next ledge. He gloated as he realized Nicole must be hiding in a temple room. Which meant she was trapped. He swaggered over to the room entrance.

"Somebody," Chief Valente yelled, as he jumped down to Nicole's level, "should have taught you that a cow does not belong in a horse's gallop."

"Someone," Nicole's voice came through the doorway, "should teach you to use your own words. Those sayings are annoying."

Rudy Valente growled as he ducked through the doorway. He was tired and beyond angry that this snippet of a girl, this American, was getting the better of him. It was time to stop the nonsense and end this chase.

Which would be easy, now that the silly girl had trapped herself. She probably assumed she could easily get back to the ledges, but the chief had played on the temple as a boy and knew that this particular room was a dead end.

He had warned her this was his territory. But being an American, she thought she knew best.

She was about to discover that Rudy Valente could outsmart her any day, even if he was a bit too stout to outrun her.

Valente entered the ten by five-foot stone room. The room was completely bare, and he immediately saw Nicole exposed with her back against the wall. Satisfied that she had nowhere to go, he smiled sadistically as his hefty body blocked the light from the doorway. Relishing this moment of success, he slowly raised his gun and took aim. But as his finger touched the trigger Nicole scuttled through a small opening. Valente grunted in disgust.

"That won't help you," he yelled, as he squeezed his rotund frame through the narrow opening to follow the girl into a much larger room with built-in stone benches, tables, and niches. Since the room's only connection to the outside world was the narrow doorway, which was currently blocked by his body, no light could get inside. It took several moments for his eyes to adjust, but when they did, he saw that Nicole was cowering against a wall on the opposite side of the room.

"Well, well, well," he snarled. "Looks like this is the end, girly. Guess you're one American who isn't going to have her own way."

As Rudy Valente raised his gun to point it at Nicole, Diaz stepped out of the deep shadows of a niche. She slammed the gun, along with Valente's hand, against a wall.

The gun fired. Nicole dove for the floor, but thankfully the bullet passed through the doorway without causing harm. Larkin jumped out of a second niche on the other side of the room to tackle Valente to the ground.

"Got him!" Larkin yelled, with extreme satisfaction.

"I was beginning to think you guys had left," Nicole complained.

"Not a chance," Diaz assured her.

Larkin handcuffed Rudy Valente, then jerked him to his feet. He shoved the rotund, little man through the narrow opening and followed.

Diaz walked over to Nicole, holding out a hand to help her up.

"So," Diaz asked, with a smile, "did you get to finish your mission before the former chief of police arrived?"

"Not quite," Nicole grimaced.

"Would you like to?"

Nicole nodded.

"Is it in here?" Diaz asked, looking around the temple room.

"I think so."

Diaz nodded as she left the room.

Using her gut to guide her, Nicole ran her hand along the wall, searching both high and low until she found an indent that felt different from the rest of the wall.

"This could be it," she whispered excitedly.

She crouched down and explored the stone further, pushing at it every so often. Finally, she found one spot where the pressure of her hand caused the stone to shift slightly. She pushed even harder and dug the opposite side with her fingers until she could pull the stone out altogether. What she was left with was a hole filled with a handful of loose rubble.

"Okay, ghost lady," Nicole sighed. "I hope you're watching. I'm giving the necklace back now."

Nicole took off the necklace and laid it on the ground. Then she took a small, brown, cloth change purse out of her pocket, dumped the change from it back into her pocket, and gently put the necklace inside the purse.

"I hope you don't mind. A beautiful necklace like this should be kept clean."

She then put the purse into the hole, examined it, and took it out again.

"No, not good enough yet," she muttered, as she used her hands to make the hole deeper. When she was satisfied that the hole was deep enough, she put the purse back in and covered it with the loose gravel.

"There," Nicole nodded. "I think even someone watching me bury it—"

She shoved the stone back into place and took time to smear the dirt around until it matched all the other dirt around it.

"—would have trouble finding this necklace. And that is about all I can do. I hope it's enough."

She stood up and brushed the dirt from her hands. The Stone Woman suddenly appeared in front of her, causing Nicole to take a step back. The two women were now only a couple of feet apart.

Nicole cleared her throat, saying softly, "I put it back for you."

The Stone Woman gazed calmly at Nicole but gave no response. Nicole feared the ghost did not understand.

"I wrapped it up nicely, dug a deep hole, and buried it."

Nicole pointed to the stone. The Stone Woman looked where Nicole was pointing.

"It should be safe now."

The Stone Woman gazed at Nicole but still gave no sign she understood.

"So...I did what you wanted. Now, I need a favor from you."

The Stone Woman looked away from Nicole, as if listening to something in the distance. Nicole stepped toward the ghost and begged, "Please stop following me. I gave you back what is yours."

The Stone Woman blinked, as if understanding for the first time. Then she touched the ghostly necklace around her neck and smiled joyfully. As Nicole watched, the ghost glowed more and more brightly until she was almost solid light, then she was gone.

Nicole melted against the wall, sighing with relief.

"Now that was intense."

She slowly exited the room and looked around, slightly dazed. A drop of sweat rolled down her forehead and plopped onto her cheek. She reached up to wipe it away.

"I just put away a bad guy and helped a ghost," Nicole grimaced. "Compared to that, the climb down the temple should be a breeze!"

With that, she headed down, and she was proud when her heart only tried to climb out of her mouth three times during the descent.

CHAPTER 30

A week later, as Nicole sat in the hotel restaurant waiting for her order of food, the reporter, Joe, appeared at her table.

"Mind if I join you?" he asked, with a smile that could only be described as hesitant.

"Sure," she nodded. Then she motioned to the waiter. "Another for my friend."

Joe took a seat and looked a little sheepish as he pulled out his notebook.

"May I?" he asked.

Nicole nodded. Now she understood the timid smile. But before Joe could ask her any questions, they were both distracted by the arrival of two huge plates of french fries.

"I thought it would be better if you had your own this time," Nicole explained, as Joe salivated at the steaming pile of sliced and fried goodness. "My treat."

As Joe dug in, the smile on his face was sincere and writ large. It was only after he had eaten about a third of his fries that he remembered why he was there and looked up at his bemused table partner.

"Sorry, I was hungry," he explained. "Mind if I begin?"

"I'm ready when you are,"

"Okay, let's get to the meat of it. At the temple, that was a setup? The CIA used you as bait?"

"It was my idea. I told them I needed to go to the temple, but they said it wouldn't be safe for me. The trap was a compromise."

Joe glanced up at Nicole in surprise but quickly looked down again. His next question was likely to upset her.

"So," Joe's voice squeaked, as it often did when he was nervous. He cleared his throat and began again. "So, have you seen it again?"

"It?"

"Umm, the ghost." Joe's face turned beet red, but he powered on. "Has it been back? I mean since you gave it back the necklace?"

"Nope." Nicole grinned. "It's been nearly a week, and not a sign of her."

Nicole craned her neck to read what Joe had written.

"You've written down almost every word I've said."

"Of course, I did! It's a great story. 'American Girl Foils Crooked Central American Cop.'"

"But I don't see the word ghost written anywhere in your notes."

"And you won't, see."

"I do see. You're a chicken."

"A what!"

"The ghost was a huge part of the story, but you leave her right out. Has to be cowardice."

Joe rolled his eyes as he tossed his pen on the table next to his notebook. He opened his mouth to speak, but the glisten of oil on fried fries caught his eyes. He grabbed a few, dipped them in ketchup, and shoved them into his mouth. He studied Nicole as he chewed.

"It's a funny thing being a reporter," he said, as soon as he was able to swallow the rather large mouthful. "You have to go out there and find that story that no one else can find. That's how you make your name."

Nicole smiled her understanding. Of course, she knew that was what reporters had to do.

"I think I might have helped you a bit there," she scoffed.

"Oh, you did," he agreed. "But not if I don't play it smart. I can still mess it up."

"Mess it up?" Nicole asked. "How?"

"Well," Joe explained, "a good reporter has to know which stories to tell, and which to keep quiet about."

He grabbed a fry and dipped it deep into the ketchup.

"I'm still relatively new at this reporter game."

"Really? I couldn't tell," Nicole teased.

But Joe failed to notice the whimsical expression on Nicole's face and continued with more sincerity than she had yet seen.

"I haven't been doing this very long," he admitted. "That's why I don't have an expense account."

He used the freshly dipped fry to write his name in the air. When he added a dot after his name it splashed ketchup on Nicole's face.

"I still need to make a name for myself. Then I'll be given an expense account, a regular salary, and all the good stories I can write."

Nicole wiped the splotch of ketchup off with a napkin, nodded her acceptance of what he was saying, and ate another of her fries. She would have argued that her run-in with an ancient Mayan woman in ghost form was one of the good stories, but the poor guy seemed to need to talk. So, she would let him talk.

Unfortunately, he seemed to also need to use his fries to make his point. He dipped another fry in the ketchup, then used it to draw a tight little circle in the air. Nicole kept a close eye on it so she could duck away from any flying ketchup that might head her way.

"Until I make a name for myself, I need to toe the line," he explained. "I've got to be cynical, hard-nosed, and ruthless."

He ruthlessly bit the fry in half before popping the rest of it into his mouth. Then he grabbed his pen and jotted down a few more notes.

"So that means no ghosts?"

"That means no ghosts," Joe declared with finality. "I don't want my editor thinking I've branched out into fiction."

"I can understand that," Nicole admitted, then she grimaced as she noticed a splash of ketchup on her arm.

Grabbing a fresh napkin from the pile the waiter had left on the table, she wiped it off.

"It's time to get back to business," a businesslike Joe prompted. "Do they have enough to put Chief Valente away?"

"Yep!" Nicole gave her own version of a ruthless bite that decimated a helpless fry. "The CIA found a laptop with names, places, times—everything. He's going away for a good long while."

Nicole picked up a twin to the previous fry and twisted it in the air as she thought back to the day Chief Valente had been arrested. She had stood to the side at the foot of the temple as a large group of CIA agents marched Rudy Valente and several of his deputies to military vehicles. Valente had stopped dead in his tracks when he reached Nicole, and a mere foot from her face, had leaned toward her threateningly, his eyes as sharp and piercing as daggers.

Nicole was proud of her response. She had not let his threatening stance frighten her in the least. Instead of cowering like she probably would have done in the past, she smiled broadly. That smile must have irritated the former chief of police, because he had growled like an angry bear. Fortunately for Nicole's nerves, the CIA agent holding his chain had no patience for growling bears and jerked him away.

Nicole shivered as she remembered just how much that bravado had taken out of her. She defiantly bit the fry she was holding, as if it proved her bravery. Joe grabbed a few more of his fries, dipped them in ketchup, and shoved them into his mouth.

"So," he asked nonchalantly, "what are you going to do now?"

"As soon as I can book a flight home, I'm out of here. I've had enough excitement for a while."

She picked up another fry and focused on it while her mind replayed all that had happened in Belize. It was a lot.

"And then?" Joe asked, a strange tenseness in his voice.

The change in his voice made Nicole look up at him. He was doodling on a napkin, quite like the little squiggles he was drawing were the most important squiggles in the world. It was obvious he wanted to avoid meeting her eyes. What was that about?

"And then, I'll start over," she finally answered, when the silence had drug out quite a bit longer than was comfortable.

She bit into the fry and chewed deliberately until every sliver of fry was macerated out of existence. Then she whispered, "Without Michael."

Joe hazarded a peek at her face. She was looking at the half fry in her hand like it held the answer to all the mysteries of the world. When she looked up at him, he quickly looked away.

"Too bad," she said bitterly, "you can't go back and do things differently. There are a few things I'd like to change."

She tossed the half fry back on the pile with its brothers and shoved the plate away.

"I wouldn't be so stupid."

Something in Nicole's voice drew Joe's eyes to her again. She was staring off into the distance, her hand on the spot where the necklace used to lay.

Joe cleared his throat.

"Nicole?"

A nostalgic smile stole across Nicole's face as memory after memory of Michael replayed in her mind. It was the first time since his death that she had allowed herself to think of him, really think of him. So many wonderful memories. So many —

"Nicole, can you hear me?" Joe asked, and his voice gave that little squeak it often gave when he was upset. Then he panicked as he realized he was losing her and needed to do something fast. He waved his hand in front of her face and yelled, "Hey!"

Her eyes regained focus and turned to him, causing him to sigh with relief.

"What?" she asked, slightly perturbed to have so many wonderful memories interrupted.

"What were you thinking of?"

"Michael, of course. What else would I be thinking of? We always had so much fun. He really was my best friend."

Nicole's nostalgic smile returned and her eyes glazed over as another fond memory drifted into her mind's eye.

Joe nodded. He realized if he didn't do something quickly, she might retreat into her memories again and he would lose his chance. He reached into his pocket and pulled out a bag, then cleared his throat self-consciously.

"My mom," he began, then he rethought what he wanted to say and started again. "People say that keepsakes lessen the pain of loss. I saw this necklace and I, well, it made me think of you."

He poured the necklace out on the table between them. It was very like the one Nicole had left at the temple, only newer.

"It's brand new, I checked. No ghosts attached."

Nicole turned the sweetest smile Joe had ever seen on him and his heart melted into a puddle on the floor.

"Thanks, Joe. It's perfect," she said, as she took the necklace and put it around her neck.

She laid her hand on it, just as she had been doing for months, and became lost in thought. Joe desperately wanted to regain her attention, but before he could figure out a way that wouldn't leave him looking like an idiot, the buzz of a mosquito assaulted their ears and Nicole slapped her leg. She craned her neck to look out the window.

"Darn it!" she grimaced. "I forgot my bug spray and the sun is setting. They're going to eat me alive!"

"Mosquitoes don't bother me," Joe bragged quietly. "I'll get it for you if you want."

"Joe, you're a sweet guy. But a few mosquito bites won't hurt me."

Joe nodded and squirmed uncomfortably. It was obvious he had more than mosquitoes on his mind. He cleared his throat.

"So, Nicole," the words came out louder than he intended, and he paused a moment to recalibrate his voice. "I was wondering about something."

"What is it, Joe?"

"When we get back to the States—"

Joe swung his arm in a wide arc, as if to encompass the entire United States, and knocked over his glass of soda. He and Nicole immediately grabbed napkins to mop up the dark liquid before it could pour off the table onto Nicole's lap.

"That should do it." Nicole grinned at the very red Joe as she swiped away the last drops of the sticky mess. "Now…what were you saying?"

Joe opened his mouth to speak, but before he could produce so much as a squeak, Diaz and Larkin walked up to the table. Joe's face turned even redder as he clamped his mouth closed. It was hard to tell if he was embarrassed by what he wanted to say, or his clumsiness in trying to say it.

"Mrs. Quinn!" Larkin's salutation was formal, but the smile was the kind given to friends. "We wanted to thank you for all your help."

Nicole smiled in return. She had learned to like and trust this CIA duo.

"We would also," Larkin winked, "like to update you on the investigation."

"Oh? I thought the investigation was over." Nicole was a bit confused by Larkin's demeanor. He was not just relaxed—which she would expect after a successful sting like the one that had just happened—but he seemed to be downright giddy. Whatever could make him act that way?

She motioned for the two agents to join her and waited patiently as Larkin and Diaz pulled chairs over to the table.

"Nearly over," Larkin grinned. "We've spent the last few days cleaning out the camps that Rudy Valente had hidden away in the jungle."

He pointed at Joe's plate of fries. "Mind?"

"Go ahead." Nicole nodded, which brought an indignant huff from Joe.

"Good!" Larkin said, after he nearly swallowed a fry whole. "I need to get a plate of these for myself."

He reached for a second fry but was thwarted when Joe pulled the plate out of his reach.

"That laptop you helped us find has been quite a time saver," Diaz contributed, with a nod to Nicole.

"Maybe even a lifesaver," Larkin grinned broadly. There was an undercurrent flowing between the two CIA agents that Nicole did not understand. It was as if they were speaking a silent language of some sort. As if—

"Mrs. Quinn," Diaz broke into Nicole's speculations. "We have a proposition for you. We want to be your lifesaver."

"My what?" Nicole asked in confusion.

Larkin jumped up from the table and sprinted out of the room.

"Where is he going?" Nicole asked in surprise.

"Mrs. Quin," Diaz continued, "what are your plans? For the future?"

"I was just telling Joe," Nicole began, then remembered that the two probably did not know each other. "I'm sorry, have you two met?"

"Do girls swoon at my good looks?" Joe quipped.

"I'll take that as a no," Nicole answered, with a concerned look at Joe. He had a very strange look on his face. What was wrong with the man?

She decided to ignore Joe's peculiarities and went on with the introductions.

"Agent Diaz, this is Joe Rogers, the reporter I told you about. Joe, this Agent Diaz of the CIA."

The two nodded to each other.

"You were telling me your plans," Diaz prompted.

"Oh, yeah." Nicole nodded. "It's simple. After I go home, I'm going to continue studying art."

Diaz looked toward the door and a quirky smile bloomed on her face, as she said, "Ah. Larkin is back."

Nicole turned toward the doorway. Then she blinked, confused, because in Larkin's hands was a badge and a bulletproof vest.

"For you!" Larkin said gleefully.

"What's going on here?" Nicole asked, possibly more confused than she had ever been in her life.

Larkin tossed the vest and badge on the table and gave Nicole a smile that wouldn't be out of place if he had just returned her long-lost puppy to her.

Joe shrunk down into his chair, scribbling furiously in his notebook. Nicole suspected he was trying to make the agents forget his presence so he could get more fodder for his story.

"You're our newest recruit!" Diaz chimed in. "You're a quick thinker, brave, no plans—"

Diaz looked at Joe pointedly. "Unattached."

Joe glared at the CIA agent. He had taught himself to be thick skinned and rarely let jibes hurt his feelings, but that didn't mean he didn't recognize an insult when he heard it.

Nicole blinked as the meaning of the CIA agents' words sunk in.

"As soon as we get back to the States, you'll start your training," Larkin declared with a grin. "We've got everything all set up."

"I bet you do," Joe muttered, under his breath.

Now, it was Diaz's turn to glare at Joe. Not exactly comfortable being the recipient of that basilisk stare, he turned his attention back to his notes, focusing on them as if his life depended on his ability to write down every word.

Satisfied that the reporter would keep his mouth shut, Diaz turned her attention back to Nicole.

"We've booked seats on the next flight," she said excitedly. She had grown to like Nicole and thought she'd make a good agent. "You'll need to pack fast. The flight is in an hour—"

Nicole cringed under the onslaught of words that were coming so fast and furious that for a moment, she wished she had an umbrella for protection. Then she pulled herself together, took a deep breath, and sat tall.

"No."

"Oh." Diaz was shocked by the negative response. "Well, I guess we can get a later flight. But CIA agents need to be flexible. You might as well start now by—"

Nicole shook her head adamantly. Diaz and Larkin looked at each other.

"Are you saying no to the flight, or no to being a recruit?" Diaz wanted to know.

"Both," Nicole replied.

"Look," Diaz softened her voice and pasted a kindly smile on her face. She wanted Nicole to know they were on her side. That they were her friends. "We're trying to help you. You've lost your husband. You're adrift. You need purpose."

"I have purpose."

There was something about the calmness of Nicole's voice that confused the CIA agent.

"I mean a real purpose," Diaz clarified. "Something that truly matters."

Diaz cringed at the look Nicole sent her way. This was not going as planned.

"Besides," Larkin jumped in, "you can't turn it down. We already turned in the paperwork."

"Then I guess you'll have to un-turn it in."

With that pronouncement, Nicole stood, slapped both palms on the table, and looked down at the agents.

"Michael always told me that I was stronger than my fear. That he believed in me."

She pushed off from the table and assumed her full height of 5 foot 4. Her right hand drifted up to touch the necklace around her neck.

"It's time I believed in myself."

Without another word, Nicole turned on her heel and marched out the door.

Larkin and Diaz looked at each other in shock.

"What just happened here?"

"This is what I'd call an epic fail," Diaz answered, with a grimace.

Larkin and Diaz turned as one to look at Joe. As they sized him up, he jumped to his feet.

"Nope!" he shouted, as he ran to the door. "I already have a job I like."

At the door, he paused to shout, "You've got ketchup on your vest!" Then he was through the doorway and out of sight.

Larkin picked up the vest. It had landed on top of a plate of fries and did, indeed, have a Texas-sized blotch of ketchup marring its formerly pristine surface.

"That comes out of your salary, not mine," Diaz proclaimed.

With a philosophical shrug, Larkin picked up a fry and shoved it into his mouth.

In Nicole's hotel room, the young woman had just folded the last of her shirts and placed them in her suitcase. She scanned the room for forgotten items, and finding none, she lowered the lid and zipped it closed.

Grabbing the suitcase, she took a glance out of the window as she walked by, but it was the mirror by the door that made her stop dead in her tracks. As she watched, almost like she was watching another person, her hand rose to touch the necklace around her neck, a necklace very like the one that had played such an important part in her life lately. A wet bead of sadness welled up unbidden in the corner of her eye and rolled down her cheek to meet the sad smile that curved her lips.

Disgusted by this dismal face she had been sharing with the world, she gave an irritated sniff and mercilessly wiped away the unwelcome tear. The time for wallowing in sadness was over. She straightened her back as she glared at the woman in the mirror, daring her to show anything but courage. Then, satisfied by what she saw, she pasted a determined smile on her face and gave a firm nod.

But when she reached the door, an invisible forcefield kept her from turning the knob to open it. Deep in her heart, she knew there was one more thing she needed to do, unfinished business she needed to finish.

Nicole dropped the suitcase next to the door and returned to the mirror. She stood there, staring at her reflection, wondering what it was that she needed to fix. What was it…?

Then, in a sudden brainwave, she had it.

Reaching to the back of her neck she undid the clasp of the necklace and removed it. After laying the necklace carefully upon the dresser, she walked purposefully to the door and picked up her suitcase.

Now was the moment of truth. She reached out a hand to the door and instantly felt the difference. A bud of a smile blossomed on her face as she turned the knob, and that same smile bloomed into a joyous laugh as she opened the door and stepped through.

At that moment she knew, given time, she would be able to get through the pain of her loss. She simply had to keep moving forward.

Nicole closed the door behind her and took several more steps, until she found herself directly in front of a beautiful flower. As she bent over to breathe in its heady fragrance, she was reminded of the old saying about stopping to smell the roses.

This flower was not one she was familiar with, and it certainly was not a rose. But its scent was heavenly. It traveled up her nostrils and down to her heart, where it wrapped that weary organ in comfort.

Suddenly the world, which had felt cold and empty without Michael, was transformed into a place of wonder. If she kept her eyes open, who knew what she would find!

With that thought, she straightened up and headed to the airport to return home.

It was time to get on with her life.